SCARLET STONE

JEWEL E. ANN

Copyright © 2016 by Jewel E. Ann
ISBN: 978-0-9972588-9-9
Print Edition

Cover Designer: © Sarah Hansen, Okay Creations
Formatting: BB eBooks

Dedication

To everyone who believes in miracles

Author's Note

This book has many Britishisms and therefore may not read "right" to American readers. My goal was to make my British characters as authentic as possible. However, since I am an American author the spellings in this book are American English and therefore may not read "right" to British readers. I hope everyone can meet in the middle.

CHAPTER ONE

*D*ON'T WEE YOUR KNICKERS.
      The kids stare at me with their owl eyes as my knees wobble with each step.

Don't wee your knickers.

The first day of school shouldn't be this scary. The other kids have rucksacks with animated characters and glitter. I have a brown leather case with a four-digit lock code keeping my spiral notepad, three #2 pencils, a twelve pack of crayons, scissors, and my packed lunch safe. Oscar promised I would fit in fantastically on my first day of primary school.

I've already been asked nine times, "Why did you bring a suitcase to school?"

"It's an attaché case that used to belong to a German diplomat. Oscar gave it to me," I reply—nine times.

Once all eighteen children find a seat and the room is silent, we're invited one at a time to share a bit about ourselves. I am the fourth to go and after bingeing on too many Jammie Dodgers and a liter of milk for breakfast, I feel ready to chunder.

I don't. Instead, I answer the same basic questions that were shared before me. "Oscar is a locksmith, but he carries a gun because not everyone respects a good locksmith." I pick at the dry skin on my lips while slowly twisting my body side to side, as everyone else stares at me. Their mouths hang open. Why do they look so surprised? His job is boring, not cool.

1

The boy who spoke before me has a dad who drives a train. That's cool.

I continue, "He's my dad, but he told me to call him Oscar because I'm not a baby." I ignore the whispers and continue. "My mum died from doctors poisoning her."

The whispers stop, leaving seventeen pairs of wide eyes on me. Even my teacher looks like she ate something that's ready to come back up her throat.

"Oh …" I continue, having forgotten the most important piece of information. "My dad calls me Ruby, but my name is Scarlet Stone."

CHAPTER TWO

My name is Scarlet Stone, and I am a third-generation thief.

26 Years Later – High Security Prison – South East London

I T'S POSSIBLE HUNDREDS of other men have worn my dad's underwear. I'm here to say a final goodbye.

Make peace.

Close the door.

Yet the thought at the forefront of my mind is communal underwear. I overheard an inmate's wife complaining about it at my last visit. She said her husband contracted a flesh-eating infection from the shared underwear.

It could have been me in communal underwear. It was my crime. For the rest of my days, that realization will always give me pause.

"I'm leaving London." There. After practicing that line for forty-five minutes on the drive here, my brain and mouth cooperate. A miracle.

His chin juts forward, eyes unblinking.

My hand moves toward my mouth. At the last second I ball it into a fist then slip both of my hands under my legs. I stopped chewing my fingernails six years ago. No amount of nerves can convince me to start that nasty habit again, especially not within the confines of these four walls contaminated with flesh-eating bacteria.

"Why, Ruby? I don't understand." On the opposite side of the metal table, my dad clenches his intertwined fingers like it's taking everything he has to keep his composure.

"I need out." My teeth grind as I deny my need to break down and tell him the crux of my intentions. The dull pain in my chest bears down with each passing breath.

"What about Daniel?"

I shake my head. "We're over." Tears sting my eyes as I avert them to the black scuff marks on the concrete floor, blinking away the weakness.

My thoughts shift to the woman beside me, talking about Joey taking his first steps. Her flowery perfume overpowers the stale, musty stench. The door behind me buzzes as another visitor enters the room. I don't know how my dad lives here. After a week, I would drown in thoughts of despair and suicide—and communal underwear.

"Ten more years. Seven with good behavior. Wait for me. You're young. Don't be rash."

Drawing in a shaky breath, my gaze meets his. "I'm leaving tomorrow."

It's impossible to miss the flinch. Oscar Stone is as steely as his name implies, and like any good Brit, he's perfected his stiff upper lip. But I am his weakness. I am the reason he is here.

"I'll find you."

My quivering lips deliver a less-than-believable smile. He won't find me. No one will find me. The weight on my chest intensifies further. Oscar isn't the best dad in the traditional sense, but he's the best dad for me. There hasn't been one day in my entire life that I haven't felt like his whole world.

It's time to say goodbye and the nod from the prison officer behind him confirms it.

"I love you, Oscar."

He rubs a rough hand over his shaven head, blue eyes

squinted, deepening the lines and wrinkles on his face. A lifetime etched into his flesh. I look nothing like Oscar. The only physical attribute I have to my Caucasian dad is my skin is brown not black like my mum's. He used to tell me we were white chocolate, milk chocolate, and dark chocolate. His word is all I have. I don't remember my mum, but she was perfect. If I have to make up imaginary memories of my mum, they're sure as hell going to be spectacular. In my mind, she was a goddess, a superhero—perfection.

My eyes drift back to reality and the man before me. Prison has aged him, but if I'm honest, running from the law stole years from him long before his stint of incarceration.

"Ruby..." his voice cracks "...I'll come for you."

I nod as we both stand. Those are four powerful words coming from the great Oscar Stone. He wasn't captured; he surrendered ten years ago. There is a purpose for everything Oscar does. Twenty years is a bargain compared to what would be a guaranteed life sentence for any other person who had committed the same crime.

My crime. Not his.

Tampering with an organ-donor list and bribing everyone who might notice is not exactly legal. Not all necessary things in life reside on the right side of the law. I did it, but he pled guilty.

The prison officer announces our time is over. Oscar clutches the sides of the table. We share a lasting look that doesn't falter as he unfolds his tall body from the chair, its legs screeching along the floor. When did the middle of life fade into this blur with 'firsts' and 'lasts' suffocating the really incredible stuff in the middle?

I'm so afraid this final goodbye will forever be my lasting

memory of my dad.

Here it is: would have, could have, should have. How many people get this opportunity to say all they've ever wanted to say? No regrets.

"I love you." Why are those my only words? My heart swells with so much pain I can't squeeze one more word past it. It's not enough. A million sentiments scream in my head: *I'm sorry. Please forgive me. I never felt normal, but I always ... always felt loved. Thank you for being both a dad and a mum. Don't hate me when you find out the truth.*

"Why are you crying? My girl never cries." He cradles my face and brushes his thumbs across my cheeks.

"Life's just ..." I whisper past the lump in my throat, "... not fair."

"No one ever said it would be, Ruby. But it's the only one you have, so go fucking live it." He kisses my forehead.

I throw my arms around his neck. If I don't let go, then this will go away. Oscar is a fixer. He makes the impossible possible again.

"Stop!" I sob as the prison officer pulls Oscar from my hold.

"I'll come for you ..." His head twists back as his feet shuffle toward the door. He's waiting for me to turn and leave, but I won't. Not this time. I watch him fade into the distance, each listless step a word in the final sentence of a book.

Goodbye, Oscar Stone.

I love you.

———— ∽∿∽ ————

THE PROBABILITY OF returning to London is zero. My name is Scarlet Stone, and I'm a third-generation thief with a one-way ticket to Savannah, an ex-fiancé on his way to Africa, and a copy of Eckhart Tolle's *Stillness Speaks* in my messenger bag. My goal is to figure out the meaning of life or die trying.

"If you have a computer in there, you'll need to take it out."

My lips curl as I wink at the airport security guard. "No computer." I zip through the scanner with a simple pair of leggings, T-shirt, ballet flats, and my ruby pendant necklace dangling in my right hand so security can see it.

An hour and a neck pillow impulse-buy later, we're wheels up. My gaze finds the white knuckles on the armrest between the first-class seats. Before I destroyed my computer and mobile phone, I hacked into the airline's system and upgraded my seat to first-class at no extra charge. It was my last illegal indiscretion.

I hope.

"You fly often?" the sandy blond asks in a shaky voice as he eases his grip, wide eyes darting to mine while trepidation continues to bead along his suntanned brow.

An American. Lovely. They can be so bloody chatty. Oscar always said I was as chatty as a Yank, but I'm not even close.

"No. I prefer rail, but if it helps, then you should know I've never been on a plane that's crashed."

His gray-blue eyes bulge with fright.

The plane dips. My neighbor clutches the armrest again. "We're gonna die."

I bite back my grin. "Just a bump in the road—a wave on the surface of the sky. If you want something to really blow your mind, I can tell you about a recent article I read about North Korea launching an EMT weapon over the U.S. If it were to detonate, then all electronics would be knocked out—

including those on planes."

Death-grip bloke gasps.

"I know. I was gobsmacked too." On a sigh, I shrug. "But hey … it sure would be one helluva ride." Okay, I may be chattier than the average Brit.

"You have a mordant sense of humor." White teeth peek from his parted lips, still taut in a grimace. Color seeps back into his fingers and face.

"You have a prodigious vocabulary." I offer my hand. "I'm Scarlet Stone."

His eyes flit between mine and my hand a few times before he releases the armrest. "Nolan Moore." He squeezes my hand like I'm holding his dangling body off the side of a bridge.

I squeeze his in return just as tight. Oscar said a handshake says a lot—do it with confidence or not at all.

"American?" I choose not to be outwardly presumptuous.

He nods.

I rest my head back and close my eyes, giving myself a nice pat on the back for being friendly.

"W-wedding."

Aannd … here we go. More small talk. "Sorry?"

Nolan's hands fist on his legs as we bounce through the clouds. "Wedding. I was here for a wedding. A friend of mine from college got married in Farnham."

"Oh. Wonderful. Very well then." I resume my napping position.

"I'm from Savannah, Georgia." Nolan's shaky hands accept the small bottle of Jack, a Coke, and a glass of ice from the air hostess. He smiles, nerves still shaking his lips a bit.

Perhaps he's only this chatty when he's nervous.

"Really? That's where I'm going. I was born in Savannah."

On a sideways glance, he narrows one eye. "You clearly sound like you're from Savannah, Georgia."

"Cheeky." I wink at him.

"Yes, *cheeky*, because we say that a lot in Savannah." He sips his drink. "Are your parents originally from London or Savannah?"

I surrender. Nolan is friendly or needy, or a mix of both.

"My dad is originally from London and my mum came to London from the Caribbean." I point to my hair, tight curls celebrating a holiday from hours of being straightened into submission. "Thank you, Mum, for the hair." I grin.

"Against doctors' orders, she traveled with my dad to Atlanta for his business trip when she was thirty-five weeks pregnant with me. They drove down to Savannah on the last day of the trip to have some beach time, and my mum went into labor. The ten-day trip turned into a month before they took me home to London. I haven't been back to Savannah since."

A flirty smile teases his lips, shedding the tension from his rigid posture. "How many years has it been since you were last in Savannah?"

My eyelashes sweep up, and I blink at him a few times before chuckling. "That's a very smooth approach to asking my age."

He shrugs, taking another sip of his drink.

"Thirty-one years."

"What's taking you back to Savannah?" This bloke fires endless questions.

Staring at my fingers drumming on my leg, I twist my lips. "Hmm ... good question. I suppose the easiest answer is that one day I realized my life was not going in the direction I thought it was. Not to sound cliché, but it was a crossroad and I had to make a decision. West. I chose west."

"Intriguing. Is this trip temporary or permanent?"

After contemplating the meaning of each word, I reply, "Both." At some point, the fact that I sold most of my belongings and decided to leave home *forever* may very well hit me; if I were leaving a large family, friends, even so much as a gold fish, I think I'd feel the impact of this life-altering moment. Daniel is gone, living the life he was meant to live, and Oscar could die of some flesh-eating disease from his communal underwear before his time is served.

Nolan chuckles. "Fair enough. I'm a stranger on a plane. We don't have to get personal. Eleven hours of small talk works for me."

Of course it does. "Fabulous." My lips pull into a tight grin.

His expectant gaze makes me shift in my seat.

I let out a controlled breath that doesn't sound too exasperated, then I smile. "Tell me what you do in Savannah, Mr. Moore."

"Well, Miss Stone, I flip homes and of recent, I've started dabbling in commercial real estate development. My father has had his hand in real estate for years, but he's getting bored with it so I've inherited his 'hobby.'"

"Do you have any houses to rent?"

"No ... well, one. Why?"

"I haven't secured a place to stay, yet."

"I could give you some names, other property owners. The one I have is on Tybee Island, a beachfront house with a single room and shared kitchen. The other room is already rented. Probably not what you're looking for."

I shake my head. "I don't need more than a room."

His nose wrinkles. "Yeah, but it's only available for six months. That's when the other renter is moving out and then the place will go on the market. It will likely sell within a day of listing it."

Six months. I can't believe he said six months.

"I'm interested. Six months is perfect."

"Really?"

I nod.

Nolan bites his lips together. "I forgot to mention ... the other renter is a guy, an old friend of mine."

"Rapist? Murderer? Weird fetishes? Smelly? Loud snorer?"

He laughs. "I can't say for sure on the snoring. We haven't slept in the same room since we were in our late teens. It's possible he has a weird fetish that I don't know about, but I'm going out on a limb and saying 'no' to the rapist or murderer. However, he does most of the construction and remodeling for me with the homes I flip, so occasionally he might smell like sweat and sawdust, but I imagine the smell washes off when he showers."

Adjusting my neck pillow, I close my eyes. "I'll take it."

"I haven't told you the price. You haven't filled out an application. I'll need references."

I smile, keeping my eyes closed. "What's the price?"

"A grand a month."

After giving it no more than ten seconds of consideration, I reply, "Done."

"What about references?"

"We have eleven hours to get personal, Mr. Moore." *Mr. Chatty.* "Let me know if you still need references once we land."

I capture a bit of sleep in the few lulls of our conversation. A true miracle. Sleep might be an overstatement. I can't stop thinking about communal underwear. Really, everything that touches my father's skin has been shared and probably soiled with every form of bodily fluid.

After the inmate's wife complained about his skin infection, I researched protocol for laundry in prisons. I came across a past inmate's blog. He said a lot of prisons send out their laundry to services that also do laundry for other businesses, like restaurants. Now, I can't use a cloth napkin at a restaurant without wondering if it was washed in the same machine as soiled communal underwear.

CHAPTER THREE

My name is Scarlet Stone, and I'm drawn to anything out of the ordinary, the crazy, the eccentric. I've been this way all my life.

"COME ON. WE'RE going to the same place." Nolan pins me with a don't-be-ridiculous look as I pull my bags toward the taxi queue along the curb. After a tiring trip, including two connecting flights, we're finally at Hilton Head Airport.

"I didn't want to be presumptuous." I grin, following him to his car, relishing the warm Savannah breeze kissing my face. And the sun—it's bloody amazing!

"Scarlet, please, be presumptuous."

The pictures of Savannah don't lie. I can't stop staring at the curvy oak trees with their saggy branches draped in Spanish moss. Oscar said my mum fell in love with Savannah and as the picturesque scenery flashes past my window, I can see why.

"Are you feeling well?"

My head jerks back. "Why would you ask me that?"

"I have this …" He taps his hand on the top of the steering wheel. "I don't know how to explain it in a way that you'd understand, but I sort of … *sense* things."

I nod slowly. "Well, you're human, so I hope you *sense* things. Contrary to what has been taught for years, humans have at least nine senses that most researchers agree on; some scientists believe we have over twenty senses."

"Wow! You're good with human biology."

I shake my head. "I'm good with random knowledge. I had an insatiable curiosity as a child—I still do."

"Well, my sense is a little more rare than the average five, nine, or twenty that you speak of."

"Oh, really?" I try to act curious, yet casual, but if I'm honest, he's got my nipples erect and not in a sexual way. "Like what? You see dead people?"

"No ... well, potentially."

"*Potentially*, wow, that would be killer on a CV. 'I speak three different languages, volunteer twelve hours a week ... oh, and I can potentially see dead people."

"I sense pain."

"Pain." I nod over and over like I'm bobbing to a beat but there is no beat.

"Yes."

I clear my throat. "What kind of pain? Emotional? Because if you must know, I left behind my fiancé—ex-fiancé. It was for the best, but I still love him so—"

"No." Nolan shakes his head, a frown and wrinkled forehead marring his pretty face. "Physical pain."

"Like ... a heart attack?"

"Yes."

"Some dogs can sense health conditions too." I shrug. So he's part dog. No big deal. It was only a matter of time before scientists crossed that line.

"Yes. I've read a lot about it. That is through smell. They can detect the slightest shift in hormones, even cancer which lets off VOCs. But I don't have a heightened sense of smell. I can just ... *feel* pain that's not mine, but it feels like mine. It took a while to discover that I wasn't dying every day of something new. I was feeling the ailments of the people around me."

Another laugh escapes me because this is absurd. It has to

be. I prefer the he's-part-dog scenario. "So, I'm causing you pain?"

He nods. "Some, yes."

"Well, your senses are off today, because I'm feeling fine."

"You're not feeling a little bloated? Nauseous?"

"What are you implying? I'm fat? Pregnant? Oh, wow, wouldn't that be something if you could detect pregnancy?"

"*Are* you pregnant? If so, then I'd say something might be going wrong with your pregnancy, and I should take you to the doctor."

Drawing in a deep breath, I reach over and rest my hand on Nolan's leg. "I'm fine. Not pregnant. Not in pain."

"I'm not usually wrong about this."

"Hey, if you're right ninety-percent of the time, that's still pretty good. Maybe today your pain is actually yours. Did you ever consider that?"

Biting at the inside of his cheek, he cocks his head to the side, eyes focused on the road. "Maybe."

It takes a few minutes for whatever the hell that was to clear from the air.

"Look familiar?"

I turn toward him, eyes narrowed.

He smirks, watching the road ahead. "Do you recognize anything from the last time you were in Savannah?"

"Funny."

"Have you been anywhere else in the U.S. since you were born here?"

"No. England, Spain, France, Italy, Scotland, Germany ... and the Caribbean where my mum has family, but not any-where else here."

"Where are you headed in six months?"

Such a brilliant question.

"Hard to say."

He takes a quick glance at me, a flirty smile curling his lips. "You're on a hiatus, huh? A break from life?"

"I'm on an extended holiday, but not from life, just the distractions."

Nolan pulls off the main road.

"This doesn't look like Tybee Island."

"So you *do* remember your last time in Savannah."

I shake my head. "Internet search."

A blanket of tangled trees seems to engulf the vehicle in every direction. The sun sneaks its way through the occasional hole, splashing light along the cobblestone drive that vibrates my seat. I squint against the morning light, my eyes desperate to close for at least a good eight hours.

"Are you the governor?"

Nolan chuckles as the red-bricked, white-pillared, two-story plantation-style house greets us in the clearing ahead. "No. He lives in Atlanta. I live here and so do my parents when they're not traveling."

"You live here and you're charging me a grand a month for one room and a shared kitchen?"

"How else would I afford to live here?" The lively glimmer in his smile reminds me of Daniel.

The last time Daniel smiled at me like that we were tasting cake samples for our autumn wedding. Life has a special way of changing everything in a blink. Love has many definitions. I'm certain I've experienced most of them to get to here.

"I see. You buy and sell houses and still live with your mum and dad. Well done, you."

"Scarlet Stone, I love your accent, even when it's wrapped

around snarky little barbs." He unfastens his seatbelt. "I have a contract to pick up here and then deliver after I drop you off. And my parents asked me to come by for a drink as soon as I got home. Two birds. One stone."

"With me?"

"I think they'd frown upon me leaving you in the car." Nolan grins but it fades as quickly as it appeared. "Savannah isn't the smallest town, but in certain circles it feels that way."

"How so?"

"Gossip. I'd like to think that during your stay you could avoid the gossip, but it's unlikely. I don't want you to believe everything you hear, especially about my family."

My probing gaze implores him, my curiosity reaching its summit.

Nolan chews on the inside of his lip for a moment. "My parents have an … *unconventional* relationship, and my mother is not well. Hasn't been for quite some time."

"Do you know what's wrong with her?"

"No. She's not in physical pain. Hers is emotional … I think. We don't really know. But I want you to meet them so you can see for yourself that they're just a married couple living in Savannah. Sure, they have a few *issues*, but who doesn't. Right?"

My name is Scarlet Stone, and I'm drawn to anything out of the ordinary, the crazy, the eccentric. I've been this way all my life. Excitement runs through my veins.

Nolan jogs around the car. "My lady."

My brow raises. "Chivalrous." I rest my hand in his.

"I'm a southern gentleman."

"Hmm, we'll see about that."

"Mr. Moore." A Hispanic lady with silver-streaked black

hair pulled into a tight bun welcomes us before we even make it up the white-painted steps to the spacious wraparound porch.

"Sofia." He hugs her, pressing a kiss to her cheek.

"Did you have a nice trip?"

I survey her black dress that falls just below her knees, black leather flats, and a crisp white apron.

Nolan nods. "I did. Thank you. I'd like you to meet Scarlet Stone. She's renting the other room on Tybee."

"With Mr. Reed?" Sofia's russet eyes grow with surprise and her jaw goes slack.

I'm missing something here.

"Yes. She'll be staying with Theodore."

Sofia purses her lips to the side, eyes inspecting me. "Have you met Mr. Reed?"

I shake my head, shifting my attention to Nolan. He motions with his head for me to step inside.

"My parents?" he asks.

Sofia clears her throat and shakes her head a bit. "Yes, sorry. Your parents are out back. Bourbon?"

"Yes. Thank you, Sofia."

"And for you, Miss Stone?"

"Room-temperature bottled water."

Sofia blinks several times. Nolan raises a brow.

"Tap is fine," I whisper.

"Ice?" Sofia smiles like all is well again.

"No, thank you."

Mr. I'm Not The Governor—but bloody hell this house is a mansion—guides me down an expansive hallway of exquisite white and gray marble flooring ending at a set of glass doors that open to a red-brick patio overlooking acres of rolling pastures and several horses grazing in the distance. The smell of fresh-cut grass hangs in the thick summer air.

It doesn't look like a single wrinkle imprinted on Nolan's mint green polo or black jeans hugging his lean legs down to his black loafers. I, on the other hand, look like I've slept in this T-shirt for months. My wiry black hair is pulled back into a ponytail but half of it has escaped, dancing in every direction.

"Hey, Son."

Nolan nods at his dad, the epitome of the anti-fashion icon with his salt and pepper hair parted down the middle and feathered back. His brown trousers cinch his indulgent waist-line about two inches too high, the crotch tight and outlining his wee willy. Poor Mrs. Moore.

I shift my gaze to her after I've had an internal snicker over Wee Willy. I stand corrected. She's worse and better at the same time. Her fiery fringe hangs in her eyes like a sheep dog, the rest of her wavy mane is pulled into a high ponytail—really high—like a sprout on the top of her head.

Her crooked lipstick is too orange.

Her pink shirt is too short, revealing the pale skin of her belly.

Her black trousers look capri-length, but I don't actually think they are capris.

The socks? I call them the masterpiece of her outfit. Brill. Just brill. She has fabulously paired white socks with rolled-over red lace edging and Birkenstocks.

What universe is this? Nolan's warning was a gigantic un-derstatement.

However, beneath the layers of her hideous fashion, she's beautiful—petite facial features and a slender frame with a few curves in the right places. A few freckles speckle her nose and

CHAPTER FOUR

My name is Scarlet Stone. I am the smallest kid in the playground. I kick bullies in the balls because they never see me coming. My self-defense skills—zero. My hundred-meter sprint time—thirteen seconds.

NOT EXPLAINING THE bizarre conversation that took place with his parents is not allowed. Yet, it happens. He can't honestly expect me to be satisfied with *unconventional marriage* and they have *a few issues,* as an adequate explanation for what I witnessed.

Nolan doesn't say one word about them during the drive to Tybee. He points out the best places to eat, the oldest buildings, the ghostly history, and the significance of each square—and there are *a lot* of them—but not once does he offer a single word of elaboration for Harold and Nellie Moore.

He doesn't know me. I love mystery and trivia. Horror films are my love stories. Risk is my drug of choice. The purpose of being here, in my place of birth, is to let go of everything I thought I knew about myself—about life—and discover something deeper, a greater meaning. However, this new development, aka the Moores, tempts the hell out of me. My head screams, *I have to know!*

Nolan helps me with my suitcases up to my room, then we return to the kitchen. "The stove is gas therefore the exhaust fan has to run when it's in use. The floors are ripped up because tiling is Theo's next project with the house. The bed has clean sheets and a quilt, but I recommend getting your own sheets if you're a germaphobe."

I'm not a germaphobe—communal underwear being the exception. I'm desperate for him to give me more of an explanation about his parents. He doesn't, and I can't bring myself to ask any more.

"Here's the key. Theo is not here unless he's working or sleeping. He doesn't say much, but he notices everything, and he's an anal-retentive perfectionist when it comes to his job. So you best stay out of his way when he's wearing a tool belt."

I take the key and place it on the worktop.

Nolan nods to the key then jerks his head in the direction of the hooks by the door. "Weird stuff like that will drive Theo crazy."

"Sorry? Like a key … one single key on an otherwise empty worktop?"

Nolan nods. "Your bedroom and bathroom are yours. You can live as messy as you want in those spaces, but the shared spaces such as the kitchen, living room, and garage will need to be kept tidy if you don't want Theo losing his cool."

I laugh. "How do you work with him?" Oh that's right … you were born into crazy. A crazy I'm dying to solve.

"I handle the business part. Theo does all the manual labor. He does his thing. I do mine. That's why we work well together. We've been friends for years, but he's become really withdrawn in his life, so I respect his space."

"He sounds like a lovely bloke."

Nolan shrugs. "He's just quiet and looks a little rough around the edges, but he's a hard worker, pays his rent on time, and makes me a shitload of money because every house he renovates ends up in a bidding war."

Slipping the key onto the hook, I get my first good look around the place, no longer letting Harold and Nellie consume my mind. The dark-stained cupboards and shiny marble worktops look brand new. Beveled-edge, wide, dark trim accent the doorways and floors. It smells like wood in here. I like it.

"Your man—Theo—is good. Did he make the cupboards himself?"

"Yes, ma'am. He has sick talent."

I nod. "Well, I plan to keep to myself for the most part, and if I can remember to hang up my key, then I think Mr. Reed and I shall get along fine."

"Get some sleep. I'll be by tomorrow to see if you need anything."

"Thanks, Nolan."

He waves before closing the door. As I turn to go unpack, I hear Nolan's muffled voice and that of another man's. I inch closer to the back door where a window is cracked open.

"You're never here," Nolan says.

"Well, when I am, I like to be alone. A woman, Nolan? Are you fucking kidding me?"

"Yes, a woman. She's from London, and I think you'll like her. Besides, she's agreed to pay double what you're paying for rent, so play nice."

"I don't need a goddamn woman making a mess around here and smelling the place up."

I lift my arm and drop my chin, taking a whiff. "I don't smell," I whisper to myself.

"Smelling the place up? I didn't pick her up off the street, Theo. I think she practices good hygiene."

"Even worse. That's what I'm talking about. All that girly crap: perfume, shampoo that smells like fruit, lotion that smells like a donkey's ass, and every damn piece of clothing saturated with fabric softener. Candles, crap-smelling oils plugged into every outlet, and incense shit—it all gives me a fucking headache."

Nolan's voice begins to fade. "A thousand bucks, Theo. If you want to pay her part, then I'll evict her tomorrow. If not … she's staying. Get some nose plugs."

"We'll see if she's staying," Theo mutters.

The back door flies open, sparing my life by less than an inch as it nearly squashes me behind it. I can't breathe as part-man, part-beast Theodore Reed stalks into the house. He's ten feet tall and maybe thirty-five stones of solid muscle and anger—at least that's how my five-three, seven-stone self perceives him. My immediate assessment could be a little inflated, but there's no denying he's built like a brick shithouse.

The average hummingbird's heart beats 1,200 times per minute. I'm a humming bird trapped in a corner.

He runs one hand through unkempt, long blond hair. My eyes shift to his other hand, half-expecting to see a hammer, because he looks like Thor. His skin peeks out from scattered rips and holes in the denim wrapping his tree trunk legs. The tattered sweat and dirt-stained rag he wears as a shirt does nothing to hide his thick muscles and inked skin.

Inhaling a deep breath, as if he *smells* me, he turns. I wait for red eyes and six-inch fangs dripping with saliva to greet me before I become his evening snack.

The eyes aren't red. They're blue—just like Thor's.

"Stay out of my stuff and don't make a mess."

Another interesting fact about humming birds: despite their size, they rank as one of the most aggressive species of birds, attacking hawks and crows without hesitation.

"Or what?"

My name is Scarlet Stone. I am the smallest kid in the playground. I kick bullies in the balls because they never see me coming. My self-defense skills—zero. My hundred-meter sprint time—thirteen seconds.

"Don't push me, little girl."

Standing ramrod straight, I tip my chin up. "It's recently come to my attention that I'm paying double the rent you're paying. I'm splitting the house into thirds; each bedroom/bathroom space is a third, and the kitchen and living room together are the final third. You're only paying enough to cover your sleeping and bathing space. So unless you're coming or going, I don't want to see you in my kitchen or living room. Understood?"

"Go to your room." Steely blue eyes narrow into slits, giving a more chilling vibe instead of the warm ocean.

Yet … I love how I feel right now. Nolan is gone. This man could move two steps, snap my neck, and throw me into the Atlantic. That morbid possibility, no matter how remote it is, thrills me. I want time to stop so I can enjoy the rush this fear gives me.

"Sorry?" I laugh, trying to hold back the level of excitement that runs through my veins.

"I think we need to establish the ground rules, which should be easy since there's only one."

Crossing my arms over my chest, I flip my hip out and cock my head to the side. "And what's that?"

"I am the law."

Time stops while we have a stare-off. I blink first, but it's been a long day and I wasn't prepared for this moment. I'm usually quite good at stare offs.

With the concentration of walking a tightrope, I ease past him. In the spirit of not killing my housemate within seconds of meeting him, I decide to go to my room and give him some space to cool his tits.

Until … he has the audacity to let his lip curl into a smirk at the last minute. I redirect my path, stopping at the fridge.

"Don't. Open. It."

"Or what?" I grin and tug on the door.

"Last warning."

Theo must not have gotten the memo on America being the land of the free. Snatching the green apple on the middle shelf, I breathe on it, wipe it against my shirt, then sink my teeth into it.

Before I have a chance to savor the taste, the apple is ripped from my grasp and thrown on the worktop.

"Hey—"

He slams my back into the fridge door, cuffing my wrists in his massive hand while shoving them above my head.

Gasping, I nearly choke on my bite of apple. On my attempt to yell, he plunges his finger in my mouth and digs out the bite of apple.

He did not just do that. He. Did. NOT. JUST. DO. THAT!

"Rape!" I scream.

Theo quirks an eyebrow.

Twelve hundred beats a minute. I can't catch my breath. My eyes dart around the room for something, anything to use as a weapon. He's gone completely mad!

"Put me down!" My plea comes out on a whoosh of air when my stomach connects with his iron shoulder as he lifts me off the ground.

He takes the stairs two at a time. I yank and pull at his hair, still fisting it when he throws me on the bed.

"Rape!"

"I'm not raping you," he grits through his teeth as he pries my hands from his hair.

Like the humming bird, I don't even think before lurching toward him as he strides to the door.

"You cuntpuddle!" I yell as he slams it shut.

The knob won't turn. He's holding it shut. What are we? Seven?

"Let me out!" I yank at the handle.

"Take a nap."

"I'm not a child. You can't send me to my room and tell me to 'take a nap.' Who the bloody hell do you think you are?"

"I told you. I am the law." Every word he speaks is slow and controlled—barely. There's a natural edge to his voice that could slice a person in half.

I don't want to be sliced in half.

I don't want to argue with a madman. Okay, I *shouldn't* want to argue with a madman.

I also shouldn't be grinning like a fool, but I am. Theodore Reed is one fucked-up bugger, and I couldn't be happier.

Sleep. He's right. I'm so knackered. I need a nana nap and a few more chapters of Tolle.

THE NERVES IN my ears rip apart in painful torture with the screeching sound coming from downstairs. Lifting my heavy head from its facedown position on the bed, I blink open my eyes. The analog clock on the bedside table reads: 8:35. Morning or night? I don't know. My brain is not awake. I'm not in London.

I had this crazy nightmare about Thor plunging his troll-sized fingers into my mouth because I took a bite of an apple. Maybe it was biblical, a Garden of Eden thing. I was Eve and

Thor was Adam.

The lining of my stomach feasts on itself. I don't think I've had any food for almost twenty-four hours. It's time to end my fast. Easing open the door, I peek through the crack.

"Shit!" I grimace, covering my ears as the piercing sound of Satan's symphony fills the air again.

Snatching my handbag off the floor, I make my way down-stairs. My ears get a reprieve as it's now quiet again. On his hands and knees, Theo arranges tile on the floor like he's piecing together a puzzle. He looks up, sweat dripping down his face, disappearing into his bronzy beard. It's a shame he feels the need to taint his beautiful face with such a narrow-eyed glare. Behind him, out on the porch, there's a saw. That explains the horrific noise.

"I'm going to a supermarket. I'll replace your apple even though your manners are anything but those of a southern gentleman. What are the chances that you wash your hands after using the bathroom?"

He resumes his puzzle like I'm not here.

"Is there a supermarket or even a green-grocer in walking distance?"

"It closes in fifteen minutes."

Nibbling on the inside of my lip, I nod. It's apparently af-ter 8:30 p.m., not a.m. "Where's the phone? I'll call a taxi."

Plucking the pencil behind his ear, Theo makes a small mark on the tile. "How the hell should I know where you put your phone?" Without looking at me, he stands and walks out back to the saw.

I plug my ears as he makes a cut. "Not my mobile…" I say when he comes back inside "…the house phone."

"What the fuck are you talking about?" He fits the newly

cut piece into its spot.

"You know. The kind that plugs into a phone socket in the wall."

"They don't have cell phones in the land of kings and queens?"

Why does he look at me like I'm the stupid one? If I had a computer I'd drain half of his savings and donate it to the Queen of England's favorite charity to teach the dumb arse a lesson in manners. But I don't have one.

I don't have a mobile.

I don't have a television.

I don't have any access to anywhere but my new little island.

This is my life now. I didn't exactly choose it, but I've chosen what to do with it for the next six months and it doesn't involve electronics.

"You could have said you only have a mobile. I'll pick up a landline phone tomorrow. Can I borrow your mobile to call a taxi?"

"No."

"No? Are you serious?"

Grabbing another tile from the box, he positions it on the floor.

I sigh. "I'm hungry. Is there someplace in walking distance I can get some food?"

Have I really ruined his entire life by being here? How can he be so rude as to not even answer me? He's taking all the fun out of my growing addiction to his madness. There's food in the fridge and probably some in the pantry. I'm not in the mood to explore Tybee Island for the first time, in the dark, by myself. I'll save that adventure for another night when Mr.

Reed isn't here to entertain me. But … I'm so hungry.

Banana.

Three bananas on the worktop call to me. My eyes dart between Mr. Huffy, the bananas, and the stairs. It's possible the apple incident was a rare moment of madness. Maybe he was in an off mood earlier. There really has to be a logical explanation for attacking me the way he did over *an apple.* I should just ask. *Hey, mind if I have one of those bananas? I'll replace it tomorrow.*

If I ask and he says no, then what?

The struggle is real.

I'm only two books into my library of "fifty inspirational books everyone should read before they die," so I have yet to master the skill of peaceful coexistence.

Ask.

If he says no, go to bed.

You won't starve, Scarlet.

Theo glances up at me for a brief second as he lines up the tile on the saw. It's like he can read my thoughts. I already feel the stomach-wrenching "NO" ready to bark from his mouth.

He flips down his safety glasses and turns on the saw. The noise and his deep concentration on the blade spinning toward the tile is my chance. I seize it. Slow at first, I creep toward the worktop, watching him the whole time. The second the banana is secure in my hand, the noise evaporates.

Theo looks up, pinning me with a scowl.

Gulp.

"Run, Forest!" rings in my mind. That's exactly what I do, not wasting even a backwards glance to see if he's chasing me. It's a stupid banana. Why would he?

"Ahhh!" I scream. My heart catapults into my throat as a

strong hand shackles around my ankle. The banana tumbles toward my bedroom door as I fall forward on the landing.

Theo is the killer. I'm the innocent victim. The banana is the gun. Flailing and kicking, I wriggle from his hold on my leg, sacrificing one of my shoes.

Banana.

Door.

Slam it shut.

Lock it.

With my bum on the floor, back against the door, knees to my chest, and breathless—I peel the banana. I should be freaked out. The man is possessive of his fruit but as he jiggles the doorknob, all I can do is grin. I feel *alive*. That might classify me as my own breed of crazy.

"Don't come out—ever," he grumbles.

CHAPTER FIVE

My name is Scarlet Stone and the reasoning behind most everything I do is—because I can.

THE SUN.

After a long night of fighting sleep, reading, and fighting more sleep, I shower then throw open the curtains.

"Well ... shit." I laugh at the ridiculousness of yesterday's charade with Thor—Theo.

The curtains don't cover windows; they cover French doors leading to a small, private balcony and *stairs*. He 'locked' me in a room with another exit. The white noise of rolling tides in the distance greets me as I step out onto the deck and ease into the sun lounger with a faded-red seat cushion and a small round table next to it. A thin layer of sand and salt is caked to the top of it.

"Well done, Nolan," I whisper. This place is exactly what I need.

Here I can just *be*. At least that's what Echart Tolle and Wayne Dyer have been inspiring me to do. Everyone should stop their forward momentum long enough to contemplate the words of these great spiritual teachers. It really doesn't matter where we're going—it's about where we are. I hope here, on this deck or somewhere along the miles of sand emerging from the ocean, I'll find clarity, acceptance, and ... peace.

Too bad Zen wasn't an "in" thing years ago when my dad presented me with long lists of jobs. *Sorry, Oscar ... this is my meditation day. I'll be busy all day nurturing my spiritual health ... in a chair ... by the pool.* We didn't have a pool, except in my dreams.

If everyone spent more time doing that, I believe we could achieve world peace.

However, contemplating life is not an easy task. For me, it's overwhelming right now. It feels like a game that I don't know how to play. Is it all luck? Does skill mean anything? What are the rules? And what happens when it's over? I close my eyes and let those thoughts play in my head while seagulls cry in the distance.

"Scarlet Stone?"

I open my eyes and sit up. "Yes?"

The little, old Asian man at the top of the deck stairs, wearing baggy linen trousers, a matching frock-type shirt, and black Tom's sandals, presses his palms together at his heart and bows. "Good morning."

"Sorry, uh ..." I share, at best, an awkward smile. There's an uninvited stranger on my deck. That's ... *strange*. I knew only one of my neighbors in London.

One.

And we only talked on rare occasions and only about the weather.

I'm short, but this man is definitely shorter—five feet max. "So, uh ... sorry, how do you know my name?"

"Nolan."

I nod.

"You come for breakfast. Yes?"

"Uh ..." It's food. Why is my brain hesitating? "Do you live close by?"

He nods and points to the small, pale yellow house over the grassy dune, maybe a hundred meters away.

I look down at my white satin dressing gown. "Give me

five minutes?"

A nod and another bow as I stand.

I slip on a long, white T-shirt that used to be Daniel's, over my rainbow-striped bikini, then shove my feet into my flip-flops.

"I'm at a disadvantage," I say, slipping on my sunglasses. "I don't know your name."

"Yimin." He moves his hand toward my face.

I pull back a fraction.

"May I?"

After a few seconds, I return a slow nod. Yimin eases off my sunglasses.

"Eyes need a little sun too."

"O—K."

He nods once and walks down the stairs. I follow. I've been in Savannah for twenty-four hours, and I've experienced weirder—as in complete mad—moments than I have the previous thirty-one years of my life combined: Nolan's parents, Theo the angry giant, and now the little Asian man leading me to breakfast. People who live in the U.S. demonstrate more peculiar behavior than I'd imagined.

Yimin slips off his shoes. Then he wipes his feet on a grass mat before opening a warped screen door that resists his first attempt. I kick off my flip-flops and brush the sand from my feet before stepping inside.

"Please. Sit." He nods to the table by the window with only two wooden chairs: one painted red, the other gold.

"The red one."

I pause before my bum hits the seat to the gold chair.

"Drink tea."

I can do this. I like tea.

After moving to the red chair, I wrap my hand around the teacup. It can't be more than a hundred milliliters and there's no steam rising from the surface. I bring it to my nose. It smells pungent. Maybe I don't like tea after all.

"Drink." From the worktop, he glances over his shoulder with a warm smile and easy nod. He's quite commanding with his nods.

What if he's poisoning me? Does it matter? No.

"Oh … wow." I try to suppress my gag reflex, which is odd because I've never had much of one until this tea coated my throat. He's making me drink his diarrhea. That's the only explanation for what's in the cup. "What is this?"

"Herbs. Mushrooms."

The soft hum of a motor sounds, followed by deeper grinding sounds. Straining my neck, I catch a glimpse of him shoving carrots into a juicer. After a minute or so, he turns it off and glances back over his shoulder.

"Finish tea?"

My nose scrunches. "Not yet."

"Finish."

I imagined bacon and eggs, maybe fresh squeezed orange juice, tea with sugar. But this? This is torture. My stomach will not approve of this liquid waste. However, for reasons I can't understand, I finish the tea with one big gulp.

Don't gag!

"Good." He hands me a tall glass of carrot juice.

I've never had plain carrot juice, but anything—an-y-thing—is better than that tea.

"Slowly."

I cease my gulping.

"Chew it."

I frown. What does that mean? Chew the juice?

Yimin takes a sip of his drink and swishes it a bit then swallows. "Chewing. Assimilating. Digestion starts in your mouth."

"Are you a doctor?"

He shakes his head. I *chew* my juice.

"What do you do?" I ask.

"I live."

"I live" is not an answer, until I think about it. Maybe it's the perfect answer.

"I guess it's better than the alternative." I shrug.

Yimin eyes me, and he then nods slowly. "Mr. Moore should not have let you stay with Mr. Reed. He carries a negative energy. It's not good for you."

I laugh. Negative energy from Theodore Reed? Why ever would anyone think that? "No need to worry about it. I don't think his negative energy will kill me."

It's impossible to escape Yimin's gaze. His look makes me feel like he knows more about me than I do. *Is* Theo's negative energy going to kill me? Or just his bare hands wrapped around my neck?

"Do you think he's dangerous?"

Yimin nods.

Well, shit! I didn't expect that. In spite of the Nellie and Harold incident, I trusted Nolan to not put me in danger. Clearly my circumstance in life has affected my judgment and all instinct for self-preservation.

"Do you know why he's dangerous?"

"He doesn't value life."

I perk an eyebrow. "His own or anyone's?"

Yimin nods. I assume that means all of the above.

"Why do you say that?"

"A feeling."

After a few seconds of attempting to get my own "feeling" about Yimin's intuition, I narrow my eyes and lean forward. "How well do you know Nolan? Have you met his parents?"

"I know them very well. Nolan is special. He has a heightened awareness."

"Yes. He told me. Do you believe it?"

Yimin slides my carrot juice closer to me. I take the hint and chew another swig.

"I do," he replies.

My conscience shakes off the uneasy feeling and the whole weird vibe that lingers around us. "Tell me about his parents."

"The Moores have been through a lot."

"You don't say." I bite my lips together. That thought wasn't meant for actual words.

Yimin's brow draws tight, slaying the curiosity beast inside of me. I stand. I've overstepped a boundary, and now I feel uncomfortable.

"Thank you for the tea and juice." Really just the juice. "I have a few jobs to do."

"Again, tomorrow."

"Oh, well ..." My objection is weak because I don't have any other plans for tomorrow or any day after that.

"Here." He moves past me to the kitchen and retrieves a mason jar from the cupboard, and then he pours the rest of the carrot juice into it. "Drink today."

"All of it?" My eyes widen a fraction at the filled liter jar.

"Yes."

"Uh ... okay, thank you." I take the juice. Changing my diet is on my life-changing to-do list. I didn't see it starting with a juice cleanse—especially since I'm so hungry.

"Tomorrow." Yimin calls as a dusting of sand from the wooden walkway clings to my feet while I make my way to the beach.

"Tomorrow."

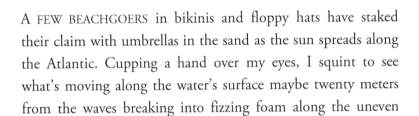

A FEW BEACHGOERS in bikinis and floppy hats have staked their claim with umbrellas in the sand as the sun spreads along the Atlantic. Cupping a hand over my eyes, I squint to see what's moving along the water's surface maybe twenty meters from the waves breaking into fizzing foam along the uneven shoreline.

At first I think it's a dolphin or shark, but as the figure nears the shallow waters, it morphs into a human figure, like I'm witnessing a modern-day evolution.

It's not. As the creature stands erect, fighting the last few waves, I notice he's wearing trunks. He's been human for a while. I gawk at his tight, black briefs that hide nothing. Who the hell swims that far out in the ocean in the early morning during prime shark-feeding time?

Long hair slicked back.

Tattoos.

Thor's body.

Bloody hell! It's Theodore Reed. Yimin was right—he has no regard for life.

A young woman runs up to him, boobs bouncing with each step. I sprint toward the house, hoping she distracts him long enough for me to grab my handbag and get out of sight before he makes it the rest of the way up the beach.

I run up the deck stairs to my balcony two at a time, shimmy into a pair of denim shorts, grab my handbag, and hustle down to the kitchen to deposit the carrot juice in the fridge.

Unbelievable. I laugh, quite possibly harder than I've laughed in a long time. There is a chain and padlock on the fridge doors.

My name is Scarlet Stone and the reasoning behind most everything I do is—because I can. My grandfather died in prison, but not before he robbed five of the highest security banks in Germany and the UK, only to prove they were not truly 'secure.' My father is the great Oscar Stone who could steal the crown from the Queen—while she was wearing it—without anyone knowing for days. If Theodore Reed thinks his hardware shop padlock is going to keep me out of the fridge, he's sorely mistaken.

Forty-five seconds.

The first twenty I spend digging through my handbag. Picking the lock swallows the last twenty-five. I'm not as fast as I used to be when my father drilled me over and over. I wasn't a traditional thief, much to his displeasure. I chose the gray-hat hacker lifestyle. Now I'm a woman in need of refrigeration for her carrot juice.

"Shit!" I grimace when my face is shoved against the fridge, wet flesh pressed to my back.

"You just don't get it. One rule. You can't follow one rule."

"Am I interrupting?" Nolan's voice fills the air like a whisper from God.

My lungs search for breath as Theo releases me. I whip around. Nolan's amused smile greets me, but it's the death look from Theo that holds my attention.

"She's a thief. You invited a fucking thief to live in my house."

Clearly, the humor is lost on both of them. I am a thief. *Was* a thief.

"Really?" I cough out a laugh. "A banana? Are you going to call the police to whisk me off to jail because I took one of your bananas?"

"And an apple." He gives me his signature slit-eyed glare.

I wet my lips and nod, taking a quick glance down at the rest of Theodore. Dear god, he's a wall of muscle and ink. "One bite. And you retrieved it by finger-raping my mouth. So technically, I don't owe you an apple."

Nolan's eyebrows lift and his lips twist into a cheeky grin like he's watching a comedy sketch.

I sigh, taking a moment to channel some inner peace. Theo and his overprotectiveness of his food doesn't matter. "But in the spirit of housemates, I'll replace both the banana and apple. In fact, I was getting ready to go to the supermarket, but I needed to put *my* carrot juice in the fridge."

"Theo, man … why is there a padlock on the refrigerator?"

"Where's your juice?" Theo ignores Nolan, keeping his attention solely on me. Lucky me.

I tip my chin up. "In the *shared* fridge."

"How did you get in there?"

"Nice Speedo." I wink at Theo as I brush by him. Nolan's presence gives me a jolt of confidence that I have no doubt I will regret upon my return. "So an apple and a banana? Anything else I can get for you while I'm out, Mr. Reed?"

Theo mutters something before sulking off to his room.

"I see you two are getting along well."

"Sorry?" It takes great strength to keep my control. "I'm paying double the rent as Mr. I Am The Law. He is completely bonkers." I resist the "then again, so are your parents" remark.

"I've been locked in my room. Twice. And there's a padlock on the fridge. But yeah, we're getting along wonderfully. Thanks for asking."

"Carrot juice? I take it you saw Yimin this morning."

"I … did."

Nolan doesn't give anything away in his expression, much like he didn't yesterday with his parents. "That's good. You need a ride?"

"I do."

"You can set up grocery delivery here. Did you know that?" Nolan holds open the door.

"Really?" Perfect. I was considering a bike, but now I have no reason to go anywhere my legs can't take me, which leaves me more time here with Theo. I might have to rethink my mode of transportation.

CHAPTER SIX

My name is Scarlet Stone and one day I will harness the power to read minds.

OVER SEVEN BILLION people live on Earth, over seven different continents separated by the seven seas under a rainbow of seven colors. There's a belief, most likely a myth, that the average person has 70,000 thoughts a day in a seven day week. Six shouldn't be my number. It should be seven. What if I need an extra month? Will I be broke and homeless?

It's possible my thoughts exceed 70,000 a day. If I read a book, do those thoughts count as my own? Maybe I'm obsessing over seven today because this is my seventh day on Tybee Island. I haven't left the house or beach behind it—except to have tea and juice *every* morning with Yimin—since Nolan took me to the supermarket where I set up weekly delivery.

"There's fresh-pressed juice in the fridge, more than I'll drink today. Help yourself."

Theo ignores me as he has since I made the Speedo comment. I think Nolan must have said something to him because I haven't been put on the naughty step since the banana incident. I also haven't heard him breathe a word in my direction.

It still astounds me that there was ever a *banana* or *apple incident* at all. Any other person in their right mind would have bailed way before now. The man physically attacked me. I'm adventurous and daring. I like risk, but I've never considered myself crazy—until now.

Eyeing the white towel around his waist, I wonder if he's wearing anything beneath it. The view inside the house is almost as breathtaking as the one outside. I should feel some sort of guilt for having that thought, but Daniel still consumes half of my 70,000 daily thoughts, so I think it's fine to have one or two about Theodore Reed. The enigma standing at the hob, breaking eggs into a pan, feeds my curiosity more than anything or anyone ever has. That's saying a lot given my background.

Seventy thousand thoughts.

I'd give my right boob to have a five-second glimpse into his mind.

My name is Scarlet Stone and one day I will harness the power to read minds.

"Chicken or the egg?" I put my book facedown on the table and pop a blackberry into my mouth as the smell of sizzling oil and eggs fills the air. "I suppose it depends on if you believe in evolution or creation. I can see both sides. I'm inclined to say chicken. I like the idea of there being something after this life—Heaven, reincarnation. I don't know. Something." Listen to me rabbit on. I'm fitting in quite well here.

The muscles along his back make subtle shifts as he scrambles the eggs. How can a man who says nothing be so damn distracting?

"I bet you're a Buddhist," I continue. "I'm working on finding peace in the midst of silence, listening to what the universe is trying to say to me. It's hard, you know? I think we're social creatures by nature. The average person uses five thousand words in their speech and over double that when writing. Seems like a waste of brain capacity if we're meant to spend so much of our life in meditation, trying to silence the voices in our head."

Theo riffles through the cupboard of spices.

"Are you looking for the salt?"

He whips his head around. Salt? So that's what it takes to get his attention. Duly noted.

"The one with the blue lid. Use that. You had non-iodized table salt. Not good. Sea salt is the way to go." Within my library of inspirational books, I have a few on proper nutrition as well. Knowledge is addictive.

"Why are you here?" Theo's voice is rough with each uneven word, like he hasn't spoken in days.

"Why are any of us here?"

His eyes narrow.

My lips twist to keep from smiling. My curiosity exceeds the average human's. I've been told as much for years. Amongst my desire to figure out what my purpose has been in life, or continues to be, I can't control my need to solve the mystery of Theodore Reed.

"Sorry. I've been immersing myself in these inspirational books and daily meditation. My brain is stuck in a philosophical state. You want to know why I'm here, in this house, with you. Correct?"

Theo's word frugality is quite commendable. I begin to feel a little envious of that trait as the weight of his stare bears down with each passing second.

"I'm a thief. *Was* a thief."

I didn't think his stony face could harden anymore, but it does.

I roll my eyes. "Not apples and bananas, so enough with the look. My dad was a thief and so was his dad. We've all officially retired—my grandfather to the grave, my dad to a prison cell."

Theo returns his attention to the frying pan.

"I decided to spend my retirement here since this is where I was born. Well ... in Savannah."

He sits across from me. I can't believe it. It's the first time he's stayed in the kitchen to eat. He usually takes his food to the private balcony outside of his bedroom that overlooks the beach. When he's out there, I give him twenty minutes before going out to my private balcony, adjacent to his. As soon as I sit in my sun lounger, he goes back inside.

"You're a strong swimmer."

His chin stays tucked to his chest as he shovels in his eggs.

"It wouldn't kill you to answer me."

He looks up, fork paused a few inches from his mouth. "Was there a question in all your incessant talking?"

"I said you're a strong swimmer."

"That's not a question."

"Fine. It's a compliment. You should say 'thank you' or 'thank you, ma'am,' isn't that correct?"

The corner of his mouth twitches, not a smile, more like he's ready to bare his fangs again. "Yes. Ma'am is used out of respect."

"But you don't respect me?"

"No."

"Because I stole your fruit?"

"Yes."

Unbelievable.

"Well, I wouldn't have a problem calling you 'sir' even though you finger-raped my mouth."

"I didn't finger-rape your mouth. If you'd like me to show you what it feels like to have your mouth *finger-raped,* then I'd be much obliged, but I'd rather stick a sock in it and cover it with duct tape."

Wow! Why am I still here? Crazy is not a strong enough word—for either of us.

He glances over his shoulder when there's a knock at the door.

"That's for me." I smile while standing from my chair, shuffling across the partially-tiled floor in my flip-flops.

"Ms. Stone?"

I nod with a huge grin.

"Where would you like them?"

"Uh …" I look back at Theo, but he's resumed eating his breakfast again like I don't exist. "If you wouldn't mind taking them to the front room for now, I'll put them where I want them later. Thank you."

"Yes, ma'am." The deliveryman carries in the first plant— one of seventeen that I ordered.

Theo gives him a quick glance, but he doesn't say a word until the fifth plant is ushered past him to the front room.

"What the fuck is going on?"

"Oh, um …" The deliveryman looks back at me as I continue to hold open the door.

Theo follows his gaze.

"Did you order all of these?" Theo pins me with his usual scowl.

"Yes, sir." I wink. "He has twelve more to bring inside."

The deliveryman jumps when Theo's fork clanks against his plate two seconds before his chair screeches along the floor as he unfolds all, seemingly, ten feet of himself.

I don't blink. Not even as *the law* approaches me. He can't murder me with a witness in the room. What if his towel fell from his waist? Something tells me he wouldn't move. Why the hell did that thought go through my mind? If he takes one more step, I'll be nothing more than something he flicks off the bottom of his giant foot.

"Listen, woman, this isn't your house. You will not fill it with a bunch of fucking flowers."

After I'm convinced his towel is secure, my eyes retrace their path back to his. The name Kathryn is tattooed in elegant script along his bicep, under a gray gravestone with a single red rose across it. I'm going to assume Kathryn died.

"Scarlet."

"What?" His face contorts with irritation.

"My name … it's Scarlet, not woman. We've lived together for a week and you've never asked my name. Our opportunities for a proper introduction have been squashed by your …"

His eyes widen a fraction. "My?"

I shrug. "Your barmy attitude, like you've lost the plot."

"Lost the plot?"

My attempt to hide my exasperation is rubbish. A deep sigh breezes past my lips. "Yes, like … you've been acting ridiculously."

He gets in my face, really in my face. "Every word that comes out of your mouth drives me fucking crazy, but not as fucking crazy as the way you say everything."

"Sorry? How do I say everything?"

"Like you think you're the fucking Queen!"

"I'm not the Queen. I'm just British."

"Then just don't speak."

"Please ignore Mr. Prick and bring in the rest of my plants." I duck out of Theo's visual hold on me.

The deliveryman moves in slow motion, keeping his wide

eyes on Theo the whole time. "Y-yes, ma'am."

The second we're alone, I feel the shadow of Theo's foot getting ready to squash me. I should run. But … fuck him. For the next six months this *is* my house.

"I'm sorry Kathryn died."

He steps forward so fast, I stumble backwards. The wall saves me from falling onto my bum.

"If you ever say her name again, I will end you."

My heart takes up permanent residency in my throat. I bet he can see it pulsing in my neck. Once I manage to find a sliver of space to speak past it, I whisper, "Sorry, I'm afraid there's a queue."

I blink for the first time since he backed me into the wall. His eyebrows pull tight, like my response somehow confuses or pains him. It can't be pain. Monsters don't feel pain.

As the deliveryman brings in the rest of my plants, Theo and I stand toe to toe, sharing thick, tension-filled air. Why is he so sad? Because that's what he is. Beneath the brute anger, jagged words, and threats, Theodore Reed is a sad man. What does he see when he looks into my eyes? I can't find myself. I no longer see my own reflection in the mirror. It's unimaginable that he sees anything beyond my dark skin and unruly hair.

All I see before me is a ridged man with a hardened soul and symbols of his grief etched along his skin in bold ink. My dad never inked himself, but he used to say that people tattooed their skin so the rest of the world could see their hopes and dreams, their fears, their past, their grief.

There's not enough skin on my body to let my emotions bleed through for the world to see. I'm a bit envious of everyone who can do that.

"Thank you, ma'am. Have a nice day."

The trance is broken. Theo steps back, his eyes averting to the floor for a brief moment before he turns and disappears to his room.

"Thank you," I reply in a shaky voice that mirrors the way my body feels after yet another indescribable encounter with Theodore Reed.

When the back door clicks shut, I close my eyes, a breath of a whisper desperate to release. "Oh. My. God." Seven billion people over seven continents and I land on the other side of the ocean in this house with this man. My life may very well end in the presence of the beast of a man who seems to truly hate me.

Why? It would seem, simply because I exist.

CHAPTER SEVEN

THEODORE

ANOTHER DAY CLOSER to the end. I make an X on my calendar, and then I stare at the photos and news clippings.

Scarlet.

There is a reason I didn't ask her name. It doesn't matter. She doesn't matter. I don't want to see her. Hear her. Smell her. How could Nolan be such an asshole to let her move in after everything I've done for him?

What is her purpose anyway? All she does is go to the crazy guy's house for breakfast, take long walks on the beach, lounge on the deck reading books, pray the world's longest prayer with her nonexistent ass perched on a pillow, eyes closed. It's probably some meditation shit. But it's the things she says that drives me to want to kill something or someone—stupid fucking shit that makes no sense. *"Sorry, there's a queue."* What the fuck does that mean?

Wash. Rinse. Repeat.

No job. No real purpose except to piss me off. I should snap her twig body in two and send her to the bottom of the ocean. Clearly she has no one. No one to miss her. No one to suspect anything.

"What the fuck are you thinking?" I mumble, pressing my palms to my forehead. I don't want to hate her. The truth is I don't want to have any emotion toward her at all. Emotion is a luxury I gave up years ago. I exist for one purpose and one purpose only: revenge.

There's a knock at my bedroom door. Great. Can't she leave me the hell alone? I open the door with enough anger to make the hinges scream in protest. One of her fucking plants is on the ground with a note attached to it.

Theo –

Peace Lilies are one of the few houseplants that bloom. I ordered three. This one is the best. I named her Phoebe. She will remove VOCs, benzene, and formaldehyde from the air. She doesn't need that much light, but she loves water. Phoebe is my peace offering to you. Don't eat her leaves, they are poisonous.

There's still juice downstairs. Help yourself. What's mine is yours. "Things" don't really matter to me. I'm only here for now.

~Scarlet Stone

I tear up the note and slap the pieces onto my dresser, then I grab the plant and deposit it in front of her bedroom door at the opposite end of the hall.

Big brown eyes greet me as I turn. They shift from me to the plant. She doesn't say anything, only nods once, lips set in a firm line. I open my mouth to tell her why I don't want the stupid peace offering, but I clamp it shut, choosing to not say anything while walking back to my room to get ready for work. She's already wasted half of my morning.

CHAPTER EIGHT

My name is Scarlet Stone. I was offered useful traits the day I entered this world. I passed on common sense, opting for the-edge-of-a-knife journey.

SCARLET

SEVEN WEEKS.
I've gone seven weeks without saying a word to Theo. I'm not sure why I thought we could be friends. When he returned my peace offering without a word, I knew he was not what I needed in my life. His rejection doesn't quell my curiosity but within the pages of my inspirational books, I find ways to at least silence the voice of it.

There's a monotony to my days, and I've come to find comfort in it. Mornings start with an hour of meditation. When I first began meditating, I lasted maybe ten minutes. Now I find peace in nourishing my mind, focusing on the part of myself that is so much greater than my physical body. We are so much more than the sum of our parts. For that hour I don't see pain and suffering. I see joy and happiness for not only myself, but all life. Wayne Dyer said, "When you change the way you look at things, the things you look at change."

I don't think Wayne ever met Theodore Reed.

Nevertheless, the things I look at are changing. With each passing day, I feel less physical suffering and less emotional anxiety. I'm intrigued by the words I read. At university, I thought I knew everything. My grades were perfect. The world was mine, and I thought I had it all figured out.

Now, I question if I truly *know* anything. The assumption

that a good education equates to intelligence is not necessarily true. A lot of highly-educated people have been told what to think, therefore, they think they know it all. The other segment of the population has to figure out how to think, therefore they question everything.

"You're better—focused. Finding peace," Yimin says as I finish my tea that now goes down without any gag reflex, not even a slight grimace of disgust.

"You think I'm in pain, like Nolan. That's why you give me this tea and juice every day?"

"I think you're navigating a difficult journey. Must nourish body on difficult journey."

"Why do you think I'm in pain? Why do you think I'm on a difficult journey?"

Yimin sips his own tea. "Doesn't matter. I see you in a better place. That's all that matters. The mind is very powerful and so are words."

"Yeah, well, I think my skin is orange."

He laughs.

"I'm serious. Two liters of carrot juice a day for almost two months. I haven't worn my glasses or contacts in weeks. I don't need them."

He nods. Nothing seems to surprise or shock Yimin. His belief in the unimaginable, the unbelievable—miracles—is something I envy.

"Do you think it's working?" I ask. "*Hypothetically*, if I were in pain, do you think it's working?"

I used to shy away from his gaze. Not anymore. He says so much to me without saying an actual word and when he does speak, it's usually very few words with cryptic meaning that I've become quite good at deciphering.

"Does it matter?"

Wow. That's a heartbreaking question. I've come a long way over the past seven weeks, but … am I ready to answer that question? Does my physical existence matter? Tears burn my eyes as the mental truth collides with the very real physical emotions I still possess.

"Don't be afraid." He rests his hand on mine.

The waves dive into the shore, holding back nothing, submitting to their fate. I envy them too. My lips roll between my teeth. I believe fear drives everyone—fear of suffering, fear of pain, fear of the unknown. At the very core of humanity is an innate intelligence that makes us work for shelter, steal for food, kill for that last breath. I'm not sure I can rise above that fear … at least not in this lifetime.

"Afraid of what?" I ask.

"Life."

I nod.

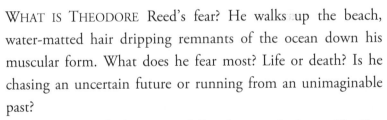

WHAT IS THEODORE Reed's fear? He walks up the beach, water-matted hair dripping remnants of the ocean down his muscular form. What does he fear most? Life or death? Is he chasing an uncertain future or running from an unimaginable past?

Keeping a safe distance, I follow him to the house like I've done for the past seven weeks. Theo swims with the sharks every morning while I have breakfast with Yimin. He goes to work for Nolan, remodeling homes, while I read, enjoy long walks down the beach, and water my plants that now number twenty-seven. Maybe I need more oxygen to breathe than I ever did before. Maybe I don't feel as lonely with so much life around me. This life—coexisting with someone who won't even look at me on the few occasions we sit and eat at the same table—it's lonely. I'd feel less lonely if I were actually alone.

I miss Oscar. I miss Daniel. I miss London. But more than anything ... I miss the touch of love: a gentle hand wrapped around mine, an embrace to hold me together on the days I feel like I'm falling apart, lips ghosting along my skin, a whisper of forever, a smile signifying my presence makes another human feel happy.

Human. That's it. I miss all the things that define the best part of humanity. I don't want my biggest regret to be wasted time.

Today I make a detour from my routine and clean every inch of the house until Theo's handiwork looks its best. Then I cook dinner for two, complete with candles and music from a radio. He actually has a plug-in radio. As I start to descend the stairs after a shower, wearing my hair down in long, ironed-straight black strands, and a touch of lip gloss, I hear a woman's voice.

A curly-haired brunette, bubbling over with giggles like she's had too much to drink, gawks at me with her hand over her mouth as I stop at the threshold to the kitchen. "Oh, my god, Theo! You had your maid make us a candlelit dinner!" She hugs his chest still clad in his tattered gray work tee.

Maid? Really?

Theo inspects me with unnerving thoroughness, dragging his hawkish gaze down my body dressed in my nicest pair of white shorts, a black halter top, and flip-flops with silver rhinestones. I even painted my toenails a deep chardonnay.

"It's not for—" His eyes meet mine.

"It is." I smile. "It's for the both of you. It's all keeping warm in the oven. There's salad in the fridge and a bottle of wine chilling as well. Enjoy." I turn and navigate the stairs slowly, evenly, not giving away anything.

"Sit. I need to take a quick shower," he says to her.

I pick up my pace, feeling him closing in on me.

"Why?" he asks before I close my bedroom door.

I turn, but words escape me.

"Another peace offering?" He says it with such disgust.

I flinch as his tone delivers each word like a smack across my face.

"I…" I shake my head "…I thought we could be human for one night."

"Human?"

I nod, focusing on the floor between us, feeling foolish. A nervous smile trembles along my lips. "Food. Small talk. Maybe I say something that makes you grin. Maybe you say something that makes me giggle. Maybe the food is crap, so we drink too much wine. Maybe the full moon beckons us to the beach where we walk in the shadows of the night. Maybe you tell me something about yourself. Maybe it's a lie, and maybe that's okay because we're both going our separate ways in four months. But maybe … just maybe for one night we feel *human*."

He blinks several times. "I didn't bring her here for dinner."

I laugh a little, still focused on the old, scratched-up wood floor between us. "You brought her here to sleep with her."

"Not sleep."

My laugh grows even more. This could not be more awkward. "Of course not." I clear my throat. "Well, she seems pretty excited about dinner, so you really should feed her before you …" Risking a glance up, my nose wrinkles. "*Not* sleep with her. I'll leave and give you some privacy." I turn and shut my door, drawing in a shaky breath. "Scarlet," I whisper, "what are you doing?"

∾

BOISTEROUS LAUGHTER, CLINKING of glass bottles, and friendly smiles surround me at the pub down from the pier. I should have checked out the Friday-night scene on Tybee way before now.

"What can I get ya, hun?" the older lady with leathered skin asks as she slides a white cocktail napkin in front of me.

"Wine."

She laughs. "What kind?"

I shrug. "Doesn't matter, just something red."

"You got it."

I haven't had a drop of alcohol in months. Tonight, I'll have a few sips to ease the disappointment of my stolen dinner. Okay, I gave it away, but I had no other choice. We hadn't talked in seven weeks. Theo had absolutely no reason to think he'd come home to a candlelit dinner with the woman who he unequivocally despises for reasons I have yet to understand.

"This seat taken?" Glassy hazel eyes look at me.

A handsome bloke with messy brown hair, who is clearly a little over-served, wants to sit by me. A hundred red flags pop up in my head. It's a really bad idea.

"No. Have a seat."

My name is Scarlet Stone. I was offered useful traits the day I entered this world. I passed on common sense, opting for the-edge-of-a-knife journey. When I die, I want my gravestone to have the word 'epic' on it somewhere.

Epic thief.

Epic daughter.

Epic adventurer.

Epic risk-taker.

Somehow I don't think the word epic can be placed before the words beach dweller or meditator.

"Your accent…" he grins and signals to the bartender "…it's British."

I smile when she puts my wine down. "It is." The red liquid burns my tongue a bit before it slides down my throat, dry and spicy. I used to like wine. Now I fear Yimin's juice and pungent teas have ruined that for me. It should be a good thing, but right now I need a buzz.

"I'm Rowan."

"Mmm …" I rub my lips together. The alcohol immediately enters my bloodstream since I missed dinner. "I like that name. I'm Scarlet."

Rowan takes a swig of his beer. Sure, he's drunk and soon, I will be too. But I haven't seen muscles fill out a shirt so perfectly since the day I met Theodore Reed, and everything about the place my mind goes right now seems really wrong. That's what makes turning toward him so my leg rests against his seem so right. I'm due for an *epic* mistake.

His eyes shift to my bare leg for a prolonged second as a smile grows behind the neck of the amber bottle paused at his lips. "Well, I like the name Scarlet, but not nearly as much as I like the way you say it."

"And how do I say it?"

"Gah!" he says with exasperation as he presses his beer to his chest, head thrown back. "Just like that. Don't stop talking. I could listen to you forever."

I laugh, a real, honest, spontaneous laugh that feels so damn good. "My housemate doesn't agree."

"Well, she's crazy."

My head shakes as I swallow my sip of wine. "*He.* My housemate is a bloke."

"Boyfriend?"

"Hahaha! No. He seems pretty angry that I'm using up some of the oxygen on Earth."

"He's a prick, then."

Sucking in a breath, I prepare to agree with him but at the last moment this foreign emotion prevents my words from forming.

Protective.

I feel protective of Theo. He is a prick and so much worse, but I don't like Rowan saying it.

"He's … troubled. But he's also so amazing. You should see him work. He's a carpenter, and everything he touches turns into the most beautiful creation." I take another drink of wine then my finger traces the rim of the glass. "Sometimes I watch him when he doesn't know I'm watching him. He's an artist. I love how his hands skim over a newly-sanded piece of wood, the subtle nod he gives himself when he's satisfied with something he's done, or the way he sits back on his heels while kneeling on the floor, worrying his upper lip between his teeth while he contemplates his next move."

Rowan puts his empty bottle down and grabs my legs, scooting my stool closer to his, so his legs cage my knees. "So he's a talented prick, but if he doesn't treat you well…" he leans forward until his lips brush my ear "…then he's still a prick."

I shake my head, intensifying the heavy fog seeping into my

brain from one glass of wine. "He's just … he's …" I continue to shake my head as I pull away and drop some money on the bar. "I have to go. It was nice to meet you."

"Wait." Rowan pays for his drink and follows me out of the bar. "Where are you going?"

"My house." I continue to make my way to the beach.

"Scarlet, I thought we had a connection."

His hand clasps my arm, stopping my momentum.

Run, Scarlet!

"Please don't."

"I'm not going to hurt you. I just want to talk."

My narrowed eyes attempt to focus on his hand still gripping my arm. Now who's the prick? "If you're not going to hurt me then why are you gripping my arm so tightly?"

He chuckles. "Sorry. If I let go, promise not to run?"

My heart screams, "Giddy-up!" Adrenaline dances in my veins.

"If you don't let her go, some early morning jogger will find the remnants of your dead body washed up on the beach after I bloody you up and feed your pathetic fucking ass to the sharks."

Theodore.

I don't have to look back to know that my housemate must look quite intimidating because Rowan releases me and stumbles backwards like he can't get out of here fast enough.

"Three … two …" Theo's voice jabs through the air.

"Dude, I'm going." Rowan turns and runs back toward the pub, tripping a few more times before clearing the sand.

"Thank you—" I turn, but Theodore is already a tall figure in the distance. I chase after him. "Stop!"

He doesn't.

I hop on one foot and then the other, pulling off my flip-flops, then I continue to close the distance between us. "Thank you."

Theo keeps walking as I try to match his long strides, my winded breath louder than the waves along the dark shore.

"You stubborn arse! Did you hear me? If you hate me so much, then why save me back there?"

"Go to bed," he says as we walk into the house.

My eyes shoot daggers as he continues to the stairs without even looking at me. I blame the wine or maybe the lack of food, but before my mind fully registers what I'm doing, one of my flip-flops connects with the back of his head.

He stops, turning ever so slowly.

I shake my head. "Don't look at me like that. I don't care how fucked-up you are. I'm not a child you can order around. Why were you on the beach? Were you following me? Why save me? Is it because you think I'm *your* toy and no other man except you is allowed to manhandle me? Well, I have news for you, Theodore Reed, I am not your—"

CHAPTER NINE

THEODORE

I'M FED UP with this woman running her mouth.

Seven weeks.

I had seven weeks of quietude, but now she's back to irritating the living hell out of me, distorting every word with her I'm-a-fucking-queen accent. Her eyes widen as I swallow the distance between us in two, quick strides. At the last moment, she holds up her little fists that wouldn't dent a piece of bread. She can't be serious. I'm not going to fight her with my fists. I take her with my mouth. The instant our lips meet, she sucks in a breath so big I'm shocked her tiny lungs hold that much air.

Anger boils in my veins. I need to stop. I've made my point—she doesn't want this. She *can't* want this. Why the hell doesn't she move? Push me away. Slap my face and tell me to fuck off.

The warm body I can't tear my fucking mouth from falls limp as my hands cup her face. This is by far the dumbest thing I have ever done. Her hands cover mine, clawing into my skin like she's trying to release my grip on her, but her hungry mouth begs for me to keep going. Why is she kissing me back like she's trying to crawl inside of me?

I hate that her taste quenches something hidden deep in the dark shadows of my soulless being that's been starving for so long. I hate that her warm touch feels like a jagged knife stabbing the pain I've tucked away for the day when I can avenge it.

If we don't stop, she could awaken something that *cannot* be brought to life. Not ever.

I hate Nolan for planting her in my world. I hate this life.

I really. Fucking. Hate. This. Life.

CHAPTER TEN

My name is Scarlet Stone and I love sex. I believe if all emotion and reason were stripped from human existence, the answer to all physical questions would be sex.

SCARLET

I DIDN'T SEE this coming.

    At. All.

The candlelit dinner wasn't foreplay or some sort of seduction. I wasn't lying when I told him I wanted a human connection. Apparently, to men, a human connection is sex. So why am I kissing him back like I've never wanted anything more in my whole life? I skipped dinner. It must be my misplaced hunger. I planned on ravaging the leftover Japanese yam that's on the top shelf of the fridge. My mouth has confused his for a yam.

"This means ..." His lips brush along my jaw as he whispers in a shaky voice that sends waves of chills over my skin.

My head falls back, eyelids heavy. "Nothing," I whisper or really *moan.* Of course it means nothing because it's not happening. Dear lord, my body is misbehaving tonight. His right hand slips under my shirt.

Don't beg, Scarlet.

I'm a cat leaning into his touch.

Don't purr, Scarlet.

Until the warmth of his hand slid along my flesh, I had no idea how much I *needed* it. I do.

So. Very. Much.

We have to stop, and we will ... as soon as he makes it to

second base. Then, I will grab that yam from the top shelf and bid him a goodnight.

"Oh!" I don't mean to yell, but he forgot second base, and I know this because he has ripped open my trousers—and by ripped open, I mean the button pinged against the tile and my zip will never work properly again—and his hand is down my knickers vying to capture third base. He can't skip a base.

"You … you're m-marking me," I protest with a weak whisper as he sucks and bites at my neck like he didn't have dinner either.

"You're fucking driving me insane," he growls into my neck.

No. He was insane before me. However, I'll wait a bit to make that case.

Two of his fingers plunge into me, and I forget about hickeys, bite marks, and Japanese yams. My knees forget their job is to keep me standing. I didn't like his finger retrieving food from my mouth. But its current location? I like it—a lot. Damn my knees for giving out because it forces him to remove his hand from between my legs to steady me. That's unfortunate. Bollocks!

That thought did not go through my head, did it?

My name is Scarlet Stone, and I love sex. I believe if all emotion and reason were stripped from human existence, the answer to all physical questions would be sex. I know it should be food, too, but I'm starving right now and still, I choose sex.

He lifts me up and I wrap my arms and legs around him as he attacks my mouth again. So deep. So hard. So … angrily.

He carries me upstairs to my bed, and we become a frantic storm of clothes being ripped and discarded. This man hates me. His touch does nothing to hide it. Yet the second my back hits the bed, he plunges his hard cock into me with a deep grunt, knocking the wind out of my lungs.

No easing. No acclimation. Foreplay be damned. He's punishing me. I can feel it. My existence pisses him off and this is his way of trying to scare me away.

While he fucks me, he whispers in my ear over and over, "*This ... means ... nothing.*"

I cling to him, because fuck him ... I can use him the way he's using me. He's looking for a release, I'm looking for human touch. It's not love, it's not even sex. It's ... nothing.

But ... as I hold him to my body, the bed creaking, the headboard knocking against the wall, I realize, for me, this is *everything,* and that makes tears escape the corners of my eyes. I miss Daniel. I miss my dad. And right now, I'm drowning in the feeling of Theodore Reed's naked body pressed to mine, the full warmth of him moving inside of me, the buildup of my orgasm, an orgasm I don't even need. Just the *touch.*

"The—ooo!" I squeeze my eyes shut and hold my breath because even something as basic as breathing distracts from this feeling: my body temperature rising and a heavy tingling radiating deep inside, starting right where he's hitting the most perfect spot over and over. Oh. Dear. God.

"Theo ..." his name on my lips drags on forever, like this orgasm. I didn't need it, but sometimes good things happen when you least expect it. Karma.

The wall takes three more unforgiving collisions with the headboard before Theo collapses on me, releasing the same deep grunt with which he entered me.

The man is not human. I've never been manhandled and flipped and fucked so thoroughly in my life. He's obliterated every emotion I had.

Should I be mad?

Grateful?

I don't know.

I bet myself he'll pull out of me and be gone within five seconds. I lose. He waits a full ten seconds before leaving me covered in his sweat. No eye contact. No words. *Nothing*.

That's fine because he gathers his clothes from the floor and walks away *naked*. I declare Theodore's naked backside to be the eighth wonder of the world.

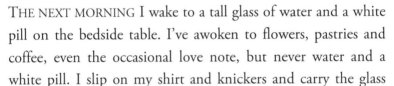

THE NEXT MORNING I wake to a tall glass of water and a white pill on the bedside table. I've awoken to flowers, pastries and coffee, even the occasional love note, but never water and a white pill. I slip on my shirt and knickers and carry the glass and pill to the kitchen. Theo's at the table eating porridge, already dressed in his work jeans and T-shirt.

I face the sink, my back to him. "What's this pill?"

"Emergency contraception—Plan B."

My soft laugh sounds more like his grunt as I shake my head, drop the pill down the drain, and drink the glass of water. Did he send off his date with a pill and bottled water before he decided to follow me up the beach? "You're not worried about STDs?"

"No."

I nod slowly, letting the echo of his monotone voice settle into my conscience.

"Are you?" His aloof tone does little to make me think he actually cares about my answer.

Am I worried about STDs? "No." I deposit the glass in the dishwasher and go back upstairs to shower before meditating and breakfast with Yimin.

I suppose I should replay the previous night's event over in my head, try to make sense of it all, but … it was *nothing*. And by nothing, I mean the roughest sex, yet best orgasm I've ever had, which was only by chance because Theo's goal was not to pleasure me.

My meditation proves to be more difficult than it's been in weeks. The physical part of my world has reared its head again, distracting from my real purpose. Yimin doesn't say much during breakfast, but that's nothing new. I'm content to eat in silence since I have my thoughts from last night to keep me company.

I miss seeing Theo swimming this morning. Why did he go straight to work before his swim? To avoid me? Does it matter?

My father used to ask me that all the time. When kids in school made fun of my hair, because in spite of my dominant black traits, I navigated through a disastrous blond-home-bleaching-kit phase in school, I'd come home in tears and my father would ask if what those kids thought of me really mattered? Even when I was sad about not having my mum, he asked if it really mattered. Maybe that's why I'm in search of what *does* matter in life because my years have been filled with days and nights of … nothingness.

Daniel was my chance to have something that really mattered. Now he's gone and I'm left with the same introspective question. Does it matter? I don't think it does. I think I've passed a critical point in my life where anything can ever matter again.

I go for a walk along the beach, relishing everything from the cool, gritty sand beneath my feet to gatherings of seagulls awaiting the beachgoers and their picnic scraps sure to litter the shore by midday. I seem to notice everything. Only a couple months ago, I'm certain the sky could have turned green and I wouldn't have noticed it past my computer screen.

As I approach the house, I spot Theo on a tall ladder, replacing some siding that blew off during the storm a few nights ago.

"I noticed you and your date didn't eat the food I made last night. If I warm it up, would you eat some of it?"

Theo hammers at a nail, hair pulled back into a low ponytail, sweat beading along his tight, tan skin. "We're not doing this."

My hand shields my eyes from the sun as I squint up at him. "Sorry? Doing what? Eating?"

"I told you last night meant nothing."

"You did. You told me on every single thrust and once more before you pulled out. Don't get your knickers in a twist. I agree, it was nothing. Frankly, it was the least memorable sex I've ever had. A weak two out of ten. Now, come down and I'll make us an early dinner, and we'll discuss all the animals in the world that have better sex skills than Theodore Reed."

I reheat the leftover curried rice and beans, fluff up last night's tossed salad, which does little to revive the wilted lettuce leaves, and I crack open a beer for Theo, bottled water for me. To my complete surprise, he comes inside as I retrieve the baking dish from the oven.

"I need a shower."

"You do. I'd join you but I don't want to eat a cold dinner."

He stops two steps beyond the kitchen. His panic is palpable.

"I'm kidding. Two out of ten ... I don't have sex twice

with a two. Life's too short and the men are too plentiful for that."

"Two out of ten?"

"Yes." I whisk the balsamic dressing in a bowl. "When you basically use a woman as a wanking vessel while whispering 'this means nothing' in her ear over and over, you get two stars."

He pauses, I assume to contemplate the proper response to someone telling him he was shit in bed. "So why a two and not a one?"

I shrug. "You didn't have to take a pill for ED, which got you one star, and you didn't call out some other woman's name ... that secured your second star."

"And the orgasm?"

I still. "What do you mean?"

"You orgasmed. That doesn't get me a third star? You yelled my name—twice. That's another two stars. We're up to five."

"I didn't orgasm." I resume my whisking, refusing to let him fluster me.

"You did."

"And how would you know?"

"I could feel you milking my cock while your eyes squeezed shut and your heels dug into my ass."

Bollocks! Mr. Reed is pretty damn observant in bed.

I snicker. "Maybe you're remembering your first shag of the night. Don't forget, I wasn't your first."

His lips purse while a chill slithers along my spine. "You were my only 'shag' of the night." My head snaps up, but he's already halfway up the stairs.

THEODORE EATS LIKE a caveman. His right arm rests on the table, curled around the perimeter of his plate protecting his food while he shovels it in with the fork fisted in his left hand.

"You're a lefty." I lean back in my chair, after maybe two bites of food. Observing Theo satisfies my appetite more than food.

"Sometimes."

I chuckle. "Sometimes?"

He shrugs, giving me a brief look before returning his focus to his endangered meal. "I'm ambidextrous."

So he's good with both hands. That wouldn't make headlines, yet it fascinates the hell out of me. I want to know everything about this man, but I don't know why.

"Nolan said you're moving in six months ... well, four now. Where are you going?"

He pauses then drops his fork onto his plate. "Why?" he asks with exasperation as his cold eyes meet mine.

"Curiosity, that's all."

After a good five seconds, he resumes eating. "You know what they say about curiosity," he mumbles over a mouthful of food.

"It kills the cat?"

Theo keeps shoveling food.

"Fine. Then make something up."

He wipes his mouth with the back of his hand then takes a swig of his beer. "Make something up?"

"Sure. Make something up. Make everything up. We're going our separate ways in a few months, so make something up ... but make it good. I love a good story."

He's mastered the you're-crazy look. It's possible I've helped cultivate its perfection.

Leaning back, he blows out a long breath. I freak out on the inside because he's really going to do it. Theodore Reed is going to make up some bullshit story and share it with me. Life is good.

"I'm the lead singer in a band and we're going on a world tour."

My eyes double in size like he's telling me the truth, but I know he's not. I didn't expect him to say something so *cool*.

"Do you play an instrument?"

"Guitar." He gets a gold medal for the fastest answer ever. He's good at this.

"Genre?"

"Country Rock."

"How many band members?"

"Five."

"First tour?"

"No." He keeps a straight face the whole time, eyes glued to mine.

"Favorite part about touring?"

"Getting laid."

I laugh and one corner of his mouth relinquishes the slightest twitch of a smile.

"Why do you act like you hate me?"

That tease of smile vanishes. "What makes you think it's an act?"

Before my head or heart, or whatever the hell seems to control my emotions these days, can react, he stands and takes his plate to the dishwasher.

"Don't you want to ask me anything?" I grasp for something that will keep him from walking away, even though he's halfway up the stairs and, really, I should be pissed off about his reply, but I'm not.

"Did you shut off the oven?"

"Yes."

His bedroom door slams shut. That was the only question he wanted to ask me? *Oh, Theodore Reed ... what happened to you?*

CHAPTER ELEVEN

THEODORE

I DON'T WANT her story, real or fictional. It won't change mine. It won't bring back the lives that have been taken. I cannot change who I've become, what I need, and where I'm going.

Nolan letting her live here is like someone offering me a chip. I say, "No, thank you." But they insist. Finally, I give in and take a chip. Now I want to eat the whole fucking bag of chips and rip Nolan apart for offering me the stupid chip to begin with.

"Aaaah!!!"

I spit out my toothpaste and wipe my mouth. "For the love of god, woman," I mumble to myself.

"Theo!"

Two seconds after I open my bedroom door, Scarlet is stuck to me like a koala to a tree. "What the fuck?"

"There's ... there's ..." With her face buried in my neck, she fights to speak each labored word. "An angry lizard in my room!"

"Off. Me. Now."

She shakes her head, tightening her arms around my neck and her legs around my waist. I walk down the hall with a complete nutcase in a dinky T-shirt and threadbare panties, clinging to me.

"Where?"

"Bathroom." Her nails dig into my skin as I approach her bathroom.

"It's an anole."

"What are you doing?" Her shrill voice pierces my ear.

I bend over, koala still attached, and grab the lizard. Then I walk out onto her balcony and give it a toss. "Gone. Now get off me."

"What if there's more?"

"Then toss them over the balcony."

Her head jerks up, eyes ready to pop out of her head. She smells like all the girly crap I hate. Her skin is too soft. Her lips are too full. Her breath is too warm against my face.

Why is she looking at me? Why isn't she climbing down? One of her hands releases my neck as her gaze moves along my face, following her hand that brushes along my cheek, her fingers ghosting over my eyebrows, down my nose and over my lips. My eyes close and my dick hardens. I don't care if she can feel it.

Damn chips. I could fucking eat her up in more ways than one right now.

"Tell me …" I whisper, "… tell me a lie." I need her to talk, anything to keep from stripping her and taking what I want. I thought once would scare her. I thought it would satiate me. It didn't and I'm not sure it ever will. So, this can't happen.

She swallows hard. "When I leave here, I'm going back to London to get married. I've picked out a lovely forty-five piece handmade tableware set with cobalt blue trim. The guest list is two-hundred and seventy-three."

My hands go from limp at my sides to wrap around her,

but I don't open my eyes. "What's your fiancé's name?" If she hesitates, then it's made up.

"Daniel." She doesn't hesitate.

He's real. Where the fuck is this guy and why is he allowing this woman to have her body wrapped around mine?

"What does he do?"

"He's a highly-sought-after wildlife photographer and videographer."

"Did he give you that necklace."

I don't have to open my eyes to know that her hand moves to the ruby pendant dangling from the gold chain around her neck. I've never seen her not wearing it, but when she gets nervous, her hand moves to it, like a talisman.

"No."

"What's the most valuable thing you've ever stolen?"

I can't remember the last time I felt someone's heartbeat against mine. Why is she here? I get it, God. You know what I'm planning and you think she's going to distract me. It's too late.

She releases her grip on me, and I let her slide to her feet. Letting her go isn't easy, but it's necessary. That single, most unexpected thought gives me pause. Leaving behind an unsettling pain that I fucking hate.

I open my eyes to the many flecks of brown and gold in hers.

After several blinks, she whispers, "A life."

DAYS AND WEEKS pass in more silence. Scarlet seems to disappear emotionally. After days of nonstop jabbering, she closes off from the world. She spends more time with the crazy Asian guy, takes longer walks, and devours more books that have cluttered the house, only outnumbered by the fucking plants. I don't say anything about the mess, it's a fair trade for her silence.

She's all skin and bones. I haven't seen her eat solid food in weeks. She drinks juice, lots of juice, and really potent teas that she makes from some weird weed-looking crap brewing in a ceramic pot. Clearly, she has an eating disorder, but it's none of my business. If she wants to starve to death, who am I to change the course of *her* life. I sure as hell don't want anyone trying to change the course of mine.

However, the most disturbing part is how much she watches me. When I work around the house, I feel her eyes on me. She thinks I don't see her, but I do. I see her peeking over the top of a book, giving me quick glances at the kitchen table, and I feel her footsteps in the sand a safe distance back every morning when I return home after my swim. She's everywhere and nowhere at the same time.

In my head.

On my nerves.

Gnawing at my conscience.

I hope she's not waiting for me to save her. I'm no one's savior.

"Where are you going?" Her voice halts my forward motion.

I've succumbed to the real possibility that one day I'll come home to her wasted-away body dead on the floor.

I slowly look back over my shoulder to her standing at the bottom of the stairs in a white beach-looking dress, hair curly, like what black women look like when they don't try to deny the fact that their hair is meant to have life. It distracts a bit from the gauntly look in her face, much like the loose dress hiding her bony body, except her arms. They still look like a skeleton covered in a thin layer of brown skin.

"I'm going to town for some supplies."

"Mind if I ride along?"

Of course I mind if she rides along. "It's just the hardware store."

"Works for me." She smiles.

She has no life.

As soon as we pull out of the drive, she slips off her sandals and tucks her legs underneath her, staring out her window. Since weeks of silence has been broken, I expect her driveling to commence, but she seems quite enamored with the view as we make our way off Tybee.

"So beautiful," she whispers. I don't think her comment was meant for me to hear.

I clear my throat along with the unwelcome thoughts of her in my head. "I'll be starting on the upstairs in a few days. It's the last project before I leave. So all of our bedroom furniture will need to be moved out so I can work on the floors. You can take the sofa sleeper."

She turns to me. "Where will you sleep?"

"I'll stick a cot in the kitchen."

She laughs, looking back out the window. "You can put your 'cot' by the sofa. I'm used to your snoring."

"I don't snore."

"You do. I hear it when both of our bedroom windows are open."

"I don't—"

"You totally do. It's so loud it could be its own instrument in your imaginary band."

Rolling my lips together, I keep my focus on the road, but I can feel her looking at me, and I know she's smiling.

"Oh, Theodore Reed ..." She sighs and leans back, seemingly quite content. "You are a labyrinth—an onion with infinite layers. If given the chance, I think I could really miss you someday." Her eyes close with a soft smile gracing her face.

What does she mean by that?

CHAPTER TWELVE

My name is Scarlet Stone and I steal random stuff and plant it in the sparkly rucksacks of mean girls, then report them as thieves so they get in trouble. Karma is my religion.

SCARLET

"'LL BUY YOU lunch." Theo pulls into the car park of a café.

"You don't usually eat lunch."

He turns off his truck and pins me with a serious look.

I shrug. "Fine. You're hungry today. I'm just along for the ride." I get out.

He opens the door to the café for me.

"Thank you, sir." I wink.

He shakes his head and mutters something I can't quite understand.

The waitress seats us by the window and gives us the specials. Theo orders a bacon avocado cheeseburger with fries and iced tea.

"Have you decided, ma'am?"

"Do you have spring water in a glass bottle?"

"Sorry, just tap."

I nod. "Fine. I'll do that, no ice, and several lemon wedges."

"Food." Theo glares at me with narrowed eyes. "Order food."

"I'm on a cleanse." I smile. "It's good to give your body a break from constant digesting."

"She'll have what I'm having."

"I don't eat meat anymore." I keep smiling at him. "I think

meat is too acidic for my body."

He sighs. "Grilled cheese for her."

"Or dairy." I cringe. "It's too acidic too. I read that our bodies have to rob calcium from our bones to neutralize the acidity. It's crazy how milk is touted for helping build strong bones when really—"

His jaw tenses.

I bite my tongue and shrug. "Sorry. I'm … sure you don't really care."

The waitress clears her throat. "I can get you a garden salad, no meat or cheese."

"She'll take it." He continues to glare at me.

"Ranch, French, Italian, Caesar, or Balsamic dressing?"

"No dressing … just bring extra lemon." I hand her my menu.

Theo focuses out the window. His jaw remains clenched. "You look like shit."

I laugh. "Why thank you. Day. Made."

"If I find you passed out, *when* I find you passed out, I'm not calling for an ambulance. If you want to kill yourself, a gun would be a helluva lot easier."

"You think I want to die?"

He looks at me, expressionless.

"Fair enough." I shrug. "But for the record, if I find you passed out, I will call for an ambulance, check for a pulse, and administer CPR if necessary."

"And if I put a bullet in my head?"

The waitress serves our drinks. I squeeze my lemon wedges into my water. "Would you? Would you put a bullet in your brain?"

He takes a swig of his iced tea then licks his lips. "If I wanted to die, yes, I'd put a bullet in my head."

"Are you sure you wouldn't just swim with the sharks every morning knowing that statistically one day you'll be breakfast?"

He grunts. As usual, my words only aggravate him more.

"Do you own a gun?"

"Why?" He strokes his beard while shooting me a beady-eyed glare.

"I'll make you a deal. If you show me where it is, and how to use it, I promise if the day ever comes that I want to die, I will place it at my temple and pull the trigger. Deal?"

Theo doesn't make the deal. In fact, he doesn't say another word for the rest of our lunch. He might be my unsolvable mystery and when he studies me like he has been today, I think I may be his, too. If I didn't know better, I'd say Theodore Reed cares about me. I know better.

"Oh, shit!" I grab the back of Theo's shirt as we exit the café.

"What?"

"That's Harold Moore *and* a woman who is not his wife," I whisper, peeking around Theo's body like I have some reason to hide.

I'm not the one pressing a younger woman up against my black Range Rover, sticking my tongue down her throat and my hand up her shirt. His charcoal suit looks designer too. Not the charity shop getup he wore the day I met him.

"What's your point?" Theo continues to the truck as I shuffle behind him, like he's shielding me from gunfire.

I hop in and shut the door. "What's my point? Nolan's dad is cheating on his mum. That's my point."

"That's not news around here." He backs out and waves, yes *waves*, at Harold as we pull out of the car park. Harold waves back like he's not at all trying to hide his affair.

"Does Nolan know?" I think back to Nolan's comment about *unconventional marriage.*

Theo chuckles. It's uncharacteristic of him, and normally I would find it endearing, but he's laughing about an affair. "Yes. He knows. Everyone knows … except Nellie."

I open my mouth then clamp it shut and repeat it several times before words find their way out. "Why doesn't he leave her? Why make a fool of her?"

He gives me a quick glance with a quirked eyebrow. "You've met Nellie. Right?"

"Yes. She's … she's … a little …"

"Crazy."

"I was going to say simplistic. It doesn't mean she deserves to be cheated on."

"No, she's crazy, and they have a doctor's diagnosis that confirmed it."

"Oh … well, what happened?"

He shrugs. "Don't' know. Don't care. Nolan had some accident. She lost her shit. The family is richer than God, but she doesn't have any clue as to her social status. Before she lost it, she was the epitome of a southern, uppity rich bitch. Big parties, charity events … they own half of Savannah and one of the most lucrative horse ranches in Kentucky. Now, she's the equivalent of a child."

"Why isn't she someplace receiving special care?"

"Rich people don't live in institutions."

"It makes no sense. He dresses in secondhand clothes when he's with her … but …" I shake my head. "He's cheating on her. Why stay?"

"The money is all Nellie's. If anything happens to her, everything goes to Nolan. The old fucker just wants the life. Nellie's content, so Nolan's content. Harold gets to stay. End of story."

"So, Harold lives two lives? Crazy-dressing husband to Nellie one minute and rich businessman shagging younger women the next?"

"Yup."

I'm buzzing inside, trying to play it cool like I'm not dying, seriously *dying* to solve this mystery. "Just like that? Nolan has an accident and Nellie goes mad? How does that make any sense?"

"Don't know. Don't care."

We park in front of the hardware shop, and he jumps out, not waiting for me and my ten-second delay from my head stuck in detective overdrive.

"Wait!"

He doesn't.

I chase him around the store for ten minutes. He's quick and precise with his shopping. His lack of patience to browse shouldn't surprise me. I'm mesmerized by his concentration while loading his trolley with paper bags of nails, screws, caulk, some big roll of paper, and other random stuff.

"I love these." Plucking a windmill from the checkout display, I blow on it as we wait in queue. "When I was younger we had to get out of our house in a hurry because …" I peek up at Theo and grimace "Let's say for *reasons.* Anyway, my dad told me I could bring one toy. I grabbed this red and silver windmill that I stole …" I glance up at him again.

He regards me with wide eyes.

My name is Scarlet Stone and I steal random stuff and plant it in the sparkly rucksacks of mean girls, then report them as thieves so they get in trouble. Karma is my religion.

I clear my throat. "That I *borrowed* from Piper, a girl who made fun of me in school. I had far more expensive options, but I chose the windmill." I blow on it again and smile.

"Pinwheel." Theo loads everything onto the conveyer belt at the checkout.

"Sorry?" I deposit the windmill back in its cardboard display and squeeze past him to wait at the end of the checkout.

"It's a pinwheel, not a windmill."

"I don't know what you mean by pinwheel." I cross my arms over my chest.

"Of course you don't." He shakes his head.

"You're making fun of me."

He smirks.

After the cashier scans the last item, Theo reaches over, grabs the 'pinwheel,' and swipes it past the scanner himself. He holds it out to me like a long-stemmed rose. Expressionless.

I gawk at it, then at him for a few seconds before my grin wins over and I take it. "Thank you."

He considers me with a tense brow and eyes that make a slow trip down my body and back up to meet my gaze. It's not sexual, it's confusion, conflict—maybe even wonderment. For a moment so brief I can't fully make sense of it, I think he sees my truth. I could cry because it's … I inhale a shaky breath … not his to see. He nods once and swipes his credit card.

My hands fist. I haven't had the urge to chew my nails since saying goodbye to Oscar, but Theo could break me before I get the chance to let go on my own.

I clear my throat. "You shouldn't use credit cards. They're not secure."

He glances over at me while I blow on my windmill.

"Our system is secure, ma'am. I can assure you," the cashier says.

Keeping my focus on my proverbial long-stemmed rose, I shake my head. "It's not. If I had a laptop, I could bring up every credit card number that's been swiped through that exact machine in the past thirty days."

"You can load your lumber around the back, just show them your receipt." The clerk hands Theo his receipt then gives me a dirty look like I said something wrong.

"What?" I say as Theo continues to scrutinize me while we walk to the truck. "Cash. Pay cash, Theodore. It's safest, unless you keep your wallet where someone can pick your pocket."

"I'm going to feel someone sticking their fucking hand in my pocket." He gets in the truck.

I open my door and throw him his wallet as I get inside. "I'm not so sure you would."

He leans to the side and feels his back pocket, like there's really any question that I lifted his wallet.

"Fucking thief," he mumbles as we drive around back to get his lumber.

"Ex-thief." I grin, holding my windmill out my rolled-down window.

It's a good day. Scratch that. It's a great day. Theo loading heavy lumber into the back of his truck is a visual treat. I lean against the side of his truck. My windmill takes a backseat to Theo's muscles. My insides warm as my mind drifts back to the feel of his hard, naked body pressed to mine.

Human touch—oxygen to the soul.

"You're drooling."

I wipe my mouth but nothing is there. Theo chuckles.

Laughter—music to the soul.

"Cheeky bastard." I glare at him, but my grin doesn't give it much merit.

I offer a silent thank you to the creator of my universe for allowing me to see life in slow motion so I can appreciate the moments that have passed me by for so many years.

He continues to load everything, giving me an occasional glance that quickens my pulse. I don't *know* him at all, but it's impossible to share space with someone for this long and not feel attached to them in an inexplicable way. Familiarity via cohabitation osmosis—I'm labeling it a real thing.

"The leaf-cutter ant can carry fifty times its body weight. That's like you or me carrying a small car above our head. Isn't that amazing? Well, I can actually see you being able to do that. Me ... not so much."

"Get in." He lifts the hem of his dirty shirt and wipes the sweat from his brow. "You're drooling again."

My gaze snaps from his abs to his eyes. "You're being an arse again." I grin and he does too. I've never seen so many of his teeth at once. Theodore Reed is truly a beautiful man.

Stop.

Stare.

Give thanks.

Let go ...

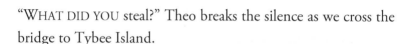

"WHAT DID YOU steal?" Theo breaks the silence as we cross the bridge to Tybee Island.

"I didn't steal anything. You bought the windmill."

He shakes his head. "In London."

"Oh. This and that. Nothing too exciting. Mostly money."

"So you're rich?"

I chuckle. "No. I didn't steal it for myself. Well, I kept a small percent to pay rent and food, but it was more of a recovery fee. A fair number of my clients were poor and unemployed. So, for example, when corporations downsized to make sure the rich bastards at the top didn't have to take pay cuts or even worse, didn't have to forego their raises, I made sure the unemployed were *properly compensated* until they found new employment."

"Robin Hood."

"Sometimes." I smile.

"And other times?"

"And other times I was a weapon to the highest bidder. I got paid to expose certain people, provide information to blackmail others."

"And you did this all from a computer?"

"Yes."

"But you picked my pocket."

"My grandfather and dad taught me survival skills at an early age."

"Survival skills," Theo says like he's testing out the meaning of the words.

"No credit cards?"

"No."

"No debit card?"

"No."

"So you're paying for rent, utilities, and food with cash?"

"Yes." I return a resolute nod.

"Where is all this cash?"

"Wouldn't you like to know." I grin.

"You don't have a job. What are you going to do when the money runs out?"

"Six months. I brought enough for six months." That's a half truth. I brought enough money for six months if my rent was reasonable. My accepting Nolan's offering of a thousand dollars without so much as a counter offer was very unlike me. In all fairness, I wasn't myself.

"Then you're going back to London to get married?"

I hop out as he parks the truck. "That was plan A," I whisper to myself as I walk up the wood-plank ramp to the back door, carrying my windmill and a guilt-ridden conscience.

YIMIN BOWS AS he does every time I walk in his house.

"Good morning."

"Good morning."

He puts my tea and juice on the table.

"I had lettuce yesterday. I didn't want to, but I did. Then I added some cooked veg to my broth last night. I feel good, but I look like hell. I'm going back to solid food. It's just a body and I know it, but I have this … itch." My nose wrinkles.

Theo was right. I look awfully gaunt since starting my liquid cleanse. Nolan was also right, as much as it freaks me out to admit it. I had been experiencing some pain, but over the past few weeks the pain has disappeared. Looking in the mirror lately, it would appear that I've been doing the same thing.

Yes. I look like hell, but I've never felt better.

"Your books? They tell you to expect these symptoms. Yes?" he asks.

Yimin has been supportive of my desire to test out some of the theories I've found in my plethora of books. It started with eliminating everything that wasn't a plant in an attempt to make my body more alkaline. Disease flourishes in acidic bodies. The next book discussed the miracles of fasting and liquid diets. The theory being that the body heals itself when it's not busy digesting food all the time.

"Well, yes. There can be side effects to liquid fasts, but that's not exactly what I'm implying."

Yimin nods once, but I don't think it's because he understands. "Toxins leaving your body can cause rashes. I can give you a salve for it."

"No. Um … I don't think you have a salve for my itch. It's more of a *need*."

He nods again. Still, there's no way he gets my point yet. This is awkward.

"I want to look physically more appealing so that a man might be willing to … scratch my itch."

His eyebrows lift a fraction. "Sex?"

It's my turn to nod.

He leans forward, placing his hand over mine. "Let your body live. That's why you're here."

I blink back the tears. "I hope so," I whisper.

He nods to the table. "Eat. Don't eat. It's your journey. But for now, drink then scratch."

I laugh. Yimin has a sense of humor beyond making me drink piss tea. I never would have guessed. He smiles. It makes me wonder if he ever has an *itch*. For some reason when I meet completely put-together people, or people of high power, I have trouble imagining them scratching an itch—letting go of all inhibitions and succumbing to something so purely animalistic.

CHAPTER THIRTEEN

My name is Scarlet Stone and I like theatrical masks. My father gave me a real gold mask that he "borrowed" from a museum. He said I should wear it when I need to feel brave. I wear it a lot.

OVER THE NEXT week I eat solid foods, keeping my meals nutrient dense but high in calories. I also do squats and pushups to nurture my neglected muscles.

We move everything from the bedrooms to the main level and garage. The garage is filled with tools and weights. Lots of weights. I now understand why Theo is solid as a bull.

Clearing the upstairs has forced all of my plants onto the main level. He seemed to tolerate them fine, until they all had to be shoved in the kitchen and lounge.

He grumbles as he makes room to set up his camp bed for the night. I can hear him through the thin walls of the bathroom that we now share off the kitchen. I'm up over half a stone but my reflection in the mirror still looks a little gaunt. My hair has been au natural for a while, no more straightening, but Theo hasn't said anything. There's no way he hasn't noticed. I'm tempted to cut it off soon, like really short. Maybe if I can gain another half a stone, I'll do it.

"You can do this," I whisper to myself as I open the door, wearing only a black bra and matching knickers.

Theo's head is bowed, looking at the screen of his phone from the comfort of his camp bed in the kitchen, surrounded by plants. He's in exercise shorts, no shirt, and his hair is down instead of tied back like it is when he works.

"Theo?"

"These fucking plants have to go." He doesn't look up.

I clear my throat. "Theo?"

"What?" He still doesn't look up.

I maneuver my way through the jungle. He stills his hand, and I know he sees my bare feet and legs. Ever so slowly he allows his gaze to make its way up my body.

"I have an itch."

His lips part as his heavy eyelids blink once, like he's drunk on me. "Where?" It's a deep, throaty whisper that sends chills along my skin.

Reaching down, I grab his warm, calloused hand and place it between my breasts. *Touch.* I close my eyes for a second. How can something so simple make me lightheaded and breathless? As I start to slide it under the edge of my bra, he curls his fingers and … *scratches* me.

"Better?"

I don't know if I want to cry of embarrassment or laugh because somewhere along the way I lost my seduction mojo. Theo gives nothing away. He could have simply said no, but he didn't … so there's that. However, it does little for my bruised ego and my *itch.*

"Yes," I say with a frog's voice and a slow nod. "Thank you."

My lips twist to the side. He remains stoic Theodore Reed. I turn and make two steps toward the living room, stopping when a hand slips down the back of my knickers, fisting them like I'm his property. My heart slams against my chest as I suck in a quick breath and my body goes up in flames.

Theo pulls on my knickers, making me retreat a step at a time. I'm glad my back is to him so he can't see how scared and excited and *turned on* I am in this moment.

He releases my knickers and … oh dear god … he claws his

hands down the back of my legs. His fingernails aren't long but they bite into my skin just enough to awaken every cell in my body. When he reaches my ankles, he slides his hands around and scratches his way up the front of my legs.

Slow.

Controlled.

Dominating.

My muscles flex beneath his touch.

My lips part, releasing erratic, heavy breaths as he curls his fingers into my knickers and slides them down my legs. I jump, a grin stretches across my lips as his beard tickles my backside. He presses his mouth to my skin while his hands rake back up my legs, my stomach, my arms, my neck—scratching and touching me everywhere but my breasts and the pulsing center between my legs that's heavy and in dire need of that proverbial scratch.

Every kiss along my backside becomes more intense.

Lips.

Tongue.

Teeth.

Theo's fingers dig into my skin more and more. There's something uniquely erotic and equally torturous about him touching me everywhere but where I'm begging for it the most. He removes my bra and guides my arms above my head. I fist my own hair to keep them from falling back to my sides. He drags his nails slowly along my arms, down my torso to my abs, and up to my breasts where he finally touches them, squeezing so hard I nearly explode.

My breath seethes through my teeth. It feels like he poured gasoline over me. The second he touches my breasts it's like striking the match.

Theo stands so fast I have to fight to keep my footing. I grab his hair to pull his mouth down to mine. He fists my hair to stop me—our lips almost touching. The space between us fills with hot, labored breaths.

"You gave me two stars." His words come out as a growl.

Oh that …

I swallow hard. He's angry. My rubbish assessment pissed him off. Do I want to have sex with angry Theodore Reed?

"That means I have eight more to give. Think you can *steal* them from me?"

Oh. Fucking. Hell. YES! I want to have sex with angry Theodore Reed.

He backs me into the worktop.

Crash!

He shoves one of my plants onto the floor.

Crash!

Another plant.

Crash!

My bare bum meets the cold worktop when he lifts me up. The breath in my lungs whooshes out as he slides down his shorts and briefs. Just the sight of his naked body is worth ten solid stars.

My hair feels like it's being ripped from my head as he fists it, crashing our mouths together at the same time his cock completely fills me. I want to scream, but his tongue consumes every part of my mouth. He thrusts into me slow and hard. My fingers dig into the hard muscles of his arse, guiding—begging him to not stop.

The cupboard doors clank over and over, vibrating the dishes behind them like an earthquake. I'm so close, and I swear he knows it because he stills and wraps one hand around my waist while the other lifts me off the worktop.

Crash!

He shoves two plants off the kitchen island.

Crash! Crash! Crash!

There goes the rest of my plants. I want to protest, but he has me spread out on the island with his head between my legs, his hands pushing them open as wide as they will go.

His tongue makes a thorough introduction to my clit. Oh. My. God!

There it is. It's … it's … No!!!

He stops. I look down. He looks up and *smirks*.

"What are you—"

He flips me over with the ease of turning a page. My cheek rests against the worktop. My hands grip the edge of it. Theo lifts my hips, a knee on both sides of my legs, and drives into me again … and again … and oh fucking hell … Stars. It's all I can see as I hold my breath, letting my body seize with an orgasm.

Our fingers intertwine on the edge of the worktop as he speeds up, drawing out every last possible sensation I can have, then he stills, buried completely. Warmth fills me. A guttural moan vibrates his chest that's pressed to my back.

"Take the stars …" I pant. "Every. Single. One."

WHAT HAPPENED? WHERE am I? What time is it?

I lift my head from the pillow to assess my situation:

Sofa bed—sheets half-ripped off.

Naked Thor facedown on the floor with dirt and leaves stuck to his skin. Nice view.

Plants.

More dirt.

Broken porcelain.

I lift myself to sitting. Dirt trickles down my back, but most of it stays stuck to my skin. Well, shit! I'm naked too and covered in dirt.

The brain fog begins to lift. We had sex. I think lots of sex.

Sex on the worktop.

Sex on the camp bed. Oh, my aching back. That's right. We broke the camp bed. That might account for why he's on the floor.

The floor. We had sex on the floor too.

Good sex. *Really* good sex.

My ten-star wonder begins to move and grumble like a bear waking. Theo pushes himself to his knees, tattooed back to me. I can pretty much read his mind as he looks down at himself and around the room—because I had the same thoughts. He glances over his shoulder at me, gaze trailing along my body while he scratches his beard-covered chin.

"Mornin'," he says in a raspy voice.

"Morning." I don't know what else to say. Theo's moods are something much more complex than simply unpredictable.

He continues to stroke his beard. "That was a military-grade cot."

A smile grows across my face until I can't hold back my laughter. "I think half of my plants need CPR."

With a shrug, he lumbers to standing. "Toss them."

I push to my feet, giving my best effort to not stare at his morning erection. "I'll save them and when you finish the upstairs, I'm going to put all of them in your room."

He stretches his arms above his head and yawns.

Good lord … that body.

"When I'm done with the upstairs, this place is going on the market."

Is that his way of reminding me that this is nothing? I know this is nothing. I think I know it better than he does. "And you'll go on tour."

He regards me for a few seconds. I'm not sure if the sadness in his expression is my imagination or if he's really letting his mask slip. "And you'll go back to London to get married."

If Theo thought that was anything but a lie, I think I'd crawl into a hole and die. I'm not a cheater. Right now, I'd give anything to erase that look from his face. I am *not* a cheater.

"Tell me another lie." I need him to remember what we've shared is a lie.

Theo runs his hands through his hair, shaking out dirt as he chuckles. He looks at the floor. "Another lie, huh? Fine. I don't want you to go back to London and marry some guy who will never be a ten."

"Ha!" I shake my head and laugh as I tiptoe through the mess to reach the bathroom. "You're cheeky, Theodore Reed."

My name is Scarlet Stone and I like theatrical masks. My father gave me a real gold mask that he "borrowed" from a museum. He said I should wear it when I need to feel brave. I wear it a lot.

As soon as I'm behind the safety of the locked bathroom door, I fist my hands at my heart and slide down the smooth wood to the floor. The tears fall. "Oh god …" It's incredibly difficult to let go of the physical world with our souls trapped in bodies that do nothing but *feel* everything.

Pleasure cannot exist without pain. My heart needs to stay out of this, and Theo needs to stop saying things that lead me to believe he's letting *his* heart have a say in any of it.

CHAPTER FOURTEEN

My name is Scarlet Stone. I have 70,000 thoughts a day and they are mine. My human right. I will not be ashamed of having an opinion.

NOLAN WANTS TO meet me for lunch. I've been here for months and since he took me food shopping, I haven't seen him. Paying him six months' rent at once probably doesn't give him much of a reason to visit. That's why I have to question what makes today so special.

Theo busies himself to the point of working over twelve hours a day. I think he has been avoiding me since our sex-in-potting-soil night. I say "I think" because I've been avoiding him, too, for the past week. Saying goodbye to Daniel was the last painful goodbye I ever wanted to have. Part of me hopes that one day I'll wake up and Theo will be gone. In reality, I think he may wake up one day and I'll be the one who is gone.

Nothing lasts forever. *That* is the only truth we are guaranteed in life. When someone says they will love you forever, what does that really mean? Then again, what really is love? I think that's why we're here. For each of us to discover what love means to us.

I love Daniel and that's why I left. But what if he doesn't see it that way? My dad is in prison because he loves me. I still lose sleep over communal underwear because I love him. Love is so fucking painful.

"Hello, stranger. So, I pay you rent in full and you bugger off with it? Mr. Reed could have sliced and diced me and fed me to the sharks by now and no one would have known."

"Scarlet Stone. Don't you look lovely." Nolan takes my

hand and kisses the back of it. "I like what you've done with your hair."

I laugh. "You mean what I *haven't* done with it. I've given up on my vanity. Well, most of it."

"How un-southernly of you. Are you ready?" He holds open the car door.

"Thank you, kind sir."

We head to town, not talking about much more than the weather, specifically the rundown of the most devastating storms to hit Savannah. Weather I'm good at; it's a favorite topic of most British people.

He takes me to lunch at what I believe is an exclusive club with men dressed in suits and a few women wearing perfectly-tailored designer dresses accented with plenty of flashy jewelry.

"So tell me, how are you feeling, Scarlet?" Nolan asks behind his menu.

I have a feeling Yimin said something and that's what prompted this unexpected lunch invite.

"Underdressed. How is Harold and his young floozy?"

He stiffens, lowering his menu enough to glare at me. "I warned you not to believe everything you hear."

"We saw Harold with his tongue down some young girl's throat, in the car park outside of the café where we had lunch."

"You and Theo had lunch? Is there something going on between the two of you? Are you the beauty to his beast?"

"No. Why are you blackmailing your dad?"

Nolan chuckles. "Does he know?"

"Who?"

"Theo."

"Know what?" Why is he changing the subject?

"About your illness?"

I remember when men with badges and guns raided our place. Life was over ... at least the life I had always known. Then my father confessed to my crime. It was like everything in his life had led him to that point—the day he would sacrifice himself to save me. He promised no one would ever know it was me. He promised to take my secret to his grave.

But now no one is here to save me from the truth.

"Is it cancer?" Nolan drives the knife a little deeper.

"How do you know?" I wait for his simplistic sixth-sense explanation. He gives me more.

"I died," he says matter-of-factly.

I shake my head. "Sorry? I don't understand."

"I had an ... *accident.* I died. Doctors pronounced me dead. Three minutes later I took a breath and opened my eyes. You know those unexplainable miracles that modern medicine can't explain? That was me. Something happened to me, and I can't explain it ... no one can. But ever since that day, I've been able to sense things. I can feel things that people around me are feeling. Most of the time it's just that—a feeling. Sometimes it's specific and I can pinpoint it like a heart attack or aneurysm or—"

"Cancer," I whisper.

Nolan nods.

London – Three Months Earlier

Dear Diary,

Today I was offered a legit, six-figure salary, picked out a lovely forty-five piece handmade tableware set with cobalt blue trim for my wedding in seven months, came across three pennies in the car park, and found out I have termi-

nal cancer and a year to live—six months without treat-
ment. I'm regretting the extended warranty I purchased for
my new car last month …

"Scarlet?" Daniel glances over his white dress-shirt clad shoulder while steam rises from a pot of Heaven in front of him. He greets me with a lopsided grin and the voice that often has my clothes falling to the floor. Roasted garlic and rosemary dance in the air with Sarah Brightman's version of "All I ask of You."

"You didn't wait for me." I throw my keys on the hall table then work the buttons to my red, double-breasted peacoat.

We always make meals together.

We always listen to opera.

We always talk about our careers.

We're always in sync.

"It's your day, love. That glass of wine is waiting for you. Sit down and tell me about your day."

I shrug. "I chose the cobalt trim for our tableware instead of the red like we had originally discussed."

"Stop playing with me. You know all I want to hear about is the job."

The searing meat in the frying pan drowns out the music like the white noise between radio stations. The death sentence from a "minor" follow-up to a physical I had several weeks prior kicks my senses in the gut. A wake-up-last-call-you've-officially-been-stamped-with-an-expiration-date revelation.

"Earth to Scarlet."

My finger stops tracing the rim of the wine glass as my gaze shoots up to the dirty blond who looks sinful yet completely out of place in his black pressed trousers and semi-pressed shirt.

"Sorry." I shake my head. "Why the suit today?" My hand

moves to his chest, fighting the urge to fist his shirt. The need to hold on to him—to this life—overwhelms me.

"Scarlet Stone ... stop! I'll tell you about the suit after you tell me about the job." His playful grin stabs my heart. I already miss him.

I shrug, relinquishing a hint of a smile that I hope doesn't look half as pained as it feels. "They offered me the job."

"Yes!" He pulls me into his arms and swings me around in circles. "My little thief has gone legit."

"I'm not a thief."

He lets me slide back down to my feet and devours my mouth. "You'll always be a thief for stealing my heart." He means it figuratively ... if he only knew.

My eyes close as his nose brushes mine. "The suit." I clear my throat while the words fight past the thick emotion. "Why the suit?"

Daniel wiggles his eyebrows then turns back to the hob. "I have a job announcement too."

"Oh?" I take a sip of my wine. "What is this wine?" I swirl it around in my glass.

"It's on the table."

I turn and narrow my eyes at the bottle, moving closer to read the label. "Bugger! This bottle of wine costs over six hundred quid!"

"As I was saying ... I have job news too. I've been asked to film that documentary. It's going to be huge. A serious once-in-a-lifetime opportunity. But I'll be gone for five months, and ..." He slides the pan off the burner and turns toward me. "I leave on Monday." His nose scrunches but it fails to hide the excitement in his eyes.

Our ambitious and career-oriented personalities brought us

together. Kids? A doctor told me, several years ago, I would never get pregnant thanks to endometriosis. Daniel doesn't want them anyway. The fake grimace is theatrical; he knows I won't blink before jumping for joy to celebrate his professional accomplishment. That's us. Two independent people who happen to be in love. At least that's who we were until today. This very moment.

"Say something." He grunts a laugh of disbelief. "I bought this bottle of wine for six hundred quid to celebrate *our* day, but you look like you're ready to cry." His hands cradle my face. "Scarlet Stone, I've seen you cry once. *Once* in the ten years I've known you. What is this all about, love?"

For a brief moment, which feels like an out-of-body experience, I think I could make it disappear if I don't say the words. With one blink my tears fall, and I say the words anyway. "I have cancer."

"Sorry? No ..." Daniel shakes his head, brow pinched tight. "What are you talking about?"

My tears taste salty on my lips as I rub them together, drawing in a deep breath. "The off and on pain in my abdomen? The bloating? The weight I've lost without trying over the past six months?"

"You went to the doctors and they said it was stress or the endometriosis."

"They missed it."

"Sorry? They *missed* it?" Daniel's head jerks back. "What the bloody hell is that supposed to mean?"

I shake my head. "They're human. It happens."

"What kind of cancer? They ... they caught it early. Correct? You'll go through treatment, and you'll be fine." His voice cracks. "Answer me." My man who defines tall and ruggedly handsome, looks utterly broken and defeated with his eyes reddening behind his own tears, shoulders curled inward.

"It's ovarian cancer." I grab his hands and squeeze them. The lines along his brow deepen. "It's terminal."

He jerks his hands from mine, spinning around with his back to me; his hands fist his hair as he releases a growl. "FUCKING HELL!"

A numbness blankets my body. I don't even jump when he yells. All I can feel is the soft trickle of more tears sliding down my face. I know no pain will ever compare to this moment. The victims of cancer reach far beyond those with the disease.

"Okay ..." He turns back to me, his eyes wet with emotion. "We'll fix this. Chemo, radiation, whatever it takes. Cancer is not a death sentence anymore. They're coming out with new treatments every day."

"Daniel—"

"Or surgery. Can't they just remove your ovaries?"

"Daniel—"

"There has to be something, there's always—"

"DANIEL!"

He snaps out of his incessant rambling, his pointless grasping for something that isn't there.

"It's *terminal*. I talked to an oncologist. She gave me a year tops *with* treatment, six months without."

His Adam's apple bobs, like he's finally swallowing what I said. "A year," he whispers, his eyes affixed to me with a blank stare.

I shake my head. "Six months."

"Scar—"

"I'm not doing the treatment."

His head juts forward. "Sorry? Please tell me I didn't hear

you right."

"You heard me."

"No." Daniel shakes his head. "I didn't hear you right. I didn't hear the woman I'm going to marry imply that she has no intention of fighting this. Because *that* woman's mother died of cancer. *That* woman watched my father die of cancer. *That* woman held her best friend's hand while she battled breast cancer for three years. And you never once told my father or Sylvie that they shouldn't have the treatment. Hell, you even took Sylvie to the hospital for her surgery. You took her to her chemo and radiation appointments. You cried over her grave, saying there should have been more we could have done for her!"

"I don't believe in cut, poison, burn," I whisper.

"Cut. Poison. Burn?"

I nod.

Daniel laughs—the painful, condescending kind of laugh. "You don't believe in modern cancer treatment?"

My name is Scarlet Stone. I have 70,000 thoughts a day and they are mine. My human right. I will not be ashamed of having an opinion.

I shake my head.

His jaw drops. We've discussed almost everything over the years but never this. The look in his eyes is one of complete confusion, like he doesn't recognize me.

"You have to make me understand, Scarlet, because I don't."

I wince, feeling ripped apart by his endless head shaking. I feel like his nightmare, one that he can bring himself out of if he shakes his head enough.

"It's just my opinion."

"Well, it's wrong—completely fucked-up!"

Drawing in a deep breath, I fight for control. He's hurt and the devastation he's feeling is what's coming out in his angry words. It's not his fault.

"I would never tell you what to believe, Daniel, so please don't tell me that my opinion is wrong. We should be allowed a few basic human rights in life: the right to decide what goes into our bodies and the right to have an opinion without feeling shamed for it."

"Where was this 'opinion' when my father battled cancer or when Sylvie was dying before your eyes?"

"It was their lives, their opinions, their decisions. Not mine. They never asked my opinion."

His sinister laugh cuts through the air again and gouges my heart. I never wanted to have this discussion with him or anyone. I wanted to take my very unpopular opinion to the grave with me.

"If you don't do this, you're going to die." He grips my shoulders, his face a breath away from mine.

His reaction is fueled by pain and fear. My brain knows this but it still triggers something defensive inside of me. I yank myself out of his hold. My skin heats with anger, and I don't want to say something I will regret, but I can't stop the words. I feel pinned to the ground and my instinct to free myself overtakes every other emotion.

"My mum died. Your dad died. Sylvie died! Everyone is searching for the goddamn cure, but no one is searching for the cause. There is no money to be made in eliminating the *cause* of cancer."

"Scarlet, that's not true."

"It doesn't have to be true! It's just my own opinion. The

cure is *prevention*. If we prevent cancer, then we don't need a cure. But there's no money in prevention. I've hacked into research databases, email, and financial records of the largest pharmaceutical companies. Cancer is no longer a disease, IT'S A FUCKING BUSINESS! And we buy it hook, line, and sinker. 'Hurray! My cancer is gone.' A year or two later—at best—I'm dead because the chemo and radiation obliterated my immune system, so the next time those cancer cells start to divide, they spread like wild fire because there are absolutely no defense mechanisms left. But … here's the silver lining … the pharmaceutical companies make money with round two of cancer treatment as some last-ditch effort that they know won't save me at this point. Instead, it leaves my family with false hope and two seconds later I'm dead!"

Shock. That's all I see in Daniel's lifeless expression. A toxic mix of regret and relief war somewhere between my head and my heart. I've shattered his hopes of changing my mind and for that I feel terrible. At the same time, I feel liberated. Never, ever have I said those words aloud. For years I've watched people I love die, and I've always held my opinions to myself because they are not an answer for anyone but me. But now it's *me,* and all I want is for the people who love me to respect my wishes without trying to change my mind or make me feel irresponsible or crazy.

"This is complete madness." His voice becomes weaker with each word.

"I always go with my gut. If a thousand people are in queue for door A but my eye is drawn to door B with no queue, I choose door B. The most brilliant and innovative people throughout history have shunned the norm, questioned authority, charted new territory, and challenged beliefs that no one before them had ever dared to challenge."

"Cut. Poison, Burn. Call it whatever you want, Scarlet. It's your only option for staying alive." He looks up.

"Those three years … Sylvie wasn't living. She was dying, and it was a fucking miserable death sprinkled with a few moments of false hope." I take in a deep breath, relishing each one that I have left in this life. "Go take a poll, Daniel. Ask every cancer survivor, if given the choice would they have chosen their 'lifesaving' treatment or to never have had cancer in the first place. It's so messed-up. We are a corporate run world. Medicine is a business. Follow the money, Daniel. There is *no* corporate incentive to prevent cancer or even find a true fucking cure!"

He blinks at me over and over. "Jesus, Scarlet, you're jumping off a cliff without a parachute." Daniel pulls me into his arms as all my fight is drained, leaving me with nothing but my sobbing emotions.

"It buys me six more months at best," I whisper. "Six miserable months of having poison in my veins killing me as fast as the cancer. Six more months of practically living in a hospital. Six months of waiting to die. I won't do it. I feel fine today, and I might feel fine tomorrow and the next day."

"The wedding …"

I frown. "There's not going to be a wedding."

"We can move it forward."

I laugh, pushing him away and wiping my tears. "We could. But really … why?"

"I'm supposed to leave next week."

I press my salty, tear-stained lips together as I shake my head. "I'm not asking you to stay."

"Fucking hell, Scarlet! What is that supposed to mean?"

"All the reasons you fell in love with me no longer exist. All the reasons *we* fell in love no longer exist."

He shakes his head. "That's not true."

"You almost married another woman, but you didn't. And why was that?"

"Scarlet, don't do this."

"You didn't marry her because you knew that her dreams of babies and big fluffy dogs would lead to missed opportunities. You were, and still are, unapologetically married to your career." I fist my hands at my heart. "That's what made me love you—your ambition, your desire to live every single second to the absolute fullest. Don't give that up for me or anyone else. It's not selfish, it's admirable and commendable and … beautiful."

I hug his back, he laces our fingers together over his chest.

"If you stay. I will die. If you leave. I will die." I move around to face him.

He blinks and big, fat tears roll down his cheeks. He's seen me cry once since he's known me, but I've *never* seen him cry until now—not even when his father died.

I brush my thumbs along his cheeks. "Daniel, I won't be responsible for your missed opportunity. Do this for me. It's my dying wish."

"Jesus Christ, Scarlet…" his voice breaks "…I'm not leaving you to die alone."

"If you don't leave … I will." It's cruel, I know it, but I hope someday he will not see this as me being selfish. I hope he will see this as exactly what it's meant to be—my love for him, a quick break instead of a long suffering for both of us. I hope by the time I'm dead, he will have already grieved my loss and found his footing in life again with a brilliant career.

He collapses to his knees and hugs my waist. I run my hands through his hair, memorizing how it feels against my skin. Touch. I will miss his touch.

"Fuck you, Scarlet Stone. Fuck you for taking my heart. Fuck you for … for …" he sobs.

"Fuck me for dying," I whisper as I fall to my knees and hug him.

I. Really. Fucking. Hate. This. Life.

CHAPTER FIFTEEN

My name is Scarlet Stone and my first concert was Rod Stewart. In the front row, where the sweat dripped from the sexiest man alive and the roar of the crowd shook the stadium, I vowed to one day marry a rock star.

S ALMON MAKE THE long and grueling journey up their natal river to spawn once and die where their life began. No one tells them to do it. They have this instinct that drives them.

Nolan can't explain how he senses things that no one else can. He just does. I can't explain why I chose to leave London and return to my place of birth to die. I did it on instinct. Maybe this is where my circle of life ends. All I know for sure is I want to know why. Not why do I have cancer. Why am I here? What is the purpose of life? Did I do what I was placed on this earth to do?

Nolan stops the car in my drive. "My father is a terrible husband, and I'm not sure he has that many redeemable qualities in general. But … she loves him. He will never change. I could take him away from her. I could give him exactly what he deserves, but losing him would be the final straw, and … I think she's barely hanging on. One day she's going to remember what happened and that will obliterate her whole world."

I shake my head. "I don't understand."

Nolan's hand rests on mine over the console. "You don't have to. I just needed to say the words aloud to remind myself why I let this go on. Have you ever had this desperate need to say what's been going through your mind for years and it didn't even matter if anyone else understood?"

Yes. I don't understand a word he said about his parents, but his *need* to say it connects with me on a very personal level.

"Scarlet?" he calls before I close the car door. "I think you should see a doctor. It's time."

I smile. "Thank you for lunch."

I HAVEN'T SPOKEN the word *cancer* aloud since I've been here. Yimin has been treating my body for something that he may or may not know exists. The word-filled pages of books written by spiritual teachers have made my reality emotionally manageable.

Shit happens.

All we have is now.

Better give thanks.

I don't know if I drank too much or if the summer I spent with a Frenchman, who convinced me to smoke with him, had some monumental impact on where I am right now. Maybe random sex wasn't the best form of recreation in my late teens. An STD sat in the back of my mind during my recklessness, but never cancer. Maybe in this toxic world my body burden hit a tipping point and my wake-up call came a little too late. But it all comes down to this: does it matter?

All I have is now, and I will take every single now I'm given.

As soon as I open the back door, I hear a voice—someone singing. I creep up the stairs, not wanting to make a noise, fearful the voice will disappear. That would be tragic because I could listen to this voice—*his* voice—forever.

I stop at the top step. Theo has nailed down some sort of underlayment for the tile. I don't know if I'm allowed to step on it, so I sit on the top step and listen to him. He's on his hands and knees with his back to me, several feet away, earbuds in his ears, and he's singing a song I have never heard before.

My name is Scarlet Stone and my first concert was Rod Stewart. In the front row, where the sweat dripped from the sexiest man alive and the roar of the crowd shook the stadium, I vowed to one day marry a rock star.

It's a love song and it's dark and … heartbreaking. I don't recognize the voice, it's tangled with emotion and veiled by sexy grit that is so not the Theodore Reed with whom I've become acquainted. The longer I listen, the more I feel like I'm intruding on something personal. Is he singing this for Kathryn? As I ease to my feet to leave and give him privacy, he stops singing. I halt and wince, feeling his eyes on me before I even turn.

"Hey," he says. I feel zero hatred toward me at the moment because his "hey" is said in a friendly, un-Theo way.

It's the first word we've shared since my breakdown in the bathroom the morning after we had sex. Lots of sex. I don't know what scares me more—our uncontrolled physical attraction or our mutual need to not talk about it, at all, like it never happened, like it was … *nothing*.

"Hey. Sorry. I heard a voice so I came up to see what it was and then …" I shrug as if I've been caught doing something wrong.

Theo stands and pops one earbud out and then the other. I came to Savannah to see where it all began … where I began. But right now, I swear to God I flew to the other side of the pond just to see Theo in a dirty white T-shirt and faded blue jeans with holes in the knees, a red bandana wrapped around his head, and the most vulnerable look in his blue eyes. In this moment, I don't even recognize him.

"You're fine. Did you just get back?"

I nod. "Nolan asked me to lunch."

He leans against the door frame, boots crossed at the ankle. "A date?"

I smile. It feels painful on my face and even more unbearable in my heart. "No. Just lunch. I'm quite possibly the most un-datable person on Tybee Island."

"Because you're engaged?"

I shake my head. "Your voice. I'm starting to think your lie is the truth. If I have…" I bite at my lip, wincing at my likely fate "…a little extra *time*, maybe I can be a groupie for your first concert."

He pushes out a long breath. "Maybe we can play at your wedding reception."

Ouch. This hurts. Does he have any idea how much pain I feel right now?

"The Amazon river has a species of freshwater dolphins. When they get excited they turn pink. Very human of them, don't you think? Anyway, they have this mating ritual. The male throws a piece of driftwood around—which he can do because unlike other species of dolphins, they can turn their heads from side to side. If the female catches it, that means they will mate."

Theo smirks.

"My dad told me that. He fed my insatiable hunger for knowledge more than anyone. Books. He gave me books. Some quite rare."

I look up just as Theo quirks an eyebrow. "And he purchased these books from some little hole-in-the-wall bookstore that happened to have some hidden treasures?"

I grin. "Something like that." No person has ever loved me like my dad. If he knew about the cancer, he would be here. He'd steal a thousand lives to save mine. "I don't…" I shake my head "…I don't know why certain random things pop into my head. But I can't *not* say them. I've been so enamored with the unique, the crazy, the unexpected … I assume everyone around me surely finds this information as fascinating as I do. My dad did." I furrow my brow, staring at my feet. "At least I think he did."

"Dolphins …"

I glance up as Theo speaks.

"Driftwood … mating … fascinating." He rubs the back of his neck, eyes on me, and a boyish grin claiming his mouth.

Who is this man? And where has he been? And why do I feel his hand reaching into my chest, trying to claim something he cannot have?

"Sharks …" He continues. "Sharks kill, on average, ten humans per year—worldwide. Humans … we are responsible for the death of over one hundred million sharks per year. So … statistically, I'm not going to die by the jaws of a shark."

I did not know that. I'm equally saddened by the morbidity of his statement and excited that he has his own random-facts bank. In another life, Theodore Reed would make my heart do flips. A part of my soul would gravitate toward his. However, in this life, I will be satisfied with moments like this, stealing as many nows as I can. Surely, a third-generation thief can do that. Can't I?

"I don't have an eating disorder. Never have had one. I like cheese and cream sauces, anything fried, pints of lager, wine so old it's a crime to drink it, and the occasional puff of a cigar because it reminds me of my grandfather. I obsess over large chocolate bunnies at Easter and sweets at Halloween. I never believed in Father Christmas, but it didn't stop me from pretending that I did so my dad would attempt to bake biscuits to put by the tree. They were the worst thing I have ever tasted.

"But I came here—*Savannah*—to see…" I shake my head and blink back the tears "…to see if I can do it better. To see if doing it better will make a difference in my life. In this life."

Theo's brow pulls tight. I can only imagine what he thinks of my sappy and cryptic view on life. I could tell him. I could say "*I'm dying*," but I don't owe him any explanation, and he doesn't owe me an ounce of sympathy. Everything between us is a lie. We are nothing and that's how it has to be.

Every kiss.

Every touch.

Every moment of skin to skin in truly stolen breaths.

It's all *nothing* but a fleeting moment—a *now* with nothing brought from the past and nothing borrowed from the future. What if life could be that for everyone? What if every moment was free from expectations and regret? What if we started counting time in breaths instead of seconds? What if I could hold my breath and stop time?

I smile. That's my ah-ha moment. When we stop breathing … time does stop. That's when we know our time is up. I think I'll keep counting breaths.

"I'm holding you up." I turn and head down the stairs.

"Maybe I can quit a little early."

I turn.

Theo shrugs. "Maybe I can make us dinner. You know … Food. Small talk. Maybe I say something that makes you grin. Maybe you say something that makes me laugh. Maybe the food is crap so we drink too much wine. Maybe the full moon beckons us to the beach where we walk in the shadows of the night. Maybe you tell me something about yourself. Maybe it's a lie, and maybe that's okay because we're both going our separate ways in a few months. But maybe … just maybe for one night we feel *human*."

I won't love you, Theodore Reed. I can't.

I nod. "I'd like that very much."

CHAPTER SIXTEEN

My name is Scarlet Stone and I would stick my hand in a biscuit barrel of poisonous snakes on the off chance that there might be one biscuit left.

THEODORE

IT'S BEEN A week since I've looked at the newspaper clippings and photos. It's been a week since I polished my knives and closed my hand around my .45 Winchester Magnum or assembled my .22 long rifle. It's been a week since I've thought about killing anyone.

"What is this?" Scarlet covers her mouth with a napkin and coughs a few times.

"Tofu. You said you didn't eat meat." I cut into my medium rare steak.

"What did you do to it?" She gulps down her water then takes a sip of Merlot.

"Fried it in a pan with some of your *sea* salt."

"And?"

"And what?"

"That's it. You're feeding me salted, fried tofu?"

I tap my fork on the bowl of steamed broccoli.

She shakes her head. "You might want to look into a steamer. This broccoli is crunchy."

"It's perfect. Had I cooked it any longer it would have been mush."

"I like mushy veg." She shrugs. "Maybe it's a British thing."

I grab the bottle of wine in one hand and our glasses in my

other hand. Then I stand. "But the wine suits Her Royal Highness?"

She rolls her eyes and pushes away from the table. "The wine is perfect, just like the company."

Don't say that, Scarlet. Don't ever say that.

I can't help but relinquish a small grin. "The beach is calling."

As she steps off the boardwalk into the sand, she stumbles a bit and laughs. "Mr. Reed, I do believe you've gotten me a little tipsy."

She's taken two sips of wine. There's no way she's tipsy. I set our glasses on the top of the railing and refill mine. Then I top off hers. "Here."

She narrows her eyes as she takes the glass. "Your response to me being tipsy is another glass of wine?"

Tapping my glass against hers, I grin. "Just seeing if alcohol makes you *itchy*."

Her wild curls whip in the breeze when she turns. Then she flips off her sandals and trudges toward the water, ignoring my comment. "Tell me a lie, Theo."

The wind presses her dress to her body, revealing small curves that weren't there a few weeks ago. She's by far the most beautiful woman I have ever seen. My life is nothing more than bad timing separated by unimaginable moments of tragedy. I'd reconciled my pain with the promise of revenge … until *her*.

She looks over her shoulder and smiles. "Did you hear me?"

I nod slowly, drawing in a breath to replenish the one she steals every time I look at her. "I grew up in Lexington, Kentucky. My father trained horses. My mother worked at the university."

"I already love this story. So you know how to ride a

horse?"

"I was a jockey."

Laughter fills the night air as she throws back her head, some of her wine sloshes out of the glass. "Aw … poor horse."

"Yes. Poor horse. They are incredible creatures. Some are treated like royalty, others … more like slaves."

She drops the glass in the sand, letting the earth drink the rest of it. "I've never ridden a horse." Her foot rips through the water, splashing it on my legs. "Well…" pinching her lower lip, she tugs on it, meeting my gaze "…except for you."

My dick hardens.

"But I do like to race, and I'm fast. Very fast."

"More lies."

She shakes her head. "Truth. Want to see? Let's race."

I drop the empty wine bottle and my glass next to hers in the sand. "I hope you're right because if I catch you, it's going to be very bad." I don't say that with an ounce of humor.

Her smile fades, eyes wide and glued to mine. She nods as if she understands but there's no way she can.

"You'll never catch me," she whispers. "It will feel like you're chasing a ghost."

She doesn't say go. In the next breath, she's sprinting down the beach. I chase her. After a while it does feel like I'm chasing a ghost. Resigned to the fact that I will never catch her, I slow down, but then she trips, clawing the sand to regain her footing. It's too late. I've caught her.

Grabbing her waist, I lift her to her feet. She's breathless and covered in wet sand.

"Theo …" The second she whispers my name the wind carries it away. I wish it would carry her away before we destroy each other.

I shake my head, grabbing her dress and peeling it over her head. Her body shivers, arms wrapped around her bared breasts as I simply stare at her. Why did she trip?

I shrug off my shirt. Her eyes drop to my chest.

"I told you, if I caught you…" I slide off my shorts "…it would be *very* bad."

She sucks in a shaky breath as I pick her up. Her eyes never leave mine when I ease the crotch of her panties to the side and lower her onto me. Her breath releases in small pants as I completely fill her, walking us into the water.

Her lips part, eyes heavy. "It's…" she blinks slowly as I move inside of her "…j-just a … lie."

Dipping down, I ghost my lips over hers, so fucking hungry for her. I feel like my entire being is ripping apart at the seams. "Is it?" I whisper a second before our mouths collide.

SCARLET

THIS FEELING MAKES it impossible to open my eyes. I'd almost forgotten how it felt to wake next to a warm body pressed to my back, strong arms wrapped around me. I think I'll leave my eyes closed and keep stealing more of these moments—more breaths.

"You have absolutely no gag reflex."

My body shakes with laughter, turning in his arms. I press my lips to his chest, keeping my eyes closed. Our legs scissor together like we're both desperate to stay as close as possible. It's not a hard feat on this sofa bed. If we don't stay hugged to each other, one of us will be on the floor.

"Rude. That's just rude." My lips curl into a huge smile against the smattering of light hair on his chest.

"It's not rude. It's a compliment. A *huge* compliment."

"A 'huge' compliment? Really? Now I get the feeling you're complimenting yourself, not me. Besides, sex stays in the moment. You don't talk about it when it's over."

"I agree."

I tip my head up to nuzzle into his neck, feeling content that he's dropped that topic.

"But, I'm serious. You have *no* gag reflex."

"Oh my god!" I shove his chest and wriggle out of his hold, stealing the white sheet and wrapping it around me as I walk into the kitchen to get a bottle of water. "The Argentine Lake duck has the largest penis of any bird—which I suppose isn't saying much because only three percent of birds in the world have penises." I open cupboard after cupboard looking for something to eat. I'm starving. "Anyway, when erect, it's as long as its total body length." I settle for an apple then lean against the threshold to the living room, taking a big bite. "Now, *that's* bragging rights," I mumble over a mouthful of juicy, green apple.

Theo sits up, resting back on his elbows, my pillow covering his junk. "Is that my apple?"

I stop chewing, images of him digging out a bite of apple from my mouth cross my mind. "Maybe." I release the sheet, letting it fall to the ground. "Is that a problem, Mr. Reed?"

Theo's gaze stretches the length of my naked body. "Not today."

"It's almost six. I'm going for a walk before breakfast with Yimin. Go swim with the sharks." I give him a flirty wink before sashaying my naked arse to the bathroom.

By the time I come back out, he's already gone. I frown at my spider plant on the floor. One of its stems with a baby plantlet has been stepped on and broken. It really needs to get hung from the ceiling, so I look for a hook. Theo has a small toolbox by the stairs, but I don't find a hook. I know he took a lot of stuff upstairs, so I check up there. My eyes affix to the tool belt on the floor in his room. Maybe he has more tools in there.

I tiptoe toward it, making sure I don't step on any of the tiles he has strategically placed in their spot. No luck. It's just a tool belt and several boxes of tile. I slowly make my way to the en suite bathroom. My curiosity is getting the best of me right now. He has everything moved out for the renovation, so I don't know what I expect to find. There's a sink, nothing on the worktop, a toilet with the lid up, and a bath-shower combination. I'm a little surprised the shower curtain is still up.

With a quick tug like I'm doing a big reveal, I slide the shower curtain to the side. Inside the bath is a black footlocker trunk with a heavy padlock on the front.

Close the curtain and walk away, Scarlet. My brain knows the right thing to do.

Not my room.

Not my trunk.

Not my business.

Maybe it's where he plans to keep my body when he cuts me up into six manageable pieces: legs, arms, torso, head.

"You're losing it," I say, rolling my eyes as I slide the curtain closed. "Don't cross that line." Vocalizing my voice of reason seems to help. I've made it back downstairs. It's time for my walk so I'm not late to Yimin's.

I mist a few of my plants by the window and think about the trunk.

I shove my feet into my trainers and think about the trunk.

I grab a bottled water and think about the trunk.

"Fuck it."

My name is Scarlet Stone and I would stick my hand in a biscuit barrel of poisonous snakes on the off chance that there might be one biscuit left.

Before reason has a chance to slay my deadly curiosity, I'm already ten seconds away from having the padlock removed. Daniel used to call me a thief. I preferred philanthropist. Perspective is a funny thing.

"Theo, if you don't want me to get into here, then you really should invest in something more secure than a discount shop padlock." I can talk to myself all I want, make excuses for my really bad behavior—even if justifying breaking the rules is ingrained in my DNA—but it still doesn't make this right. If I'm completely honest, short a lock triggering a bomb, there is nothing he could use to keep me out of this trunk.

The good news? As I ease open the lid, I don't find a cut-up body. However, as I sift through the content, I wonder if the former would be less disturbing.

"Oh my god, Theo …" I whisper.

Guns.

Knives.

Photos.

Newspaper articles.

"What. Are. You. Doing?"

University Of Kentucky's Professor Kathryn Reed Found Dead in Her Home

I skim over the words. *Murder. Survived by a son, Theodore Reed.*

Another article.

Brian Reed Dies of Self-inflicted Gunshot Wound

His parents died. *Suicide. Survived by a son, Theodore Reed.*
Emotion hardens like a golf ball lodged in my throat. My
hands feather over each sentence. I can't believe the words
jumping off the page.

Braxton Ames arrested in the murder of Kathryn Reed.

Another article.

Anonymous donor pays for University of Kentucky Professor, Kathryn Reed's Funeral and donates two million dollars to memorial fund ...

I need to walk away. In another life, one where I didn't
have a closely-estimated date with death, one where I still had
internet access, one where I felt invested in the outcome of
whatever *this* is ... in that life, Theodore Reed's secrets would
consume me.

I *need* to walk away.

"There's always your next life," I mutter to myself as I close
and lock the lid of the trunk as well as my painful curiosity.

OH MY GOD!

I'm dead. There is a hand over my mouth, my chest feels
like a grenade just exploded, and a large arm wrapped around
my waist has my back pinned to a solid body. My cancer must
be pissed off it's not going to get the chance to steal my life.

"Why are you in here?" The whisper at my ear is the Theodore Reed from my first day on Tybee Island. It's the spawn of
revenge and murder. This embrace holds no passion and even
less of a promise that my lungs will ever receive oxygen again.

The calloused paw over my mouth prevents me from answering as my tears spring free. He's going to kill me. My instincts were right.

"Are you going to scream?" The edge to his voice makes my knees tremble.

I shake my head.

His hand slides from my mouth. "Did you open it?"

I swallow back wave after wave of fear as he keeps my back pinned to his chest. "No," I whisper, unable to find my true voice. "It's locked."

"You're lying."

"Everything is a lie." My voice of reason is so much slower than my vocal impulsiveness.

"Open it."

"I don't have the—"

"OPEN THE FUCKING LOCK!"

Normal people who live sheltered lives would convince themselves that they could never die at the hands of a lover. I've known men who have killed their wives, mothers of their children, because they opened the wrong drawer in a wardrobe or arrived home from the supermarket thirty minutes too early. I hold no illusions that Theodore Reed won't kill me.

I open my fisted hand to reveal the pick I used. His body stiffens against mine, like in spite of the truth he knew, the confirmation that I did in fact invade his privacy still sends a small wave of anger—maybe even disappointment—coursing through his body. He loosens his hold on me.

I step forward and unlock the trunk, but I don't open it.

Remorse. It's all I feel right now. My journey to find the best part of my soul and live out that life for as long as I have left has failed. I am a thief. Theo was right. Curiosity will kill the cat.

I can't bring myself to turn and look at him. The last memory I have of his face was the grin of appreciation for my naked body standing in front of him. It held something innocent, beautiful, and worth holding on to forever. That's the only memory I need.

"Open it."

I do. It's not worth my effort to look shocked at the contents. He knows I know.

Easing my hand over the edge, waiting to see if he'll stop me, I reach for the handgun. Why isn't he stopping me? He doesn't move, not one inch. Maybe he's already holding a gun to my head and I just haven't turned to see it.

"I'm sorry," I whisper, wrapping my hand around the gun. I've never held a gun. My father never wanted me to be *that* thief. I close my eyes, letting my palm acclimate to the cold metal grip. "I shouldn't have crossed that line." My eyes pinch tight, wringing more tears out as I lift the gun. "I've loved every minute of our lie." My finger curls around the trigger as the blunt edge of the muzzle kisses my temple.

Every bad thing I've ever done, every failure, every moment of grief, every word of my terminal cancer diagnosis and stolen future hits me like a torrent of negativity that pulls me under, numbing my senses.

Fuck you, cancer.

I pull the trigger.

Nothing.

"Jesus fucking Christ!" He rips the gun from my hand.

My back collides with the wall as my steps falter. I blink through my tears that blur Theo's face marred with utter horror—wild eyes, mouth agape. He shakes me, hands gripping my arms to the point of pain.

Pain.

I feel it in unforgiving waves.

I'm still alive.

Oh. My. God ...

Did I just—

"What the fuck did you just do? Jesus ..." His hands go from my arms to fisting my hair as his forehead presses to mine.

I've never heard such agony in his voice.

"Did you..." each word seems to rip from his throat "...did you think it was loaded?"

Reality shatters this out-of-body experience—the glass box that separated me from life. "Y-Yes," I whisper.

I wanted to die. For one second—I wanted to die.

Pain.

Love.

Anger.

Regret.

For *one* moment ... it was all too much. I wanted out. I. Wanted. To. Die.

What's happening to me?

His nostrils flare with each breath that washes over my face. Pressing a hand to the wall next to me, he pushes off and turns toward the trunk. "You don't get to fucking take your own life." He riffles through the contents.

Numbness. For *one* second it swallowed me up. Now, I'm left drowning in an ocean of shame.

My blank stare lands on his hands shoving a loaded clip into the gun. In the next blink, he slams me back against the wall. The impact punches the breath from my lungs. Theo presses the gun to my temple much harder than I had done.

"*I* take your life. *You* don't get the fucking choice. Do you understand?" The devil dances in his eyes, cold as the metal pressed to my head. His jaw clenches while his whole body shakes, even his hand quivers as he digs the gun into my skin.

Theo or cancer?

Cancer is so unoriginal. I choose Theo.

"Then pull the trigger."

He squeezes his eyes shut and shakes his head, muscles pulsing along his arms and up his neck. "Go." His hand falls limp to his side, the gun dangles from his finger. "GO!"

I suck in a breath, suffering more from the sight of this man—eyes shut and chin down—than I would have had he pulled the trigger.

I turn and move toward the door with an unsteady gait.

"We never talk of what's in the trunk *ever* again or else ..." He leaves the end hanging in the air.

I nod once then keep walking.

CHAPTER SEVENTEEN

My name is Scarlet Stone. I think modern medicine is miraculous—as well as overrated, corrupt, and sometimes deadly. I'm not sure when doctors began to focus on treating the symptoms instead of the root cause of disease. Whenever that was, they could no longer abide by their oath to "do no harm."

I DON'T RECOGNIZE the reflection in the mirror anymore. By all predictions, I will die in about a month. Even if this life doesn't give me my formal eviction in thirty days, Nolan will.

Theo works on our place in between his other projects, and he seems to be on schedule with the upstairs renovations nearing completion.

The trunk? I let it go. I don't know what it all means. The 'Kathryn' tattooed on his arm is his mother. She was murdered. I should be dead too. I pulled the trigger and the *click* of not dying won't stop replaying in my head. Even the stubborn daughter of the great Oscar Stone can admit when she is wrong. Pulling the trigger was wrong.

My purpose in life? I haven't completely figured it out, but I'm getting closer to acknowledging my existence—albeit shorter than I'd hoped—means something. Dancing with death for months reveals many secrets of life. I don't have kids or even that many friends, but if I did, I'd want my lasting impression on them to be this: Every life matters, but never one more than another. Sometimes silence holds more meaning than words. And love … it's infinitely impossible to define, but unequivocally, without any doubt, the reason we are here.

"I'll be gone for a few days," Theo announces as he slides on his trousers, no underwear.

Sex has been a constant between us for the past few months. He didn't pull the trigger either, but that night I swear he tried to fuck me an inch from my life. It was punishing, demanding, controlling, and life-changing. As much as he tried to hide it, I felt every ounce of his pain over what happened that day.

I can't bring myself to address the depression that's been brought on by my diagnosis. It's not just the diagnosis; it's Theo. Accepting death was easier after leaving Daniel and Oscar—severing the ties that fed my guilt over wanting to live out my days on my own terms. Theo makes me want to live *all* my days, even the ones I cannot have—more than I wanted to live them for Daniel or Oscar—and that is too much to take.

Still … it's just been sex mixed with a growing web of lies that serves as a nice barrier to the truth. It's fucked-up in so many ways, yet equally perfect. The one truth we share is that everything is a lie.

I slip on my shirt and pull up my knickers as I stand. "Where are you going?"

Theo glances over his shoulder, his bronze beard a bit longer, his blue eyes a bit softer but they still hold an edge of warning.

I shrug. "Lie to me."

After studying me for a few moments, his focus returns to his zip, yanking it up while he clears his throat. "Kentucky."

A chill slithers along my skin, awakening the curiosity that I've suppressed for months since finding the trunk. "Want company?"

He shakes his head. "Don't you have a wedding to plan?"

My grunt echoes with sarcasm. "Yes. I need to firm up things with the caterer, do the final fitting for my dress, and stop fucking my bearded housemate."

Theo runs a hand through his tangled hair, walking away

from me. "Well check 'stop fucking your bearded housemate' off your list. We're done."

"Fine. I'll call the caterer."

"You don't have a phone." He slams the bathroom door.

"Fuck you." I scowl at the door.

He's right. I don't have a phone. I don't have a caterer or a fiancé either. I barely have a life.

MY MUM DIED of ovarian cancer, but not before they nearly gutted her on an operating table, injected poison into her veins, and charred her inside and out with radiation.

Cut.

Poison.

Burn.

That was my earliest lesson in cancer, a firsthand account from Oscar. Maybe I haven't seen enough miracles in my life to put my entire existence in the hands of companies whose livelihood depends on treating not curing cancer.

Mum was declared NED "No Evidence of Disease." My father took her to Italy to celebrate while my nana watched me. I was eighteen months old.

Modern medicine cured her. Cue the confetti.

Six months later, they found cancer in her liver, lungs, and brain. Thirty-seven days later, she died. I don't remember that but my mum's death has played out in the depths of my father's grief-stricken eyes since my earliest age of remembrance. He didn't want her to have the chemo in the first place.

Cancer is the effect of weaknesses in the body, not the cause of it. My mum obliterated the last shred of her immune system with carcinogens. Someone—anyone with a spark of true intelligence—has to see the irony in treating cancer with carcinogens. My opinion is wildly unpopular. Does it matter? No. It's just my opinion and it only should matter to me.

My mum wanted the treatment. As much as I feel cheated of a life with her, I could never blame her for taking the path in life she chose to take. It's a bittersweet celebration of freedom.

"Scarlet Stone," the nurse calls my name.

The air reeks of disinfectant and the temperature is much cooler than necessary. The setting supports my belief that humans go to the doctor to die, not to live. If they're going for the modern-day mortuary feel, mission accomplished.

I giggle. The timing is terrible, but I can't help it. I imagine the nurse saying, "Scarlet Stone, we'll fit you for your coffin now." Maybe the cancer has spread to my brain. At least I could blame my crazy thoughts on that instead of having to completely claim them as my own.

"Let's get you weighed, and then I'll have you deposit a urine sample in this cup and place it on the shelf in the restroom."

The nurse frowns at my weight. How professional of her.

I wee. Find my room. Undress. And sit on the folded gown.

There's a knock at the door.

"Yes," I respond.

The doctor enters with his head down, focused on his electronic tablet. When did bedside manner become optional?

"Scarlet, I'm Doctor—" He looks up, then down, then turns.

"Sorry, do you need help with your gown?"

"Nope. If your medical degree is legit, then I don't think my naked body should be an issue. Don't act like you're not going to ask me to recline back and spread my legs."

"Ms. Stone, it's protocol for you to—"

"Protocol schmotocol … I'm not hitting on you. I simply think the paper-gown peekaboo game is utterly ridiculous. Let's just get on with this."

I can't explain my behavior, because I'm not a nudist. The only good reason I have for making this poor man feel uncomfortable is Theo. Since he tried to dismiss everything between us, I've sort of run out of give-a-fucks.

He turns and clears his throat.

However, it is quite ironic how I'm the one who feels most vulnerable with that stupid gown on, yet he's the one who is clearly uncomfortable without me wearing it.

"So you're here to … *check on your cancer?*" His finger traces along the screen, repeating my *Reason For Visit* verbatim.

"Yes."

"I don't have any of your medical records. Have you had a cancer diagnosis?"

"Yes."

"Well, without your records, I can only run through standard procedure: physical exam, blood and urine tests—"

"Give me your tablet."

He shakes his head. "I can't—"

I hop off the table. There are probably not enough days left in my life to learn to play by the rules, but that's what I'm here to find out. He steps back until the wall meets him. I'm seriously questioning his medical degree.

"You can't do this," he protests as I snatch the tablet from him.

"I'm here to check on my cancer…" I access the internet "…and you need my medical records…" my finger eats up the screen, making haste with my mildly-illegal hack into my own medical records "...so I'm getting you my records so we don't have to reschedule and wait for all the ... *protocol* to be followed. Things run much more smoothly when we look at rules and laws as recommendations. Helpful—or sometimes not—suggestions."

"Ms. Stone, this is completely un—"

"Here." I hand him the tablet.

He smooths over his dark hair and adjusts his thick round glasses before he takes the tablet. I ease my bare bum back onto the table and fold my hands in my lap while he reads in silence for several minutes.

"How do you feel?" He finally looks up with a deep line of confusion along his brow.

"Amazing. That's just it. I haven't felt this good in..." I shake my head "...forever."

"Any pelvic or abdominal pain?"

I shake my head.

"Bloating?"

"A bit when I first arrived in Savannah five months ago. It was mild and disappeared within a few weeks."

"Loss of appetite?"

I shake my head.

"Urinary issues such as increased frequency or urgency?"

I shake my head.

He releases a long breath, eyes moving across the tablet again. "Back pain, menstrual changes, fatigue, pain during sex?"

I continue to shake my head.

"You're below normal weight for your height and age."

"Weight charts have been adjusted over the years to normalize obesity, especially in children. It's truly disturbing. I'm not underweight."

I don't share that a little over two months ago I was very underweight. Something tells me he wouldn't understand the health benefits of liquid fasting. Conventional medicine frowns upon anything that doesn't come in the form of a prescription.

"I'm not an oncologist, but I can say the progression and symptoms of cancer can be different for everyone, especially with ovarian cancer. We're not going to know anything definitive until we do a few tests. Then you can meet with an oncologist to discuss further treatment."

My name is Scarlet Stone. I think modern medicine is miraculous—as well as overrated, corrupt, and sometimes deadly. I'm not sure when doctors began to focus on treating the symptoms instead of the root cause of disease. Whenever that was, they could no longer abide by their oath to "do no harm."

"Further treatment? I haven't had any treatment, and I don't want treatment. I just want to know where I stand because three different doctors gave me six months to live without treatment. I sold my worldly possessions and deposited almost all of the money into my ex-fiancé's savings account." My voice escalates with each word as I fist my hands in my lap. "I buried my past—my life—in London and stamped it with a gravestone, never to return. I came here to die, but I don't feel like I'm dying. My lease is up in thirty days. I just need to know if I'm going to die on time!"

The unsuspecting doctor winces.

Something drips onto my leg. I look down at the clear moisture, then I touch my fingers to my cheek. I don't know when I started crying, but sure enough, the little bastards broke free. After brushing them away, I press the heels of my hands to my eyes and slowly shake my head.

"Just run the tests," I whisper.

CHAPTER EIGHTEEN

My name is Scarlet Stone, and I was with my best friend when she died. Her parting words to me were: "The only thing worse than living with regret, is dying with regret."

WAIT THREE days to get the results of my tests. Nolan drives me to the oncologist. I'm not sure why I was referred to a cancer specialist when I have no intention of having any treatment.

"What's the doctor going to say?" I ask Nolan as he parks in the parking ramp.

"I don't know."

"Don't tell me that. You've had a *feeling* all along. You told me months ago to see a doctor. Just say it."

He sighs, angling his body toward mine after he parks the car. "I've had five MRIs in the past two years. I've seen four of the top neurologists in the world. I don't know why I can sense ailments in the human body. It's not a gift. It's a curse and some days I want to end my own life because I *feel* the pain. Do you understand? Can you imagine what it's like to feel everything so vividly? I'm a pathetic recluse most of the time because I don't want to be around humans. Sick. Disease-ridden. Humans."

I rest my hand on his. "I cause you pain."

He shakes his head. "No … that's just it. I don't feel it anymore. And as much as I want that to mean something positive for you … there's this selfish, sadistic part of me that wants to find out your cancer is everywhere because that means I'm no longer *feeling* the pain."

I laugh and Nolan looks at me like I've lost the plot, but I can't stop laughing.

"What's so funny?" He tries to hide his own grin. "I know I'm really messed-up."

I shake my head, trying to catch my breath. "No ... four weeks. I should be dead in four weeks." I laugh some more. "Oh, hell ... I *need* to be dead in four weeks." It's pure exhilaration when hysteria takes over. "I'm about out of money. I have no job. I left my fiancé. My dad is in prison. And I'll be homeless in four weeks." I hold up my hand. "Come on, Nolie," I giggle out of control. "High-five for terminal cancer."

His eyebrows pull together. I hate that.

Regret.

He has no reason to feel regretful. We shame ourselves way too much for our most raw and true feelings. I hop out when he refuses to give me a high five.

"Scarlet?"

I continue walking and laughing all the way to the entrance. Something snapped in my brain, and I can't stop laughing.

Death I can accept. Life I can live. It's the in between, the whiplash of emotions, that's taking my last shred of sanity.

"Scarlet ..." Nolan grabs my arm a second before I open the door.

In this very moment, I know he feels everything I'm feeling. I might not feel it like he does, but I see it in his eyes. My smile fades, and as if someone flipped a switch, I fall to pieces in his arms.

I don't want this. Dying shouldn't be this hard.

"Shh ..." he whispers in my ear.

"I-I'm so scared."

"I know."

I've questioned Nolan's extraordinary ability to sense things up until this point, but right now I believe he does know. He knows I'm not afraid of dying—I'm afraid of living.

NOLAN DROPS ME off at the house. I don't say much because there really isn't anything to say. The two oncologists didn't have much to say either. Theo's truck is in the drive. I'm not ready to face him, but life doesn't seem to care about readiness.

I open the door and stop as soon as I look up. "Hey."

Theo leans against the threshold to the kitchen, tatted arms crossed over his chest, hair pulled back. He doesn't say anything, and that's okay because all these emotions that have been denied, rejected, even passed off for another lifetime, are ready to explode.

"I have something to say." My heart wants out of my chest. I can barely breathe as it tries to escape. My voice shakes, even my hands won't stop trembling as I fist them. "I came here in search of peace. I came here to find something true about my existence. I came here to …" I blink and my emotions crumble. "I came here to die."

Theo doesn't even blink.

"I had terminal cancer, they gave me six months to live."

He blinks. It's something. His gaze moves from me to the floor between us. What is he thinking?

I can't stop and wait. I have to say this. "I saw the doctor today, and he said it was stage one. It's crazy. They think it had to be a misdiagnosis, but I had three different oncologists confirm my terminal cancer diagnosis. It's going away. I left my life—I *ended* my life in London. I broke off my engagement. I said goodbye to my dad. I sold everything and left it to

Daniel. In a few weeks, I'm going to be broke and homeless."

"You need money." His eyes meet mine.

I flinch. "What? No ... I mean, yes, but that's not my point."

He shakes his head. "Then it doesn't matter. Go home."

I step closer. He stiffens. I stop.

"*Don't* tell me it doesn't matter." I grit my teeth as more tears spill down my cheeks. "We—"

"There is no we. Go home. Go get married. Go live happily ever after."

"Stop!" I swallow hard as months of anger erupt. "Don't you understand, you stubborn arse, I don't want to go—"

"Scarlet?" A man's voice stops my words—my heart—like a fatal dagger.

"Daniel," I whisper, turning slowing toward my ex-fiancé emerging from the small bathroom with all kinds of pain etched into his face that's covered in several days of stubble, bags sagging heavily beneath his eyes like he hasn't slept in months.

"You're alive."

I nod. Right now, with every cell in my body, I wish I weren't. I'm beating the most impossible odds. I've been given a second chance, but I no longer want it. He heard everything I said to Theo. I've been in that bathroom enough to know there is nothing soundproof about it.

"I came for you. I came to tell you how sorry I am for letting you push me away. I came here in hope of finding you alive, holding you until you took your last breath, whispering I love you over and over until all you feel is my love—not the pain. But ..." He clears his throat and blinks back the tears filling his red eyes as he clenches his jaw.

There is no explanation that I can give him that will ever make him understand. "I love you, Daniel."

He shakes his head. "Finish."

My eyes narrow a bit. "Finish what?"

"Finish what you were going to say to *him*." He jabs his finger in Theo's direction. "You don't want to go … where? London? With me? With Oscar?"

My gaze shifts back to Theo, but his eyes hold as much contempt as Daniel's. Apparently, I'm the worst human alive. *Alive* … I internally laugh.

"It's—"

"Don't you dare say it's not what I think!" Daniel yells.

I jump. I wasn't going to say that. My trembling lips fold between my teeth as more tears spring free with every blink.

My name is Scarlet Stone, and I was with my best friend when she died. Her parting words to me were: "The only thing worse than living with regret, is dying with regret."

"It's exactly what you think," I say each word slow and evenly, but I say it looking at Theo. "I came here to die and fell in love with another man. I didn't count on finding *him* anymore than I counted on living."

Theo glares at me, like he has some superpower stare that can break me and everything we shared. I tip my chin up, owning my feelings for him. Owning them in front of Daniel, knowing that I'm completely shattering him for a second time. Love is indiscriminate in its path—healing some people while destroying others.

Theo pushes off the wall and closes the space between us. I love this man and I know he loves me, even if it pisses him off that he loves me.

I know how he feels.

It pisses him off that his heart let me in.

I know how he feels.

It pisses him off that he needs my touch.

I know how he feels.

"Go home. I don't love you." He brushes past me and slams the back door behind him.

I turn and chase him, led only by my heart. My brain registers the look of utter devastation on Daniel's face, but my heart leads the way, and for the first time in my life, I let it.

"Theo!" I run to his truck and bang on his window as he backs out of the drive.

He ignores me. I keep banging my fists against the glass.

"Stop it. He's going to run you over, Scarlet." Daniel wraps his arms around my waist and pulls me away from the truck.

"No. No. No …" I try to wriggle free.

"Come on. Let's go home."

My eyes leave the taillights fading into the distance and land on Daniel's face. I'm stunned into complete silence, tears still clinging to my eyelashes. *London*? He can't be serious.

"Eventually, I'll forgive you. What we had can't be destroyed in a day," he mutters in defeat as he pulls me back into the house.

I wasn't cheating on Daniel. We were over. I was supposed to be dead to him. But now I feel like a cheater—a cheater who needs forgiveness.

"Where is your stuff?" He looks around, anywhere but directly at me.

My tears have stopped. My jaw is slack. My vocabulary—nonexistent.

"Here it is." He heads toward my suitcase in the corner of the room. I've been living out of it since we moved our stuff to the main level. I do nothing. He does everything, including grabbing all of my personal items from the bathroom. "Anything else?"

Blink. Blink. Blink.

"Scarlet? Is this everything?"

I nod.

I MATTER.

I love myself.

The world is a better place with me in it.

Who has to think those words? Me. That's who. I'm not sure how many more times I can get jerked around, knocked down, and kicked in the stomach before I tap out.

Daniel drives us to his hotel in Savannah. I remind myself that the hole in my soul the size of Theodore Reed will not remain forever. This is my journey. No matter who I meet on the way, it's mine and only mine.

I found out I was going to die and I wanted to live.

I found out I was going to live and now I want to die.

It's time to count breaths and give thanks for every single one. Eventually, I won't have to remind myself to take them.

"How did you find me?" I whisper as we enter the hotel room.

We haven't said a word since we left the house.

Daniel plops my bags down and sits on the edge of the bed. "Oscar."

I close my eyes and shake my head. "What have you done? I told you never to tell him."

He pulls his shoulders up and drops them with a heavy sigh. I've drained him. "It felt like a life-or-death situation. I knew he'd know how to find you."

"He's going to break out."

Daniel shakes his head. "Why do you say that?"

"Because you told him his baby girl is dying!"

Daniel winces.

I pace the room. "You have to go back and tell him I'm fine. If he breaks out, he will be a fugitive forever, but if he serves his time, then he can be free again. You have to go back. You have to—"

"We."

I stop and narrow my eyes at him. "Sorry?"

"We. *We* will go back and tell him you're fine, even though you're not completely fine. Stage one cancer is still cancer."

"Daniel ... I'm not going back." It feels like I'm giving a five-year-old instructions—soft and slow.

He shakes his head and reaches for my hand, pulling me to stand between his legs. "Scarlet ..." He presses my hand to his chest. I feel his scar beneath his shirt. "You're my heart. I lived for you. It's a miracle that I'm even alive, but I am. And so are you. We are two miracles. Don't you see that? In spite of everything, we're meant to be together. The cheating doesn't—"

"Whoa." I step back. "I didn't cheat on you. We weren't together."

"We were engaged." He jumps to his feet. I take another step back.

"*Were.* I left you—I left us. I grieved you and what we had."

"By jumping into bed with another man?"

I turn and look out the window. "I don't even know what I'm supposed to apologize for. Having cancer? Choosing to live my last days on my own terms? Finding comfort in the touch of another man when I thought I was going to die? Or not actually dying?"

"Tell me it was just sex, Scarlet. Tell me you didn't really mean what you said to him. Tell me—"

"It was nothing." I face him again, emotions burning my eyes. "It was a lie. But at some point that lie became my greatest truth. And that 'nothing' turned into something that right now feels like everything. Now I'm left with the cold reality that *we* were the lie, Daniel."

His face contorts into a mask of confusion. "What are you talking about?"

I forgave myself for this when my death seemed imminent. Now I need to let go of it in order to live.

"When you were in the hospital..." I draw in a shaky breath as the past slams into me again "...and the doctors said you needed a heart transplant soon or you were going to die, I panicked."

Daniel's eyes narrow. "We all did."

I shake my head. "I didn't just panic. I did something ..."

"What do you mean?"

All these years, he's had no idea how much truth there was to his joking about me being a thief who stole his heart.

"I moved your name to the top of the transplant list, and I deposited a sizable amount of money in the accounts of anyone who would notice the change in the list."

"You said ..." He shakes his head. "You said the recipient died before the heart arrived. You said I was the closest match, and if I didn't take it, the donor heart would be lost. You said it was a miracle."

Oscar told me to "save the boy." He said that between right and wrong, life and death, there existed a gray area called love.

In his completely fucked-up book of life principles, he insisted that love was boundless, fairness was a flaw of the weak, and morals killed more people than they saved.

Until five months ago when I left London, I was a product of Oscar Stone, equal parts nature and nurture—a third-generation thief destined to get caught. We all do, eventually.

"I lied."

"You lied? You LIED!?!"

"I'm sorry. For *that*, I am truly sorry."

"So … so …" He laces his fingers behind his neck and turns his gaze to the ceiling. "You're sorry for lying to me or you're sorry for stealing a heart that should not have been mine?"

"Both."

He laughs the most cynical laugh. "So looking back, almost eight years later, you wish you wouldn't have stolen the heart?"

I shake my head. "I wish I wouldn't have taken a life."

"Semantics."

"No. I had no issue with stealing the heart. I'd do it again. If there were some bank of hearts available to the highest bidder, I'd lie and steal from almost anyone to give you life. Even now." I need him to understand that my love for him has not vanished. It never will. "But that heart didn't belong to the highest bidder. It belonged to another human, just like you, desperate to live. So I didn't just steal your heart. I stole a life. *That* I would take back. *That* I would undo if I could. Even if …"

"Even if it meant I didn't live."

I blink, releasing my tears as I return a slow nod.

His jaw clenches several times as his glassy eyes meet mine. Before me stands a man who feels guilty for being alive. I never wanted for him to feel this way, but my guilt nearly killed me. I honestly believe it played a leading role in my body succumbing to cancer.

"I still love you," he whispers.

Biting my trembling lips together, I nod, wanting nothing more than to fall into his arms and sob. Of course he still loves me. I would never have said 'yes' to any man who didn't love me so completely. As much as the old me wants this to be an epic moment about a woman who fell in love with two men, but ultimately chose the one she loved longer, it's not.

I step closer to him and press my hand to his chest again. "I love you *always*, Daniel. But no matter what my prognosis is, the Scarlet you proposed to? She died. I'm not her. I'm not going back to London with you—to that life—to Oscar. Over the past five months, I found this person I never knew existed, and I like her and so does my body. *She's* the Scarlet who is beating cancer. *She* lives in the moment. *She* doesn't own a single electronic device. *She* sees life so differently. *She* doesn't live with regret."

My hand moves from his heart to his handsome face, wiping away his tears. "*She* ... loves another man."

Daniel collapses to the floor, hugging my waist. We've come full circle. I run my hands through his hair as he buries his face into my shirt and cries.

"Fuck you, Scarlet Stone. Fuck you for taking my heart. Fuck you for ... for ..." he sobs.

"Fuck me for *living*," I whisper as I fall to my knees and hug him.

Right now, in the middle of the worst kind of pain, I realize I'm not choosing Theo. He may *not* love me. We may forever be *nothing*. I can live with that. I will *live* with that. I'm choosing to let go of the guilt and hold on to the sound of my own breath—breathing in, breathing out. I count them. Today, I choose Scarlet Stone.

CHAPTER NINETEEN

THEODORE

FOURTEEN TRIPS.

It takes fourteen trips to the old Asian guy's place to deposit the plants that she left behind. He regards me through his screen door, wearing a "poor bastard" expression that I sure as fuck don't need. But he says nothing. I didn't ask him if he wants them. When I set the last two down, he eyes me for a few seconds, then he nods.

After three washings, I decide to burn the sheets from the pullout bed and her pillow. I refuse to smell her anymore. I throw out all of her food, even the shit that I'd normally eat. It's hers and I don't want it.

I swim.

I work.

I drink.

I get a new tattoo.

I watch porn on my computer. The really bad kind. No kissing or sensual shit—just hardcore fucking. Anything to forget about her.

Days get X'd on my calendar. My guns get cleaned and my knives get sharpened.

After two weeks, I'm still so fucking pissed. That was her plan ... screw around and die. She could have died on me with my dick buried in her. I'd have been left fucking a corpse. The thought repulses me, so much so I expel the contents of my last six beers over the edge of the balcony.

After thirty minutes of recovery, I retrieve another six pack from the refrigerator.

Unzip my pants.

And watch more porn.

"THEO?"

I'm not ready for company. Nolan has the worst timing. "Upstairs," I yell.

"Looks amazing."

I nail in the final piece of trim and turn. "Thanks. I'll fill in the nail holes and that's it."

He nods, looking around the bedroom. "I'll put it on the market by Friday."

"I'll be out this weekend."

"Take your time." He tips his chin up. "What's with the plant?"

I glance over at the damn peace lily. I should have given it to the Asian guy too, but I didn't.

"She left it."

"Scarlet?"

I nod, sweeping up the saw dust.

"You want me to take it to her?"

I grunt. "I'm sure they have houseplants in London."

"Probably, but London doesn't have Scarlet Stone."

"What's that supposed to mean?" I bend down and sweep the pile into the dust pan.

"A couple of days ago I received a call from a guy who owns an apartment in town. Scarlet listed me as a reference on her rental application. Later that afternoon, she showed up at the house, on a bicycle—an old Schwinn. Said it was all she could afford for now."

"And what did she want?" I try to sound like I don't care, because I don't.

"A job. She wanted to know if I knew of any good job openings."

"Why—" I stop myself.

"Why what?"

"Nothing." I shake my head.

It was nothing.

It was a lie.

It's over.

I'm leaving soon, and I won't be returning.

CHAPTER TWENTY

My name is Scarlet Stone and my biggest fear is that some-day I will find what I want most in life and it will be impossible to steal.

SCARLET

I HAVE A bicycle with a tire that keeps deflating, a one-bedroom flat free of anoles at the moment, and a job that pays a dollar over minimum wage because my boss is a total tight arse. He says the benefits make up for the low pay, that and it's a made-up job—one I made up.

"You're late."

I bump Nolan's arm on purpose as I invite myself inside his mansion. "I had to stop three times to pump up my tire." I hold up my small bike pump.

"You should buy a new tire or a *car*."

"When you pay me my first wages, I will get a new tire. The car will require a bit more money in the bank." I drop my rucksack and water bottle by the door and slip off my trainers.

"I offered to give you a loan—an advance."

"You did and it was very generous of you. Had I not had enough money for my deposit and first month's rent, I might have taken you up on your offer. But I'm good. I want to do things on my own." I smile. I want to do things fairly and *legally*.

"Good morning, Miss Stone. Can I get you some breakfast? Coffee? Tea?" Sofia greets me.

"Tea would be lovely, thank you."

Nolan gestures to a room off the foyer. "Mother is still

sleeping. Come in and have a seat."

"Have you told her about me?" I sit in the black and white paisley arm chair by the window. Nolan sits opposite of me.

"You mean that I've hired her a babysitter?" He smirks, smoothing his hand over his black trousers as he crosses one long leg over the other.

"A personal assistant and confidante, not a babysitter."

"Let's stick to personal assistant." Nolan narrows one eye. "Confidant implies she's going to share her secrets with you. She doesn't know she has any secrets to share, and I'd prefer we keep it that way."

Sofia serves us coffee and tea.

"Thank you." I smile before taking a sip. "I thought we could go shopping today."

"She buys everything secondhand."

I shrug. "That's fine. She can show me her favorite places. Does she have a bike?"

Nolan rolls his eyes as he pours cream into his coffee. "She has a driver. Lorne will take you. He'll be here by ten." He stirs his coffee with a silver spoon. "How are you feeling?"

My fingernail traces the pattern on the arm of the chair as my lips twist to the side. "You tell me?"

"I don't feel emotions very well. Physically, you're much better."

I nod. "Have you talked to Theo lately?"

"Yesterday. He's done with the place. I'm surprised you moved out so soon. You were paid up through the month. I take it something went wrong?"

I laugh. "I didn't die as expected. My ex-fiancé showed up unannounced and met the man I've been fucking for months—"

Nolan chokes on his coffee, holding his fist to his mouth. "You … what?"

"Oh, Theo didn't tell you?"

He shakes his head while clearing his throat.

I watch the wind whip around the tall grass in the distance. "It was just sex, boredom—nothing." Everything. It was everything.

"I didn't know you were engaged."

"Yes. I had a new job. A really good-paying job." Turning, I narrow my eyes at Nolan.

He grins.

"A new car. Money in the bank. My dad is in prison, but hey, no one has a flawless life. Then there was Daniel. We were perfect together, or so it seemed at the time. Then I got my diagnosis and that perfection just … shattered." I still can't talk about it without emotions stinging my eyes.

"To sum it up, I didn't want to ruin Daniel's career, or his life. One was enough. So I said goodbye—forever—and I came here to die. Theo was …" I shake my head. "I don't know. Something physical I needed at the time. It wasn't until I found out that I wasn't going to die—at least not right away— that I realized I …" I press the pad of my finger to the corner of my eye, trapping my tear before it falls.

"You fell in love with him."

I nod.

"You should tell him."

I laugh. "I did. I told him right in front of Daniel. I thought it would mean more if he knew I was willing to hurt one man that I loved to prove my love to another man."

"He didn't say anything?"

"He said he doesn't love me."

My name is Scarlet Stone and my biggest fear is that someday I will find what I want most in life and it will be impossible to steal.

Nolan has no response. There really is none. I fell in love with a man who never hid his complete detest for me since our first encounter.

"Mr. Moore, your mother is awake."

We both stand and nod at Sofia.

"Don't take it personally. Theo is pretty messed-up. You're better off without him," says the man whose parents define completely insane. "He's moving out this weekend anyway."

I follow him up the stairs. "Where is he going?" I'm doing a shit job of acting like I don't care.

"Nashville ... Tennesse."

He's leaving. I can't believe "I don't love you" was his goodbye. Fuck cancer. Nothing is more painful than love. But I won't feel sorry for myself. Daniel has to feel the same way right now. I gave him a life again ... and then I took it away.

Nolan turns. "I didn't tell her I hired you. She thinks you need a friend."

My head bobs a bit side to side. Then I shrug. "It's not entirely untrue."

He grins and knocks twice on Nellie's door. "Mom, Scarlet is here."

"Perfect timing." The door opens.

Nolan doesn't flinch. How is it possible that every muscle in his face remains completely relaxed? His mother has on a powder-blue felt skirt with a poodle appliqué and a pink corset. I'm not sure anyone has ever paired these two items of clothing before now.

"Be a dear and tie this for me." She turns.

I grab the corset laces and give them a gentle tug with my eyes on Nolan.

"Thanks for spending time with Scarlet today, Mother. I think she said something about shopping. Lorne will be here soon."

"Thank you, Nolie." She sucks in a deep breath.

I cinch the corset.

"Has Nolie proposed to you yet?"

I look toward the stairs, but *Nolie* is gone.

"No. We're just friends."

"Oh? He said you didn't have any friends."

"I don't have any female friends."

Nellie looks over her shoulder. "You do now." She smiles, orange-red lipstick stuck to her teeth.

"There." I tie the bow. "Shall I see if Sofia has your breakfast ready?"

"Please."

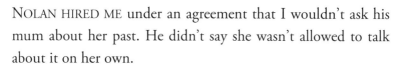

NOLAN HIRED ME under an agreement that I wouldn't ask his mum about her past. He didn't say she wasn't allowed to talk about it on her own.

"You're quite fashion forward, Nellie. I bet you've always had an eye for it." Not a question—just a statement. I watch her rummage through rack after rack of secondhand clothes, picking out only the most hideous and outdated pieces.

She stops and looks at me with her head cocked to the side like she's searching for an answer, but I didn't ask a question. It's her past. She's trying to remember if in fact she has always had an eye for fashion.

I grab a fancy wide-brimmed black hat with three soft pink

roses in the front and slip it on. Nellie's gaze moves to the hat and becomes even more intense.

"I liked hats," she whispers like she's not really sure if it's true. Her face pales a bit.

"You look like you could use some lunch. What do you say?"

Her vacant eyes shift to me, yet I know she's still sifting through something from her past that's not clear. After a few moments, she seems to let it go as her smile reappears, her eyes more focused again. "Yes. Lunch would be perfect."

We go out for lunch. Lorne drives us around town so Nellie can give me the history of Savannah that Nolan already gave me when I arrived. She can't remember *her* past, but she remembers everything about Savannah's past. I like Nellie. Theo said before the 'incident' she was a rich southern bitch, and maybe she was. However, she's not now, and I hope if or when she gets back her memory, she keeps the part of her that is grounded in secondhand clothes and supermarket coupons.

When we pull up to the house, she reaches over and rests her hand on mine. "You're welcome."

I smile, feeling a laugh building in my belly. She's sincere, as if I'd thanked her, and I had planned on it, but she beat me to that part of our conversation.

"Thank you." It's so backwards, but she doesn't seem to notice. "Maybe we can do something together again tomorrow."

She nods. "If you need me, I'm here for you."

Lorne opens her door just as mine is opened as well.

"Hey!"

Nolan offers his hand and helps me out. "Did you two lovely ladies have a pleasant day?"

"We did." I grin because it's the truth.

"You two will give me lovely grand babies."

Nolan wiggles his eyebrows in the first really flirtatious look he's ever given me. I roll my eyes as we follow Nellie inside.

"I'm going out to the house to check everything over before I put a sign up. Want to ride along? When I was there yesterday, I noticed you left a plant."

"*A* plant?" I laugh. "I left thirty odd plants. I'm sure they are dying. I should get the ones that are salvageable, but—"

"No." Nolan shakes his head as we both give Nellie and Sofia a wave goodbye. "One. There was only one plant that I saw. Something with white blooms." He shuts the door behind us.

I hike my rucksack over my shoulder. *The peace lily.*

"It didn't look dead. He's clearly been watering it."

I stop a few feet from my bike. "I'll go with you."

CHAPTER TWENTY-ONE

My name is Scarlet Stone, and I've been told I have a fiery personality when it comes to men. Of course, the only people who tell me that are men.

N OLAN LOOKS OVER at me after he turns off his car. I stare at Theo's truck in front of us.

"You good?"

I nod, but I'm far from good. This is a bad idea. So he kept the lily, it doesn't mean anything.

"If it gets too awkward, grab your plant and wait for me in the car. Okay?"

Taking in a deep breath, I open the door. "I'll be fine."

As we approach the door, it opens. I stop, Nolan runs into my back, but it doesn't distract from my focus on dinner girl—the girl who Theo brought home the night I made him dinner. The girl who thought I was his maid has something in her hands—*my peace lily*!

"That's my plant," I mutter as I charge toward her.

"Hey!" Her eyes bulge out, mouth open in shock, when I snatch the plant from her. "Theo gave me that!"

I glare at her for a full five seconds before I tear open the screen door and march inside with my plant. Nolan says something to her, but I can't register his words over the anger surging in my veins, making it difficult to hear anything but my own racing heart.

The target of my anger turns, partially hidden behind boxes on the worktop. He gives me the once-over with no discernible expression before he wraps a plate in newspaper and places it in a box.

"Did you fuck that tart then give her *my* peace lily as a parting gift?"

He ignores me. The stupid wanker has the nerve to ignore me.

"You have your plant, Scarlet. Maybe it's time for you to wait in the car," Nolan says, stepping in front of me so I can no longer see Theo.

"Maybe you should wait in the car for *me*, Nolan," I grit through my teeth.

"Maybe you both should come back after I've moved out. Technically, this place is still mine."

I step past Nolan before he can stop me. "*Ours*, you big arse. Technically it's still ours, but the lily is *mine!*" My voice proves to be double the size of my body.

"Give us a few minutes, Nolan," Theo says with his frigid glare on me.

"You okay?" Nolan asks me.

"I'm not the one you should be worried about," I narrow my eyes at Theo. The humming bird … I will always be the humming bird.

Nolan chuckles with a slight head shake. "I'll be up the way, getting a beer. Call me when you get this settled."

I still don't have a mobile but saying that would break my concentration. Nothing can distract me from plotting Theodore Reed's death.

The door clicks and Theo steps toward me. I step back.

"Where's your fiancé?"

"Daniel is in London, but he's not my fiancé. I broke off my engagement *six months ago*."

Theo takes another step. I don't move; instead, I hug the peace lily tighter.

"You gave me the plant."

I shake my head. "You rejected her, so she's mine."

"You abandoned her." He takes another step.

I can't breathe with him towering over me. "You rejected me. You basically spat on my face and dumped me. Then you fucked that tart and gave her *my* peace lily."

He laughs—the nerve of him.

"Why do you always think I'm fucking her?"

My jaw drops as my head juts toward him. "Are you serious?" I stomp past him and slam the lily onto the worktop. It's not my intention to release my frustration on Phoebe, but this man is monumentally irritating.

"Sorry." I plant my fists on my hips. "But if I'm not mistaken, that's what you implied when you first brought her here. The night your *maid* cooked dinner."

"I didn't fuck her that night. I told you that."

"But you did today."

He shakes his head, pumping his fists at his sides, the muscles along his tatted arms flexing over and over. "She showed up unexpected. Yes, she wanted to 'fuck,' but we didn't. I told her I'm moving. She seemed to like the plant, so I told her to take it. You were gone. What did it matter?"

My name is Scarlet Stone, and I've been told I have a fiery personality when it comes to men. Of course, the only people who tell me that are men.

"Gone? GONE!?" I throw my hands in the air. Then I press my palms to the side of my head. "I've been *here*! I've been waiting for you. I destroyed a good man to prove my love for you. I laid my heart at your feet and you stomped the living shit out of it. The day I found out I had a second chance at life, with endless possibilities, the only—*only* thing I knew for certain was…" my voice cracks just like my heart "…that I wanted you."

With one blink, the last shred of my composure evaporates. I didn't think I possibly had anything else to lay on the line. I was wrong. So here it goes.

"I know the words…" I can't stop my voice from shaking, my tears from falling "…were lies. I didn't want us to be *anything* because I really felt I had *nothing* to give, especially time. But what happened—every undefined moment—was the most honest thing I have ever experienced. For me, nothing has ever been more true."

There it is. No regrets. I'm counting breaths not seconds. I will no longer waste a single one on something that is not real. No more hiding behind lies and fear. Cancer or not, I could die tomorrow, and I can't imagine taking a single unspoken emotion to my grave.

I wish he'd say something. Every inch of me feels cut open, exposed … completely raw.

"Thirty-six," he whispers. "That's how many minutes passed between Daniel telling me you had terminal cancer and you telling both of us that you were going to live."

A shaky breath sends a shiver down my spine as he erases the space between us, one slow step at a time.

"For thirty-six minutes I couldn't find one single breath to take. For thirty-six minutes …" He swallows hard, clenching his jaw.

My palm presses to his cheek. He closes his eyes and leans into my touch, his hand gently encircling my wrist.

"Tell me something *real*," I whisper.

"I spent thirty-six minutes contemplating putting a bullet in my own head." He opens his eyes.

Breathe, Scarlet.

I can't count breaths if I can't remember how to breathe.

"B-but you said ... you didn't love me."

Theo cups the back of my neck and presses his forehead to mine. "I lied."

I fist his shirt. "Say it, and ... *mean it.*"

His lips brush mine.

I inch back, shaking my head. "Say it."

He reaches for my lips again, his hold on my neck tightening.

My hands release his shirt then push against his chest. "Say. It."

Theo growls, backing me into the wall, towering over me. Before I can protest, his mouth is on mine, our tongues vying for control of something that we both know can never truly be controlled.

"N-n-no!" I rip my lips from his, turning my head to the side to catch my breath.

He grabs my head and crashes his mouth to mine again. "N-no!" I yank his hair. "Say—"

His lips attack mine again.

I wriggle out of his hold once more. "SAY IT!"

Our bodies could not be any closer without actually touching, my chest rising and falling as rapidly as his. He looks like a wolf ready to attack again. I will be his sheep. All he has to do is *say it.*

His hands inch to the front of my button-down sundress. I watch them. He'd better say it.

I suck in a quick breath as he rips open my dress in one, quick jerk.

"I ..." Ducking down, he bites the swell of my breast.

"Ahh!" I cry.

His tongue makes a languid stroke over the bite mark. "Love ..." He rips my bra open.

I gasp again.

He licks a trail down my stomach, lowering to his knees. When he looks up at me, I feel nothing but gratitude for a disease that almost took my life. I see the reason I traveled 4000 miles to ... *live.*

"You," he whispers.

My eyes drift shut as he drags my knickers down my legs. I'm drunk on this moment—intoxicated by Theodore Reed worshiping my body. Breathe in ... breathe out ... one ... two ... three ...

His tongue flicks my clit.

My teeth dig into my lower lip, my knees shake.

Four ... five ... six ...

"You drive me so fucking insane." Another flick of his tongue. "Every word ..." Another, but a bit harder.

My hips jerk.

"Every look ... I feel so ... completely undone."

"Oh ... God." This is sweet, sweet torture. I grab his hair to steady myself as he cups the back of my legs and presses me closer to him. His tongue diving deeper into me.

Seven ... eight ... nine ...

Breathe in ... breathe out ...

Don't think a second past this moment. *This is life, Scarlet, grab it and don't ever let go.*

"Th-Theo ..." My head thumps against the wall as I grab two fists full of his hair.

Ten ... eleven ... twelve ...

I squeeze my eyes shut, jaw slack, breath held, so close

to … God, I'm almost …

The back door, a foot to the right, starts to open. Theo reaches his hand over and slams it shut.

"What the hell?" Nolan's voice sounds from the outside.

My eyes fly open.

Without taking his mouth off me, Theo moves us over against the door and flips the deadbolt. I try to squirm out of his hold. He shakes his head.

"Stop—"

He presses one hand over my mouth while his other hand hooks my left leg over his shoulder. I wrap both of my hands around his arm trying to move his hand from my mouth, but … Oh. My. God. It's too late. He takes my orgasm with such command, I'm certain he is the better thief.

"Scarlet, what's going—" Nolan's voice is no longer at the door—it's at the window on the other side of the door.

The blind is shut, but not flush to the window. He sees us: tits out and Theo's mouth making out with my vertical smiley face. This is bloody brilliant. I can't do anything because it's physically impossible to stop the progression of an orgasm that's already started. My abs pull tight, arse clenches, the muscles in my legs flex, desperate to capture every bit of pleasure. It's a complete state of falling and nothing can be done to rectify the situation until I hit the ground. Then I will run to the bathroom with the now-two-separate pieces of my bra and my tattered dress, only to *never* come out.

Theo releases his hand from my mouth and my leg from his shoulder, then he kisses his way up my body, stopping at my breast.

"Ow! Bloody hell!"

The cheeky bastard grins with his teeth on the verge of

breaking the skin of my nipple, then he bangs his fist twice on the door. "Go home, Nolan," he mumbles *with* my nipple still in his mouth.

Fuck the cancer. I'm certain my death will come of complete embarrassment.

"Scarlet?"

My nose scrunches. It's not like he doesn't know I'm in here.

"Are you good?"

He can't be serious. I know he *saw* just how good I am.

Theo's tongue makes a trail up to my neck as he unfastens his trousers. Nolan *needs* to leave before Theo nails me to the door. I know this look in his eyes. He's pleasured me once, and now he's ready to guarantee I won't walk straight for several days.

"Great … good … I'll make sure your bike gets back to you … uh … bye!"

I grab Theo's face, forcing him to look at me. "Say it again." I grin, needing to hear him say it once more.

He licks his lips—licks *me* from his lips—and shakes his head as he shoves his trousers down enough to release his cock. "It's not going to make me go easy on you."

I know this. I would be disappointed if he did. Some men fuck much different than they look. Not Theo. He looks like a beast and he fucks like one too. There has never been anything gentle about him. It's like riding in the front seat of a roller-coaster: I'm guaranteed to get jerked around, my body slammed in every direction, my stomach will be in my throat; I fear all the feels as much as I crave them and in the end I'll feel a bit bruised and battered, but utterly satisfied with the biggest damn smile on my face.

Theo grips the back of my legs and lifts me up, pinning me to the door.

"Say it."

He impales me, eyes on mine the whole time. I wince a bit, feeling the first jerk of the rollercoaster. Theo has no idea what it means to ease into a woman. He's everything Daniel never was. The woman I am with Theo is a Scarlet Stone no other man has ever known. If this life—this moment—is a lie, then the truth will never matter to me.

"I love you," he says a breath before our mouths crash together.

Theodore Reed is the ride of a lifetime in *every* way.

"Harder …" I mumble over his lips. "Faster …" My fingers curl into the muscles along his back.

His head drops to my shoulder.

I close my eyes and just … hold … on. "More … more of this … more of us … more breaths …" I whisper to the universe as I let him bleed me dry of every sensation and emotion I have to give.

My name is Scarlet Stone, and I love sex. I believe if all emotion and reason were stripped from human existence, the answer to all physical questions would be sex.

CHAPTER TWENTY-TWO

THEODORE

S HE CUT HER hair short. I like it, but I won't tell her that. There is no better feeling in the world than her naked body curled up to mine, but I won't tell her that either. She will never know I can't see anyone or anything but her in my dreams. I can no longer get off on porn. I spend my days in constant agitation and my sleepless nights in frustration.

She didn't die and for that I can't find the proper gratitude. No matter what happens in my life, the world is a better place with Scarlet Stone in it. Yet the fact still remains, her reason for living the lie is gone, but mine is not. The lies will fade and before long she might see my truth. She can't see it. I can't be with her. But ... I can love her.

I can love her from afar.

I can love her in my dreams.

I can love her until my life is over.

Maybe I can love her in another life.

And maybe, just maybe ... that love will be enough to cure her.

CHAPTER TWENTY-THREE

My name is Scarlet Stone, and I've always believed compassion is not earned, it's given.

SCARLET

"WHERE'S THE SOFA?" I ask, tracing the mingling lines of ink on his chest next to where my cheek rests. I want to know what each one means—in time.

"You don't like my leather recliner?"

I laugh. "It's great for watching a TV you don't own, and I loved it on rainy days when I read my books."

"I sold most of the furniture, except for a few things that were Nolan's. He had them put in storage already."

We declared some sort of love to each other, but we were nothing for so long I don't know what this love really means. It's impossible to articulate this feeling but it's like he loves me, but he still doesn't *want* to love me. It's a sad love.

"Nolan said you're moving to Nashville."

He doesn't say anything. I look up at him.

"Did you hear me?"

He nods, peering down at me.

"Well?"

"Well what?"

I sigh.

He smirks. "You have a habit of making statements and expecting a response. If you really want a response, you need to ask an actual question."

Pushing against his chest, I maneuver my body so I straddle

his lap, facing him. I look down between our naked bodies. "You're ... *awake.*" My eyes shift to his.

Theo chuckles. "Again, not a question. But yes, it's at your service. Feel free to insert it into any hole in your body, lick it, suck it—"

"Stop!" I grab my button-less dress that's barely holding on to the side of the chair and drape it over his eager knob.

He quirks a brow, looking at the dress.

"I *do* have a question and sex isn't the answer so—"

"Are you sure?" He narrows his eyes at me.

No. I'm not sure. Ninety percent of the time, sex is a brilliant answer. I'm stuck in the ten percent right now.

"Are you moving?"

He nods.

I frown.

"When?"

"Three days."

"Where?"

He stares at me.

"It was a question, not a statement."

"Nashville."

Why is this so hard? Once again, I feel it—sad love. Does "I love you" not mean I want to be with you? My heart clenches. *It doesn't.* I still love Daniel, but I no longer want to be with him.

"Is that where your tour begins?"

Theo's eyes avert to the side for a few moments. "Sure."

With each breath ... *one ... two ... three ...* I feel this deep pain, a slow carving of a Theo-shaped hole in my heart.

"Are you leaving me?"

He shifts his gaze to me again as he expels a grunt. Theo

has many grunts and they don't all mean the same thing. This grunt sounds like a sarcastic grunt.

"I have some things I need to do."

"Want some help?"

His glare hardens a fraction. The lines at the corners of his eyes deepen. "No."

"Is it tour stuff?"

The muscles in his jaw tense. "Don't do this."

"Do what? Wonder why you said you loved me but now you're leaving? I know, I have no right to ask it. I did the same thing to Daniel. Karma's usually my friend but not today. I need to know. What is the life expectancy of us? Three days? Is that what you're implying? I do better when I can prepare for things, which is crazy because I prepared to be dead by now, but I'm not and that's really, *really* a spectacular surprise, but—"

"Three days," he says with a firm finality.

I pinch my lips between my teeth and nod slowly for a few seconds. "Okay then. We have three days." I climb off his lap and kneel on the floor between his legs, dropping the dress to the floor. "I was wrong. Today … sex is the answer."

He spreads his legs wider and scoots down a little in the chair as I lean forward, grab his erection, and bring it to my mouth. I'm on my knees—naked. My tongue is giving his cock some special attention. I have *no* gag reflex. Yet … when I look up, all I see is a hint of a grimace, flared nostrils, and glassy eyes.

Pain.

Theo is in pain.

～

THEO DRIVES ME home and stays the night in my one-bedroom flat with a cheap double mattress on the floor and gaudy paisley yellow and pink sheets that were in the sale. We answer every question with sex. Then we pass out a few hours before my alarm goes off.

"I have to get to work."

Theo makes some undecipherable noise, facedown on my bed, as I shove my feet into my trainers. I ache in places that I had no idea could ever ache. I will have to ride my bike to Nolan's house, standing up the entire way. There's no way I'll be able to sit on that seat—for weeks.

"And your job is what again?" he mumbles, turning his head to the side and peeling open his eyes. His body engulfs the bed.

I may not walk right or sit on my bike seat for weeks, but that doesn't mean I'm not going to miss the hell out of this man for the rest of my life. Swallowing back that lump of regret, I smile. "I assist Nellie."

"Assist her how?"

"Well, we shopped and ate lunch together the other day."

"That sounds really helpful."

In the past twenty-four hours, Theo has found it rather fun to say everything with a British accent. He's such a cheeky bastard and his accent is total shit.

I wrinkle my nose and stick out my tongue as I grab my rucksack from the floor. "It's quite helpful. Not that you would understand." I lean over the bed to give him a quick kiss. "Bye."

I DIDN'T THINK there could be an upside to Theo leaving me but until I can afford a car, I need to be able to sit down on my bike seat. It's not possible to ride a Schwinn mere hours after riding Theodore Reed.

During the time I thought I was dying, I never once prayed to live. I never once thought I'd actually live. I meditated and gave thanks for every day I'd been granted, the people who shared the moments that had given my life great meaning, and the chance to experience so much love. However, right now, on the front steps of the Moore's southern mansion, I'm praying—begging—for Nolan to be already gone.

The door opens. No such luck.

I smile, feeling the heat reach the tip of my ears as I shove my hands in my pockets, pull them out, fidget with the hem of my shirt, then shove them back into my pockets again.

"Good morning." Nolan's greeting seems a little too suggestive, like his smile.

Without a doubt, I'd be embarrassed if I were in his position. That's the natural reaction when you witness something so personal. Isn't it?

I move up the steps like an inmate making their way to the execution room.

"You're walking kind of funny. Something happen?"

Oh bugger! My head bows, the first step toward my whole body collapsing in on itself. Death from utter humiliation is my likely fate.

"Your southern charm is slipping, Mr. Moore." I survey the foyer like I'm seeing it for the first time. Anything requires more attention than Nolan.

"I was just showing concern for your health. *Very* gentlemanly of me."

I roll my eyes as I make my way up the stairs, trying to ignore the pain and not look like I've been straddling a horse for days.

"Has Theo decided to stay?"

"No."

"So, I should expect your resignation soon?"

"No." I turn when I get to the top of the stairs.

Nolan frowns.

I shrug, fighting back the pain, which is hard to do because everything right down to my soul aches at the moment. But ... I'm alive and I will never take that minor little detail for granted. At least ... I hope not.

"He's complicated." Nolan's explanation is not news to me. "Besides, you're not cancer-free, yet."

I nod. "I know." When I notice Nellie's door is still shut, I sit on the landing and rest my elbows on my knees. "Theo is not the only reason I didn't go back to London. Something in my life shifted over the past six months and that something has reversed the progression of my cancer. I gave up my profession, electronics, bad eating habits, late nights and early mornings leaving me in a constant state of sleep deprivation. I really don't think one thing caused my cancer but rather a culmination of many things that eventually pushed my health past a tipping point. So I won't go back—not to my job, my old habits, or my life in general that seemed to turn on me."

"You're afraid if you do, the cancer will come back."

"Yes."

"Did you ask Theo to stay?"

"No."

"Why not?"

"Because when I left London, I didn't want anyone to ask me to stay. I wanted everyone to respect my need to leave—respect my decision to not go through the cancer treatment. I didn't want to explain myself. I wanted … I *needed* to leave. It didn't mean I'd stopped loving Daniel or my dad."

"You think Theo has cancer?"

I laugh a little. "No. Well … I don't know. But he knows I love him, and I know he loves me, so if there's something greater than our love that's taking him away, then …"

Nolan nods. "Then you have to let him go. No questions."

"No questions," I whisper.

Nolan crosses his arms on the spiraled top to the newel post at the bottom of the stairs.

"Was he in a band?" I ask because it's been burning a hole in my curiosity for too long.

Nolan squints at me for a second. "Yes. Why do you ask?"

"He mentioned it, but it was when we were living a lie. At the time it was easier for me to tell him my dreams instead of my reality. I guess … I don't know … I think he did the same."

"He told you he was in a band?"

"Yes. He said the reason he was leaving Tybee was to go on tour. I know it's not true, but part of his story felt real."

"He studied music theory and composition in college. His parents, particularly his mother, imagined him doing something more sophisticated than forming a band."

Theo as a music theory graduate brings a smile to my face. It's not fair to stereotype, but really … he looks nothing like a music theory graduate.

"He hasn't always looked so … unkempt."

My eyes dart to Nolan's. How did he read my mind? "I don't mind his unkemptness"

He raises an eyebrow. "Clearly."

My ears heat again as I clear my throat. "So this band …

did they tour?"

"They headlined for a few bigger acts over the course of nine months, then…" He closes his eyes and shakes his head.

"Then his parents died?"

Nolan's eyes open wide as his head snaps up. "He told you?"

"No. I accidentally came across some stuff of his. It included newspaper articles about his parents." And a few other very disturbing articles along with knives and guns. I'm not sure Nolan needs to know that. Then again, maybe *someone* needs to know. "Was Theo in the military or some type of law enforcement before or after university?"

Nolan shakes his head. "No. Why?"

"Just curious. He's very built and then there are those tattoos. I don't know. It seemed like a possibility … or me just being really stereotypical."

"Well, since I've known him he's never been a small guy, but after his parents died, he bulked up—a lot. Grew his hair out, the beard, and seemed to have a new tattoo every month or so for quite some time. The only tattoo he had before his parents died was the name of his band on his back."

"Really? I've never noticed it."

Nolan shrugs. "It's there, but I think it's camouflaged by all his other tattoos now. Probably symbolic of how his life sort of got lost after they died."

"So the band broke up?"

"Yup."

"What was the name of it?"

He chuckles. "He didn't tell you?"

I shrug. "I never asked. It was all supposed to be a lie."

"The Derby."

"The Derby?"

"Yes." Nolan laughs. "The first two members, Theo and Brodie, drove with some other friends to the Kentucky Derby in Louisville. Theo and Brodie weren't really in to fancy hats, mint juleps, and in Theo's words 'tiny men beating horses around a track,' so they walked back to the car where Theo had his guitar. The guy never traveled anywhere without it. I don't even know if he still owns one." Nolan frowns.

"Anyway, a couple hours later, their friends found them sitting on the trunk of the car, too drunk to drive, Theo riffing on his guitar and Brodie singing some song he just made up. That day was the official birth of the band called The Derby."

I'm broken. The man I've come to love and equate with my new life—my new happiness—is leaving soon. Yet I can't stop smiling. Theodore Reed was a rock star. Why couldn't our paths have crossed before cancer wormed its way into my life, before I said yes to Daniel, and before Theo filled a metal trunk with weapons and clippings of his dead family?

"I heard him singing once. He didn't know I was home, but man … I could have listened to him all day."

"You should search them up on YouTube. I'm certain there's still some videos up of them performing."

That would require the internet, a computer, a smart phone … none of which I have because I chose to unplug from the toxic things in my life.

"Sure." My smile slips.

"Here." Nolan pulls his phone out of his pocket and taps the screen a few times while he walks up the stairs. "This was their last concert."

My hand trembles as I take the phone. I know what's on the screen will multiply my pain. The roots of Theodore Reed are about to grow deeper into my soul, somehow I just *know* it.

Theo … I stare at the video. He's hunched over a bit, pressing the guitar to his body as his fingers move with effortless precision along the strings. His hair is short, his beard just a few days of stubble. There's not a single tattoo on his arms. A hot pink bra lands on the stage a few feet from him. He doesn't look up but his lips curl into a devilish grin. Four other blokes dance and sing on the stage, but I can't tear my eyes from him.

"Scarlet," Nellie says.

I didn't hear her door open. "Good morning!" Jumping to my feet, I hand Nolan's phone back to him. It takes every bit of strength I have to not run out the door, find the nearest place to buy a mobile, then crawl in bed and spend the day … or the rest of my life … watching videos of The Derby.

"I'm so happy you need company again." Nellie smiles her usual lipstick-covered-teeth smile.

My gaze stays on her teeth. What happened to Nellie Moore? She has bright eyes and pretty teeth—although smeared in a red-orange hue. The sprouted ponytail of thick hair on the top of her head could be beautiful with a little bit of help. An equally lovely and heartbreaking innocence exudes from her like one day her family gave up on her, stamped her head with "crazy," and set her on a shelf to collect dust.

"You have some lipstick on your teeth, let's—"

"Scarlet?" Nolan gives a barely detectable head shake.

I narrow my eyes at him. She may be confused, but she's still his mum, she's still human, and she's definitely deserving of compassion not pity.

My name is Scarlet Stone, and I've always believed compassion is not earned, it's given.

"Let's get you fixed up a bit." My glare continues to challenge Nolan as I lead Nellie back to her bedroom.

"Oh … thank you, dear." She pats my hand that rests on her shoulder.

CHAPTER TWENTY-FOUR

My name is Scarlet Stone, and my nana told me I won't know I'm in love until my heart is broken. Love doesn't sound so great.

Y ES. NELLIE IS quite lovely. Stunning, actually.

"You're a hairdresser."

I smile at Nellie's reflection in the vanity mirror of the en suite bathroom. "No."

She feathers her hand along her ginger hair that falls just below her shoulders. I've brushed it and added some soft curls to it, then I fixed her makeup, opting for nothing on her lips until we can go shopping for some new makeup. Whomever let her buy ten shades of orange-red lipstick should be beheaded.

"I forgot to tell you how much I like your shorter hair."

My eyes shift to my own reflection. After Daniel left for London, I decided to cut my hair short, opting for a pixie cut with the top a chaos of curls and a few rebel spikes. The hairdresser said I looked like Halle Berry. I took it as a compliment.

"Thank you." I smile. "Lower maintenance. Straightening my hair every day was too much work, and long curls with this southern humidity is not the best combination."

"Humidity? You should visit southern Florida."

"Oh yeah?"

Nellie's brow draws tight as her eyes flit around like she's trying to figure something out. "Uh … yes." Her lips pull into a tight smile. "I think … I don't really know why I said that."

"Have you been to southern Florida?"

She looks up at my reflection. "I … I'm not sure. Have

you?"

"No. Maybe we can go on a road trip sometime. What do you think?"

Nellie nods slowly, her smile working its way to one of genuine excitement.

"Nel?" Harold bangs on the bedroom door several times before he lets himself inside. He does an immediate double take.

"What do you think?" Nellie stands. Her confidence brightening the whole room.

Harold gives me a hard look. "Ms. Stone, a word in private please."

I throw back my shoulders and start toward the door, refusing to let the Moore men shame me for being kind to Nellie.

"You can have your words right here, Harold." Nellie walks past me. "I'm going down for coffee and breakfast. See you soon, Scarlet."

Harold shuts the door behind her.

"You look utterly ridiculous and I can safely say that because I know you have an expensive wool tailored suit and silk tie waiting for you at work or at the brothel where you get your rocks off."

"Watch it," he warns. His beady eyes attempt to intimidate me. "Nel likes you. That's great. It means I don't have to spend as much time here, but I can't—I *won't* have you trying to change her. She's sick. She needs routine and familiarity to keep from …" He blows out a breath and clenches his teeth for few seconds.

"Remembering."

He takes a step toward me.

I go into humming bird mode. "You don't want her to remember what happened."

Another step.

I hold my own.

"You have no idea what you're talking about or who you're messing with."

"She's going to remember, it's only a—" All the air leaves my lungs as my face slams against the wall and my arm twists around my back to the point that tears sting my eyes. I squeeze them shut.

"I won't warn you again," Harold grits through his teeth, holding me to the wall.

The pain in my arm subsides and two seconds later the door to the room opens and clicks shut again. I open my eyes, slowly peeling my face from the wall. There's a red streak on the emerald wallpaper. I touch my fingers to the corner of my eyebrow. Blood. I'm not scared. I'm angry. Even now, I have no self-preservation.

After the blood clots, I clean the small blood streak on the wall and go down to the dining room. Nellie glances up, taking a sip from her teacup fit for a queen.

"Scarlet! What happened to your head?"

Before I can answer, Harold walks out of the kitchen holding a briefcase and wearing a firm look of don't-fuck-with-me.

"I took the corner at the top of the stairs a little too sharp. Wasn't watching where I was going. I'm fine."

With his eyes on me, Harold bends down and kisses Nellie on the top of her head. "Have a good day, sweetheart."

I swallow back my vomit, disguising my utter disgust with a smile as fake as the erections I'm sure he gets in the form of a pill.

Cancer. You're still battling cancer. My voice of reason

knows I need to calm down and let this go. The Moores' business is not mine. But every cell in my body wants to bring the Moore men to their knees for what they're doing to Nellie.

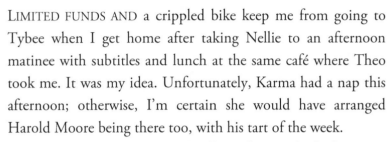

LIMITED FUNDS AND a crippled bike keep me from going to Tybee when I get home after taking Nellie to an afternoon matinee with subtitles and lunch at the same café where Theo took me. It was my idea. Unfortunately, Karma had a nap this afternoon; otherwise, I'm certain she would have arranged Harold Moore being there too, with his tart of the week.

The good news? I have a landline phone. The bad news? I don't know Theo's mobile number. I should have lifted Harold's wallet and taken enough cash for taxi fare to Tybee. We could have called it payment for injury. *Fucking wanker!*

I don't recall a time in my life when I had to live on such a tight budget. Daniel didn't offer to give me any money, even though I deposited close to fifty thousand pounds in his account before I left London. I'm sure it was an oversight on his part, but I didn't have the nerve to ask for any of it back after having destroyed his life.

I live a few streets from a library. A library with computers and internet. I've walked by it several times like an alcoholic walking past an off license. But I can't do it. Hackers can play God with a computer. A simple internet search turns into a handful of crimes within a matter of minutes. My desire to destroy the man who shoved my face into a wall is too great to give me internet access. It would be a loaded gun in my hand.

I collapse in my ten-dollar picnic chair in the middle of an otherwise empty room. "Bugger!" I wince, having forgotten that I need to avoid any sort of plopping.

There's a knock at my door.

"Unless you're a murderer, let yourself in."

The door eases open.

"Hey." I punch as much enthusiasm into my greeting as I can.

It would be easier to fall on a sword than look at the pain etched into the face of the beautiful man before me: Theo in his tattered, loose jeans, old, black T-shirt with a tear near the neck, and black boots. I can't see any life in him and it makes me, once again, question my existence. Slow goodbyes offer nothing but drawn-out pain. I did it with Daniel, and now I'm doing it with Theo.

I could cry just watching him stand here, not saying a word. My heart bangs against its cage, wanting to break out and hold on to him. I can't follow my heart, but oh, how I want to.

I didn't try to love you.

He lets the door shut behind him and walks to me, kneeling on the floor between my feet. My nose tingles. My eyes burn.

Are you my salvation or my damnation?

I open my mouth, but I can't speak. My throat swells. Breathing is its own feat. Theo lays his head on my lap and wraps his arms around my waist, but he says nothing.

Drawing in a slow breath and holding it, I roll my eyes toward the ceiling and try not to blink. Give me back the death sentence. Let me die because this kind of suffering is too unbearable. Threading my fingers through his hair, I blink and succumb to the tears that don't just fall—they come like an enormous wave, shaking my whole body.

He holds me tighter.

My name is Scarlet Stone, and my nana told me I won't know I'm in love until my heart is broken. Love doesn't sound so great.

"Don't go," I whisper around the emotions choking me. "I-I know you have to go, but I … I have to say the words." I fight the sobs. "I'm s-sorry … I had to s-say it." Leaning forward, I rest my head on his, and we stay like this until the pain becomes a numbing reality that we can no longer deny.

When my tears dry and I wonder if he's even awake, I kiss his ear. "I stole a heart. Daniel needed a heart transplant and so I … stole one. When I take things that aren't mine, I don't leave a trail. But emotions made me sloppy. I messed up. Daniel had no idea. My dad confessed, turned himself in with the guarantee that Daniel would never know what he did. But *he* did nothing. I did it. My dad is in prison for a crime I committed. He wanted a happily ever after for his daughter. I hated him for it."

I laugh. "Isn't that crazy? How can I hate him for wearing communal underwear that could have been mine? How can I hate him for giving me freedom, a future, a life? He said someday I'd have a child of my own and understand that there is *nothing* a parent won't do to give them the world."

"And your mom?" He is awake.

"She died—of cancer—before I turned two. My best friend died of cancer too."

"But you didn't."

I kiss his ear again, memorizing the feel of every point where our bodies connect, memorizing the smell of ocean in his hair, the rare vulnerability in his voice. "No. Not yet."

"Why do you think that is?"

"Why do you swim in the ocean?"

His long lashes flutter with a few blinks. "It feels natural and … freeing. It's where I let go of everything and it's …"

I sit up and press my hand to his cheek. He sits back on his heels like I've seen him do while working a million times before.

"It's what?"

His lips twist. "It's the only time that nothing has to make sense. It's just me, my breaths, my heartbeat, and the rest of the world could cease to exist in that moment and I wouldn't care." He slips off my shoes and socks and rests my feet on his legs, pressing his palms to them.

I curl my toes into the denim, never wanting to lose our touch. "That's why I left. There was never any moment of grand hope that I would beat cancer. *Anyone* who beats terminal cancer by *any* means possible is a bloody miracle. I'm many things, but I never thought I'd be a miracle. I needed for once to find my breath, feel my heartbeat, and let the rest of the world … fade away. I wanted to die without fear or regret. I wanted to find a shred of meaning to my life."

I shake my head as his hands ghost along my bare feet. "I think so many things in my life fed the disease, and when I truly let go of all of it … it had nothing left to feed on."

Theo looks up and I don't feel crazy or judged. I wish Daniel could have looked at me like this. Just once.

"I needed out, and I couldn't really explain it. I had to leave."

He nods slowly.

"That's why I won't hold on to you. If you still have to leave, knowing how desperately I want you to stay, then I won't stand in the way."

His chin dips down and his throat bobs. "I'll try to come

back," he mumbles.

I don't want even a thread of a promise, a possibility that will leave me constantly holding my breath—waiting, hoping, dying a little each day he doesn't return.

"I won't wait for you."

I detect a hint of a nod. Is it as painful for him to think about me not being here if he does return as it is for me thinking about him not returning? If so, then Karma is back on her game today.

Leaning forward, I playfully tug his beard until he looks up at me. I don't imagine Theodore Reed has shed a tear since his parents died, but right now, I swear I see tears in his bloodshot eyes.

"If there's another life after this one, we should make a date."

The corner of his mouth curls a bit.

"Food. Small talk. Maybe I say something that makes you grin. Maybe you say something that makes me giggle. Maybe the food is crap so we drink too much wine. Maybe the full moon beckons us to the beach where we walk in the shadows of the night. Maybe you tell me something about yourself. But maybe ... just maybe it's something so honest I can't help but fall in love with you. And maybe you build me a house and fill it with hundreds of plants and even a dog. I've never had a dog."

He cradles my face in his hands as I do his in mine, and we just ... breathe in ... and breathe out ...

One.

Two.

Three.

"It's a date." He smiles and I cry.

Fuck it. Life is too short to hold in a single tear, a single laugh, a single breath. Biology is how we exist. Emotions are how we *live*.

CHAPTER TWENTY-FIVE

My name is Scarlet Stone, and I see the people around me as opportunities to see different sides of myself.

"WHAT'S WITH THE chair?" Theo asks, one arm folded behind his head, his other hugging me to his side, his hand cupping my breast.

I look out the bedroom door to the perfect view of my picnic chair. "Now? Really? Now you've decided to be observant?"

"And these sheets ... fucking hideous."

Resting my chin on his chest, I bite back my grin, content with just looking at him. "Anything else?"

He dips his head toward me. "Your hair."

"It's short. Lie to me. This is one thing I don't want you to have an opinion on. I cut it. It will be a very long time before it grows back out, but had I had chemo I probably would have lost it anyway so—"

"It's fucking gorgeous."

My eyebrows perk. "Really?" I whisper.

"Really."

I smile and for this moment, these breaths, I don't feel sad. "The chair was all I could afford and the sheets were in the sale. The hair is laziness. It's easier."

"You need money?"

My name is Scarlet Stone, and I see the people around me as opportunities to see different sides of myself.

"No. My financial situation is a choice at the moment. I could get a better paying job or go back to lying, cheating, and stealing, but I'm fascinated by the whole living payday to payday thing. It's humbling and challenging at the same time. Much like the Argonaut octopus. It's a type of nautilus. Its penis, which is essentially a ball of sperm in a tentacle, can completely detach to look for lady parts to wiggle into— challenging. But … once it lets go of the goods, it soon dies— humbling."

Theo's chest vibrates with laughter. "How does 'do you need money' turn into a detachable penis story?"

"Oh … so to answer your question, I'm good. I'll survive."

"And your head?"

"My head?"

He releases my breast long enough to smooth the pad of his finger over my cut.

I frown. "Work injury."

"Nellie more of a handful than you thought?"

My chin rolls back and forth on his chest as I shake my head. "Harold."

Theo's brow knits together.

"He's worried I'm going to do something to stir up trouble."

"Your face. What happened to your face?" His voice deepens as his teeth clench.

"He had a word with me, but he thought I'd listen better if he pinned me to the wall."

Theo bolts to sitting, practically shoving me off the bed. "He fucking did this on purpose?"

"The pinning, yes. The cut was an accident. I think." My nose scrunches.

"I'm going to end that son of a bitch." He tosses the covers aside.

For a few insane seconds, I feel a bit of a rush, like I did the night he threatened the tosser from the pub on the beach. Then I think about Nellie. "Wait. No!" I grab his arm as he goes to stand.

He glares at me.

"You're leaving in forty-eight hours. Don't leave this bed now. I'll call in sick tomorrow. You can bust the windshield of Harold's car on your way out of town, but for now ... stay."

His face draws tight with pain and conflict.

I tug harder on his arm. "Me or Harold. Choose."

After a few moments, he crawls back onto the mattress, caging me beneath him. I think over the past twenty-four hours he fractured my *clamshell*. I will never bike again. But he's leaving and it's like having your favorite food for the last time ever. Consequences be dammed!

Theo bends his arms, muscles flexing as his head lowers to mine. He kisses me like mad, and I kiss him back with just as much eagerness. I can't wrap my head around Theodore Reed, music theory and composition graduate, a rather sophisticated title, fucking me all the time like a complete beast—a freight train.

The sex is nothing short of mind-blowing, but it's far from romantic. It's animalistic. When he reaches down and discovers I am dry like the Sahara because I'm so sore, his idea of gentlemanliness is to spit on his hand and rub it between my legs. I should be offended and repulsed by his behavior, but I'm not. Just the opposite. I'm turned on by this feral beast and within seconds of his fingers smearing spit on me, I'm actually throbbing for a release in spite of the pain. My nipples harden. My heels claim his back and my pelvis—my fractured clamshell—is ready for another round of torture.

I've lost the plot.

"Theo! Fuck fuck fuck!!!"

He silences me with his mouth, but I groan on every thrust. It's ninety percent pain and ten percent pleasure. I'm giving all my focus to the pleasure. When his mouth moves to my neck, I search for something else to distract me from the pain while the pleasure grows enough to take the lead.

"The male porcupine…" I pant, my heels digging into his back even more "…drenches the … the female with urine from approximately two meters away."

"What?" Theo grunts on a hard thrust, sweat beading along his brow and dripping to the ends of his hair that brush my face.

"I know. That's disgusting. But if his pheromones turn her on …" The pleasure is winning. What does this mean? Does porcupine mating do it for me? "Then they mate until he's physically exhausted …" my pelvis rocks against Theo's. I'm so close. "But it's not because of him … *she's* the one who won't let him stop."

Theo stills.

"Don't stop!" What I could barely handle minutes ago, I now *need*.

He shakes his head. "You're not a porcupine."

"Theo …" I beg.

His forehead drops to my shoulder, his labored breaths heating my skin even more. I wiggle my hips in search of some friction. Theo's chest vibrates against mine.

"You're laughing?"

"Dear god, woman …" He laughs with total inhibition.

I make one last attempt to press the play button on sex by gripping his firm arse, giving it an encouraging squeeze.

Nothing.

I'm pinned beneath two-hundred-plus pounds of laughing beast. It would seem the moment is lost.

"Pissing porcupines ..." His cackling continues.

I stare over his shoulder at the cracks in the ceiling, chewing on the corner of my bottom lip. Well, this is rather embarrassing. At the same time, I can't stop relishing the delightful sound of this man that I love or the feel of our bodies connected, our flesh pressed together.

He pulls out and rolls to the side, squeezing the bridge of his nose and ... wiping tears from his eyes.

"Unbelievable. I bawl my eyes out over you leaving, and I thought for a second that you too might shed a few tears. Nope. I'm not worthy of your emotions, but the porcupine mating ritual has you crying."

"Oh, man ..." He sighs, catching his breath. I've never seen his smile stretch so far across his face. "Please let there be another life. I need a real taste of forever with you. This ... this isn't long enough."

I know he's going for humorous and lighthearted but his words punch right through my chest and rip my heart into a million jagged, unrepairable pieces.

Sitting up, needing gravity to assist my lungs in finding air, I pull the sheet to my chest.

"Tell me about this?" He tugs at the back of my necklace, the necklace I've worn every second we've been together.

Why now? Why try to know me when we have no time left?

I rub the ruby pendant between my finger and thumb. "It was my mum's—I think." I shake my head. "Oscar, my dad, had a habit of telling me the truth when it suited him or benefited me. I'm pretty sure he stole it."

"It's worth a lot of money, isn't it?"

The sputter of a laugh escapes me. "I'm sure you're probably thinking I should sell it and buy a car or a chair that reclines not folds."

"Nope."

Twisting my torso, I peer back at him, fingers laced behind his head. I find the perfect doleful smile to match my mood. "He called me Ruby, still does. I don't think my mum ever saw this necklace."

"So why do you wear it?"

I shrug. "I make up stories about my mum; I have most of my life. In them she's perfect, of course. The truth is Oscar never liked talking about her. I think that's a good thing. It has to mean that he loved her so much it's unbearable to go back to those memories. Oscar said the ruby is from Burma, or Myanmar now, and it's older than the history of the Stone Age. Some people believe rubies are a protective stone and that they turn dark when danger looms, returning to their natural color after the threat is gone."

Theo's forehead wrinkles as he chews on the inside of his cheek. It's his thoughtful look, a little different from his pissed off look, which also involves a wrinkled brow with clenched teeth. "So, no cell phone, no computer …"

I laugh. "I was regimented. It was the most obsessive illusion of control. Up at five for my run. Shower. Breakfast alongside my computer. I traveled the world inside of a keyboard and a screen. Social media. Email. Texting. I was *connected*. I knew about things that were going to happen before they happened. There was no boundary that I couldn't cross. It was always a matter of whether I *chose* to cross it.

"Some of the people who hired me wore suits that cost

more than the average person's car. They looked the part. But it was *me* who had the control. Little Scarlet Stone at her computer with sticky keys and a dusty screen, wearing a threadbare shirt, leggings, and soft, fuzzy socks, hair in a ponytail, no makeup, and vintage Rod Stewart flowing from my speakers."

"Doesn't sound like an illusion of control."

I nod, gazing at him with a blank stare, seeing only the past six months flash through my mind. "It was. The day the doctor told me I was going to die ... that's when I realized the world would go on without me. I realized I controlled nothing, not even my body. And sitting in my flat, in front of a computer all day? It was the epitome of disconnect. People don't focus on the moment or give their undivided attention to the person sitting right in front of them. We see words and pictures on screens. The art of conversation is gone. Hell, we don't even write complete words. Life is a series of abbreviations, acronyms, and emoticons. Alcohol is stress relief instead of a toast of celebration. It's just ..."

"Fucked-up."

"Yes." I sprawl onto his stomach and press my lips to his, ending with a grin. "I'm not sure I can shun technology forever. But it's this mad addiction, maybe a lethal one. The longer I can stay unplugged, the better."

"When's the last time you used a cell phone?"

"Well, I didn't technically use it, but I touched Nolan's mobile."

"What? Like you had to *touch* it?"

"Well, since you asked," because I've been dying to have this conversation, "he showed me a YouTube video of this band called The Derby. The bloke on guitar melted my knickers right there on the spot."

Theo's brows raise as his hands grip my bare arse. "Nothing good can come of you watching that."

I bite his lower lip. His fingers dig into my skin. There's nothing I want more than to crawl inside of this man and spend eternity piecing together what I have no doubt is an ineffable masterpiece.

Dragging my teeth along his lip, I smile. "Respectfully, I disagree. But…" I twist some of his hair around my finger "…my love affair with the devastatingly handsome guitarist is over. I don't have access to YouTube and he's …"

Wow … my emotions fall somewhere between harrowing and utterly suffocating. The ones that gobble up every bit of oxygen and leave my true feelings stuck inside to drown my spirit.

Theo's hands whisper along my skin then cradle my head, bringing us nose to nose. "*He's* going to miss you every damn day. The way you smell like girly shit. The way you fuck up every word with your fancy accent. The way everything about you seeps into my space and fills it with a life I didn't ask for— a life I never needed—a life I now want so bad I'd rather die than not have it."

"Don't die," I whisper, looking into his red-rimmed eyes as my tears fall to his face.

"Don't die," he whispers back to me a breath before we kiss like there really are no words left to say.

He rolls us until I'm beneath him. Brand me, Theodore Reed. Don't you dare go slow and easy. Everything about us has been cataclysmic. Every touch so explosive it's impossible to know if we're beginning or ending. Imprint this moment so deep into my soul that in my next life I *feel* you long before we ever meet.

"Ugh!" I cry when he penetrates me—brands me—in the only way he knows how.

Angry.

Forceful.

Unapologetic.

The most poignant observation I've made over the past six months, that I failed to see over the previous thirty-one years, is that there is nothing more *phenomenal* than one human's addiction to another—and there is nothing more *devastating* than one human's addiction to another.

As Theo leaves his final mark on me, all I feel is this phenomenal devastation.

CHAPTER TWENTY-SIX

My name is Scarlet Stone, and one day I will break away from the shadows of the man who raised me. Until then—I will make him proud.

S IX MONTHS AGO, I left Daniel with a note. We said all there was to say and by the time he woke the next morning, I was gone. The way he kissed me, the way we made love … it was goodbye and we both knew it.

Theo wasn't supposed to leave for another day, but everything about last night was a goodbye. So, of course, next to me is an empty spot … with a note. I laugh.

"Oh … Karma." I hug the folded note to my chest and continue to laugh through my tears.

Three Nevers

1. *I've never been so fucking scared in my life as I was the day I laid eyes on you.*
2. *I never imagined loving the feel of something more than the wood and strings of my guitar, until I touched you.*
3. *I've written fifteen songs, but NEVER has any one person inspired my words.*

Truth: You are my greatest song.

Theo

"Fuck!" I leap from the most pathetic excuse for a mattress and rip the tangled ugly sheet from my body.

No to space.

No to freewill.

No to respecting his need to leave.

And I'm *not* even sorry.

I thought I wanted Daniel to let me go. But what if I wanted him to chase me to the airport in some grand gesture of his undying love for me? What if I wanted to be his greatest song? Why wasn't I his song?

Leggings never cooperate when you need them to. "Come ... on!"

I define hideous, but there's no time for glamour before I'm out the door.

"Sorry, sir," I apologize to the poshly-dressed gentleman on the pavement when I bump into him, but I need his wallet. I'm going to Hell—probably on a Schwinn with a flat tire, but hell nonetheless. I'll replace the money and post the wallet back to him when I can. That has to count for something. It takes me almost twenty minutes to find a taxi. Does everyone in this geometrically-obsessed city own a car? Where are all the bloody tourists?

I spit the address to the driver three times before he understands it. Apparently, he doesn't think I'm speaking English. Knobhead has Theo's honed people skills. Except, I am Theo's song, so his complete lack of southern hospitality is forgiven. I bet Knobhead can't hold a tune any more than he can hold in his beer belly.

"Can you hurry?"

He lifts his cap and scratches his head then repositions it as he gives me a confused look in the mirror. I roll my eyes. One of us speaks perfect English and the other is a knobhead.

I don't have a speech, and begging may be involved, but Theo cannot leave me. It doesn't matter what he's facing. I will walk into the storm with him. There's no way I can wait for another life that we're not guaranteed, a Heaven that no one has seen, an eternity that I can't see beyond the horizon in front of me.

Now.

We have now, and I want to share every breath of it with Theodore Reed.

"Just …" I slip a few notes from the stolen wallet. "I'm getting out here."

"We're almost there." The cabbie points to the red light like it's not his fault.

"Unlock the door!" I bang against it.

He shakes his head but the lock clicks open, so I don't care what he thinks of me as I jump out and run toward *my life*.

"Theo!" The desperation in my voice earns me a few concerned looks from people on their porches and in their gardens. I'm a few streets away from the house; my call to him may be a little premature. "Theo!" Okay, I can't stop.

His truck is gone, but he's not. He can't be. The door is locked. I pound my fists against it. "Theo!"

Where is he? Last night was goodbye to me, not Tybee. He's not leaving until tomorrow. "Theo!"

Bang, bang, bang!

A hand touches my shoulder. "Theo!" I whip around ready to jump into his arms.

"Scarlet, what's going on?"

"Nolan." I grab his shirt and shake him because my emotions have shattered all of my control. "Where is he?"

Drawing in his eyebrows, he wraps his hands around my wrists. "He's gone. What's wrong?"

"Gone? Gone where?" Every word flies out of my mouth on a labored breath; each one feels like the last.

"Nashville, I suppose."

"No. No … he's not leaving until tomorrow."

"I woke up to this text." He holds up his mobile.

I snatch it from his hand.

Theo: *Everything is out. Taking off. Thanks for the job.*

"What are you doing?" Nolan reaches for his mobile.

I turn my back to him, moving my fingers over the screen. Desperate. Out of control.

Nolan: *Where are you? Come back! It's Scarlet. I love you. I NEED you. PLEASE!!!!!*

"Scarlet—"

"Shh!" I can't listen to anyone speak. The only voice I want to hear is Theo's. "Come on!" I shake the mobile as if it will expedite his response. My patience is nonexistent, so I call the number. It's goes to voicemail and says the mailbox has not been setup. "Fuck fuck fuckity fuck!!"

Nolan: *Turn around. I'm at the house … our house. Come back to me. I'll do anything. I'll go anywhere. PLEASE! I love you … God … I can't even breathe.*

I watch the line at the top. It goes over halfway then stops.

Failed to deliver

"No." I try to deliver it again, and again, I get the same message. The first message was delivered. He's avoiding me.

"Scarlet." Nolan overpowers me, taking back his mobile. "What are you doing?" He reads the texts I tried to send.

"I love him," I whisper.

Nolan nods. "I see that. He'll call back."

I shake my head. "He won't. He's gone."

Nolan sighs, the sympathetic kind that makes me feel like a lost puppy. "Do you need money to get to Nashville?"

My gaze shifts from Nolan's phone to his concern-etched face. "He's not going to Nashville."

"That's where he told me—"

"No. He's doesn't want anyone to know where he's going. That's how I know he's not going there."

The lines in his face deepen. "I'm sorry. I'll keep trying to reach him."

I press my palm to the door, like I used to press it to Theo's chest. "I want to go inside."

Nolan unlocks the door and opens it. "Take your time. I'm going to check on a few things in the garage."

It's as if there's something invisible stopping me from going inside. All I can do is stand at the threshold and stare at the kitchen were we shared our first encounter. I can't believe he said *I* scared *him*. All I detected was this instant hatred. Theodore Reed found life in me that I never knew existed, like the gardener who sees a delicate sprout in the otherwise barren soil. I knew it the moment he locked me in my room. Something inside of me screamed, *"This! This is what I've been missing."*

"Uh … you can go inside." Nolan chuckles as he walks back toward the house.

I shake my head. "I changed my mind."

He grabs the door handle. "May I?"

Swallowing the emotion attached to every memory of my time on Tybee Island, I nod.

Shut.

Lock.

Final.

"Need a ride back to town?"

I nod again as a slow numbness encapsulates my body.

Nolan opens the car door for me. "Too many memories?"

I shake my head and get in the car. As he walks around to the driver's side, the only thought that goes through my head and my heart is: *not enough memories.*

I SAID I wouldn't wait for him. I lied. My new profession will be waiting for Theodore. Maybe I need some Tolle or Dyer. Yimin ... I need Yimin, but he's in Shanghai for the next eight months. His niece is taking care of his beach house *and* my plants while he's gone. Just as well. I don't have room for them anyway. However, he gave me his juicer and bags and bags of herbs to brew nasty tea, so there's that.

Alone. That's what I am. I came to Savannah to be alone, so why is it such a disheartening discovery that I now have what I thought I wanted?

"Ruby."

I stop before I even get the key out of my door. Oscar Stone makes my picnic chair look like a throne with his bold presence, expensive suit, unwavering confidence, and black beanie. He made the black beanie an "in" thing long before The Edge of U2 made it his mark. Oscar also makes the peppered goatee look sexy in spite of his age. My dad has always turned heads for as long as I could recognize what it meant to actually turn a head.

He would die before he took credit for my sexual inhibitions, but it was years of hearing women in his bedroom that led me to find sex a mystery I had to solve. Anything that caused a human to make those noises was worth a little research. Sadly, it was just sex for Oscar. My mum was the love of his life, and no other woman, aside from me, has even come close to touching his heart.

"No." I shake my head. "What have you done?" I jerk the key from the doorknob and shut it before falling back against it.

"I thought you'd be more excited to see me."

"Why?" I continue to shake my head. "You could have been free."

He lifts his hands then drops them back to the white plastic arm rests. "I am free."

"You're a fugitive. If they come for you, I will tell them it was me. I won't let you go back ... for even longer if they catch you."

"You worry too much, Ruby."

A sarcastic laugh rumbles from my chest. "I did. But not when I came here. I let go of it all."

"Daniel said you're getting better." He clenches his jaw. "You should have told me." The muscles in his face tense, matching the pain in his voice.

"I didn't want you to worry about something you couldn't do anything about. I didn't want you worrying about—"

"The only family I have left?"

I nod. "Why? If he told you I was better, then ... why?" I hate that he gave up his chance for true freedom for me. I add it to the long list of things Oscar Stone has done for me that has made me feel guilty for all my wrong doings. Wrong doings that he taught me.

"I was sitting in a cell for a heart that belonged to my Ruby's love. I was there so you could have a true forever."

Oh the guilt ...

"So you can imagine my surprise and *disappointment* when Daniel told me you left him."

My name is Scarlet Stone, and one day I will break away from the shadows of the man who raised me. Until then—I will make him proud.

My gaze finds the floor between us as I try to let go of the guilt as fast as he dishes it out. "The person who died because they didn't get that heart did not deserve to die. But Daniel is a good man, and he didn't deserve to die either. It doesn't matter whether we're together or not, he belongs on this earth. And I will always love him."

"But you've found another?"

I nod.

"When do I get to meet him? When do I get to meet the man who took you away from Daniel … away from me?"

"Don't …" I close my eyes. "Don't do this."

He leans forward, my bargain chair squeaking beneath him as he rests his forearms on his knees. "I'm not doing anything, Ruby, but watching out for what's mine."

"Well, I don't need you to watch out for me anymore."

He chuckles, twisting his neck to one side and then the other. "From the looks of this place, I'd say you need a lot."

"I'm paying rent—legally. I have a legit job that pays my bills. I have a bed …"

He glances over his shoulder into the bedroom. Then he returns a narrow-eyed expression.

I shrug. "It's much more comfortable than it looks." It's really not.

"So you're straight now?"

"Yes." Okay, there was the first-class upgrade and minor pickpocket incident … but other than that …

Oscar nods slowly, studying me like he always does.

"Can I give you a lift to the airport?"

He smirks, eyeing my bike in the corner of the room. "Well, I don't know, Ruby. Can you?"

Bugger!

I sigh, clenching my teeth to hide my pout. "It was code for you're not staying here. And if you must know, no, I can't give you a lift to the airport. However, I know without a doubt that you have enough cash on you to buy a car to drive yourself there or call a taxi."

"I do. But, since I'm not leaving right away, I'm going to have to use some of it to buy my own *mattress* and..." he smirks "...a matching folding chair to put next to yours. Maybe even a TV—"

"No." I shake my head. "No TVs. No electronics." I nod to the phone hanging from the wall in the kitchen. "That's it."

He twists his lips and crosses his arms over his chest. "Fine. Now ... when do I get to meet this new bloke?"

"You don't." I dump my handbag on the ground and sulk into the kitchen for a glass of water. "He's gone."

"Gone?" Oscar leans up against the fridge.

I turn, taking several long gulps, buying a few extra seconds to gain my composure. "Yes. He had to leave."

"I see. When will he return?"

I shrug.

"He's coming back. Isn't he?"

I shrug again, swallowing back the emotions that still loom at the surface, raw and vulnerable.

He studies me some more. No one makes me squirm with a single look quite like Oscar Stone. Okay, it's possible Theodore Reed had a similar effect.

"Another day? We'll talk about it another day?"

Biting my lips together, fighting to keep my composure that's ready to evaporate, I nod.

CHAPTER TWENTY-SEVEN

My name is Scarlet Stone, and I was raised by a womanizer.

OSCAR STILL SINGS in the shower—Rod Stewart, "Maggie May." For as much as I've hated him, I will always love him a hundred times more. The first time I heard a Rod Stewart song was Oscar singing this exact song in the shower. By the time I heard Rod's voice on an album, I already knew all the words to most of his songs, thanks to Oscar Stone's shower performances.

"You've still got it." I grin when he struts out of the bathroom, buttoning the last button to his crisp, white dress shirt. I hand him a cup of tea.

"Thanks." He grins his cocky grin because no one has to tell him he still has it. "So what's on our agenda for today?"

"*Our* agenda?" I eye him over my steamy cup of tea.

"What is this?" He wrinkles his nose.

"Herbal peppermint."

"*Herbal*? Really, Ruby?"

I shrug. "Caffeine is not on my anti-cancer diet." My anti-cancer diet is nothing more than nutritional theories from a handful of holistic experts—ideas that appeal to my common sense and have no negative effects on my overall health.

"I'm terrified to think of what else you've banned from your life." He puts the cup on the worktop then looks in the fridge with an even bigger scowl on his face. "You didn't answer me. What's on our agenda today?"

"I answered you by suggesting there is no *our* agenda. I

have to work and you …" I purse my lips for a few seconds. "I'd say your agenda will simply be to stay out of trouble and inside the confines of the law."

He slips on his black beanie, positioning it just right. "That's not so easy when I haven't swotted up on American laws."

"They're quite simple. Don't steal anything or kill anyone, and if you drive today, remember to stay right."

"That's so wrong."

I nod with a grin. "It really is, but … their country, their rules."

"Your country too."

"Yes, and I'm trying to fit in, but the southern accent is dreadfully painful to master. I can't make the y'all sound quite right."

Oscar laughs. "Don't." He shakes his head.

My nose wrinkles. "It's bloody awful, isn't it?"

"Yes. Don't change a thing. You're absolutely perfect." He gives a resolute nod.

"Thanks. I have to go."

"It's raining."

"I have an anorak and a change of clothes in a carrier bag."

"Scarlet." He frowns. "You are not riding that mangled, rusty excuse for a bike in the rain."

"It's only a thirty-minute ride."

"Here. He pulls a wad of money from his pocket. "Call a taxi."

"There's enough here to buy a small car."

He shrugs. "So, do that."

"No. I've got this." I put the money on the worktop next to him.

"Don't be stubborn."

"Hmm ... wonder where I would have learned that?"

"Scarlet."

I sigh and turn, skimming several notes off the top. "Just taxi fare."

"We'll share one. I do have a few places to go."

"To get a bed?" I ask while calling a taxi.

"Yes. You shoved me onto the floor last night."

"It's not really a mattress for two." Unless it's Theo and me on top of each other. God ... will my mind ever stop going to him? The taxi company answers, and I make my request.

"THIS IS YOUR job?" Oscar asks as the taxi pulls up to the Moores'.

"Yes. I assist Mrs. Moore while her husband fucks about."

The taxi driver shifts his gaze to me in the rearview mirror. Sure, this one understands my English perfectly.

"Sorry?" Oscar squints at me.

"It's complicated. Their son, Nolan, owns the house on Tybee Island that I stayed at with Theo."

"Theo?"

I glance up after grabbing my umbrella off the floor between us. "Uh ... yeah. Theo is the man."

"The bloke that left you."

I sigh. "Something like that."

He gazes back out the window. Then he hands the driver some money. "Thank you. I'll be getting out here too."

"Wait!" I start to protest, but not before Oscar steps out of the taxi and runs around to open my door.

"No. Absolutely not."

"Hurry, Ruby, before we get soaked." He grabs my hand and yanks me out of the taxi, practically dragging me to the door while my other hand fumbles with the umbrella. It finally opens up after we're already on the porch.

I frown.

"It's just a little water."

"That was my point when I said I would ride my bike."

He shakes his head. "That would have been *a lot* of water."

"I had a change of clothes," I grit through my teeth.

"Ms. Stone, good morning."

Both of us turn to the door. Apparently our bickering served as our announcement.

"Hi, Sofia." I smile and step inside. "I'd like you to meet my ... er ... dad." I bite my tongue instead of sticking it out at him. He hates to be called anything but Oscar.

"Welcome, Mr. Stone."

He leans in and kisses Sofia on each check. "You as well, Sofia. Call me Oscar, please."

She nods. "Both Mr. Moore and Nolan left this morning for a quick trip. They'll be back in a few days. Mrs. Moore is in the dining room. Can I get you both some breakfast? Coffee? Tea?"

"No we're—"

"I'll have a cup of coffee ... *with caffeine*. Thank you, and anything you happen to have to eat would be lovely as well. Scarlet's fridge is a bit ... disappointing."

I roll my eyes.

"Very well." Sofia returns a smile and a polite nod.

"Behave." I point my finger at him.

He shrugs. "What?"

We make our way to the dining room.

"Scarlet! Good morning." Nellie smiles, wiping her mouth and imparting her orange-red lipstick to her white napkin. "It's been a few days. Nolie said you were under the weather. I was worried it was AIDS since hearing of Liberace's death last week."

My eyes flit to Oscar, and I give him a slight head shake. His last minute decision to job shadow me left no time to explain Nellie's situation.

"I don't have AIDS. I was spending time with Theo before he left town." Since Nolan and Harold left town, I see no reason to lie to Nellie. "I'd like you to meet Oscar Stone, my dad."

Nellie looks past me like she hadn't noticed him. She perks up and nearly stumbles, scrambling to her feet. "Oh my ... well, welcome, Mr. Stone."

And there it is, the predictable head-turning that happens in the presence of Oscar. Although, I didn't expect it from Nellie. She's blushing and ... flirting.

"Oscar. Please. So lovely to meet you, Mrs. Moore. Scarlet has told me wonderful things about you."

I did?

She giggles. "Call me Nellie, honey."

Honey?

Oscar leans in, depositing a soft kiss on both of her cheeks, lingering a bit longer than he did with Sofia. Nellie grabs the side of the table to steady herself, causing her teacup to rattle against its saucer.

My name is Scarlet Stone, and I was raised by a womanizer.

I'd say he's putting on a show because Oscar Stone is a showman—a con artist—a thief. But that's not what I sense right now. He genuinely is taken with her—bedhead, gaudy lipstick, and all.

I shouldn't be surprised. He sees past the surface of people just like I do, and Nellie is truly beautiful. But the woman asked about Liberace and AIDS. Oscar used to prefer his woman sane and unmarried, or so I thought.

"Nellie, would you like me to do your hair and makeup this morning?"

She flutters her eyelashes at Oscar while he continues to hold her hand that's not gripping the table cloth.

"Nellie!"

She startles. Oscar releases her hand. I smile like I didn't just yell to get her attention.

"Did you hear me?"

"Uh … oh …" Her hand smooths over her messy hair. "Yes … I think I would like that very much. Maybe I'll go …" She points toward the stairs. "Maybe, I'll take a shower first or a bath. Shave my legs and whatever needs shaving."

Oh dear God. Oscar wiggles his brows at her. "If you need any help—"

"Then I'll help you." I grit my teeth, glaring at him for a second before smiling at Nellie.

"I'll let you both … or you, Scarlet, know if I need anything."

"Just give us a shout." Oscar winks as she nearly runs into the wall on her way to the stairs.

"Bloody hell!" I snatch his beanie from his head and throw it on the ground, stomping on it with each word. "What. Are. You. Doing?"

He picks it up and dusts it off. "Was that really necessary?"

"She's my boss. She's my boss's mum. She's *married* and …"

"And?"

"She's had something traumatic happen to her and that's why she's …"

"Completely delightful? Not to mention absolutely stunning. Have you looked at her eyes?"

"Have you looked at the ten carat diamond on her left ring finger?"

"You want me to steal her diamond?" He smirks.

"Breakfast?"

We both turn toward Sofia's voice.

"Now that smells wonderful." Oscar takes a seat at the head of the table like the king he thinks he is and tucks the napkin into his shirt as he smiles and nods at Sofia.

"Are you sure I can't get you anything, Miss. Stone?"

"No. Thank you."

"See what you're missing out on all in the name of—"

"Living?" I quirk an eyebrow and plop down in the chair next to him as he moans around a bite of greasy bacon.

"Don't you miss it?" He closes his eyes and moans some more as he chews slowly, savoring every bit of flavor.

"Bacon? Crisps? Cheese board? Yes, I miss it. But herbal tea, large green salads, and carrot juice are fair trade-offs for this little thing called life."

"You're probably right. Now … tell me about Theo."

"I thought we were going to wait to talk about this."

"We did. I said another day and you agreed. That was yesterday. Today is 'another day.'"

I rest my elbow on the table, propping my chin up on one hand while drumming my fingers with the other hand. "I think he's killed someone or someones, or I think he's going to."

Oscar stops mid-chew and lifts the napkin from his chest to

wipe his mouth as he swallows. "And this is the bloke you left Daniel for?"

"He's a brilliant carpenter. He's a talented guitarist with a voice that's so addictive. And he swims with the sharks."

Oscar smirks. "Daniel is a brilliant photographer who has been within feet of lions in the African safari, and he's captured video in the middle of war zones. He has impeccable taste in clothing and wine and—"

"And every moment we spent together was recorded in photos or videos. All of our holidays were spent getting the best shot. He experiences life through a lens, and I know sometimes he sees things through that lens that most of us will never get the opportunity to see, but if I'm honest, it always felt like there were three in our relationship: me, Daniel, and his camera. I desperately wanted to share a sunset or ocean view with him and not think about capturing the moment. I just wanted to *live* in that moment."

"And this *Theo* lives in the moment?"

"Well, I've never seen him take a picture of anything. I don't know how to explain it. It's not just Theo, it's who I am with him. He's so unpredictable, and grumpy, and he has this angry passion that consumes me. I'm fascinated by everything he does no matter how mundane it is, but never have I wanted to snap a photo of him. I just like immersing myself in every moment with him."

Oscar sips his coffee then shakes his head. "It's new love. Exciting and passionate. It's where everything about the other person is perfection, even their flaws." He sighs and stares off into the distance. "It's all-consuming, where you live on sex because your bodies can't get enough of each other, where you *need* each other so much you feel like you want to crawl inside of the other person. It's the most insatiable craving."

This conversation has veered off its intended path. I can't have a sex conversation with my dad, even if everything he says is spot-on.

I clear my throat and squirm a bit in my chair. "Is that what you had with Mum?"

Pain pulls at his brow as he nods slowly. "And no matter what, the newness wears off even if the love remains. However, you know you're with the right person when what brings you out of your dark days is that spark of passion you once had. It doesn't have to be a grand display of fireworks, just a spark. That tiny bit of life."

On a long sigh, I drum my fingers on the table some more. "It doesn't matter. I don't think he's coming back. My spark— that tiny bit of life—will be nothing more than an illusion, a ghost for me to chase after for the rest of my life."

His roar of laughter fills the room. "Oh, Ruby … I don't even recognize the woman before me. You could track down an ant buried in a crack of the earth in the middle of a third-world country. If this bloke is your spark, then stop tripping over your bottom lip and go find the bastard."

I shake my head. "I don't have a computer."

He tosses a wad of money on the table.

I shake my head. "I don't want that life anymore."

"For fuck's sake, Ruby! You can't do this."

Staring at the money, I blink over and over. It's not so simple.

"It's the cancer," he says in a more somber tone.

"Yes."

I expect an argument. Instead, he gathers the money and slips it back into the inside pocket of his jacket.

"You're smart—always have been. No man is worth your life. You have to choose yourself this time. It's not selfish, it's imperative. Maybe you can find yourself a suitable southern gent, buy a mansion, and give me a load of grandkids to corrupt."

I want to laugh. There's nothing more endearing than the playful side of Oscar. "I can't have children."

He studies me. "Oh? The cancer?"

I shake my head. "I had or have endometriosis. I think they referenced 'winning the lottery' when referring to my chances of ever getting pregnant."

"Why didn't you tell me?"

Now, I laugh. "Daniel didn't want kids anyway, and I don't enjoy discussing my feminine issues with my dad."

"Oscar."

I roll my eyes. "You're not 'my Oscar,' you're my dad. I don't call you 'Dad,' but when making a reference to you, you are, in fact, my dad!"

"Calm down, Ruby." He grins, sinking his teeth into another piece of bacon.

"I'm Scarlet, not Ruby." I cross my arms over my chest. It's pathetic. How does he reduce me to a twelve-year-old girl every time?

He continues to smirk at me.

"My real name is not Scarlet, is it?"

My dad has had many aliases. I've always wondered if Scarlet Stone was what my mum and *Oscar* named me when I was born. It's the name on my birth certificate, but it might not be my original birth certificate.

"I don't even care." It's the truth. "I'm going to check on Nellie." I stand. "Don't steal anything."

CHAPTER TWENTY-EIGHT

My name is Scarlet Stone and very few things in life shock me.

NOLAN AND HAROLD returned a week ago, so Oscar has been banned from the Moores' estate. Nothing good can come from Harold and Oscar meeting. The three days Oscar spent going to work with me were filled with flirtation and this unsettling sexual tension between Nellie and my dad. I don't know why I assumed Nellie's mental state would prevent her from being a woman in that way, but I was wrong. The two of them shared enough sexual innuendoes to make me want to chunder at least several times a day.

"How's Nellie?" Oscar asks the moment I walk in the door. He purchased himself a queen-sized bed that takes up half of the main room and a massage chair. My picnic chair rests against the wall, folded up. I like to go straight to my room when I return to my flat to avoid the Nellie talk he always wants to have.

"Married."

Same question every day. Same answer.

"Now, Ruby … you said it yourself. They have an unconventional marriage. I think that means an open marriage."

I stop before reaching my bedroom and turn on my heel. "No. Unconventional means Harold is a cunt and Nellie is suppressed from ever getting better because whatever made her this way seems to be quite top secret in that family. She's so close to remembering. I can feel it. Something will jolt her memory at some point, but I don't know what that will be."

I scrape my teeth over my bottom lip. My curiosity and 'need to know' has been in overdrive for weeks. It's not good. My body needs sleep, but between Nellie and Theo, I can't seem to let my mind rest.

Oscar strokes his neatly-trimmed goatee. "Hmm ... I can think of a way to maybe 'jolt' her."

"No! You will keep your trouser snake *in* your trousers. Do you understand?"

"I can't be responsible if she reaches for my knob—"

"Gross! Stop it. She won't."

His whole body shakes as he laughs. "I don't know ... that woman has a real fire in her belly ... and maybe a bit lower—"

"Ahh!" I cover my ears and stomp into my bedroom, slamming the door behind me.

AFTER A STRONG cup of chamomile tea and a double dose of valerian, I finally get to sleep. My dreams fill with Theo. Him emerging from the ocean. Him giving me that menacing scowl like he wants to eat me alive. And then ... his mouth on me, my head thrown back while he actually eats me—"

"Ruby!"

I jump.

"Breakfast," Oscar calls from the other room.

My heart pounds as I gasp for my next breath. "Oh god ..." I whisper through my panting as I pull my hand out of my knickers. I'm a sweaty mess. This could have been embarrassing beyond words if Oscar would have opened my door to make his announcement.

Sleep masturbating without a lock on my door. Disastrous.

"Coming!" I yell then slap my hand over my mouth and

giggle. "I mean … on my way," I mutter to myself, rolling onto my stomach to bury my heat-stained face in my pillow. "Theo .. Theo … Theo … this … *life* … is no fun without you."

I have a quick shower—a cold one—then peek into the kitchen, curious about breakfast made by a man who has no culinary skills.

"Good morning, Ruby." Oscar's back is to me, but he always knows when someone is behind him. I used to inspect the back of his head, quite certain he did have eyes back there. He turns. "How's this?"

"Wow!" I take the tall glass of fresh-pressed carrot juice from him. How did I not hear the juicer running? Oh, that's right—sleep masturbating. Bugger! I hope I didn't make any noise. "Mmm … very good."

He lifts a glass of amber liquid to his mouth.

"Tea?"

He shakes his head. "Bourbon."

I glance at the clock on the microwave. "It's not even seven, yet."

"I'm on holiday."

"Lucky you."

"So, what are you and the lovely Nellie doing today?"

My narrowed gaze dares him to get any ideas. "The usual. Shopping and lunch."

His casual nod puts me on guard. I can feel the cogs turning in his head and that's not a good thing.

"I'm proud of you."

"Oh?" I lick the juice from my lips.

"Yes. You didn't let anyone tell you what to do. You went with your gut when you knew everyone around you would think you'd lost the plot."

I shake my head. "I didn't think I'd live. I didn't think the cancer would go away. I just wanted to see if the suffering would be less than Sylvie's."

"And your mum's?"

I shrug. "I don't know. I can't remember her suffering, but I suppose the answer is yes because I've seen it in your eyes for ... ever." I glance at the clock again.

"I have to go. Be good."

"Yes, Mum."

"Cheeky. But I'm serious." I grab my rucksack.

"How's the tire?"

I wink. "Perfect."

Just another example of how Oscar Stone can be equally loving and infuriating. I told him I wanted to earn my own money to buy a car and instead of dismissing my wishes, like he's done so much in the past, he settled for buying me a new tire for my bike. Not a new bike—just the tire.

IT'S AMAZING HOW much shopping I do with Nellie, yet we rarely purchase anything. I think her subconscious knows that she has a wardrobe full of designer clothes on one side and secondhand bargains on the other side. She's so close to making the connection.

"I love this café," she says as we look over the menu that we both have memorized because we come to this same place every day.

Sadly, Harold still hasn't shown his cheating face here since the day I ate lunch in this same booth with Theo.

"How well did you know Theodore Reed?"

Nellie's eyebrows knit together. I shouldn't be asking her this, but lately so many things cause her to give me this exact look. It's like she's searching for something that's right there yet just out of reach.

"Nice boy. I think Nolie has known him for a long time. But ... troubled. I wouldn't get too close to him if I were you."

I frown.

She fiddles with her mammoth diamond ring, concentrating on something just over my shoulder for a few seconds before her face lights up. "Oscar!"

"God no," I mutter as my chin drops to my chest, eyes pinched shut.

"What an unexpected surprise." Oscar's voice confirms I'm in Hell.

Looking up, I pin him with my best evil glare. "Is it really?"

He ignores me and sits down next to Nellie, resting his arm on the top of the booth behind them. Her porcelain skin looks like molten glass.

"Nellie, you look lovely as always."

Internally I cringe at the eyes on our table. People know who Nellie Moore is, and while they may be used to seeing whoring Harold, Nellie cozied up to a tall stranger will make the gossip headlines.

After we order, it's like I'm not here. They laugh and flirt and touch each other while my job slips away. I've lost all control over the situation.

"I need to use the ladies' room if you'll excuse me." Nellie smiles.

The whole table jerks, rattling glasses and silverware at the same time Oscar grunts, his eyes the size of saucers. Nellie bites her lip. Why the bloody hell is she biting her lip? That's when I notice her arm close to his body, and while I can't see past her elbow, there is no doubt that her hand is on his *knob.*

"Let her out! She needs to go to the loo."

They both look at me like I'm crazy for announcing it to the whole restaurant.

Oscar clears his throat. "Of course."

Nellie wets her lips as she stands, shoving her chest into him as if she's trying to squeeze past him but there's plenty of room to get by, no need to squeeze. Why is she squeezing?

"I won't be long." She winks. "Unless …" She nips off to the loo like I have never seen her walk before.

Oscar's gaze follows her tight-skirt-covered arse the whole way.

"Stop it!" I whisper.

His eyes snap to mine as he takes his seat.

"You need to leave, *now!*"

He smirks. "Told you she has a fire in her belly."

"The only fire there is going to be is me getting *fired.* So, please, go."

On a long sigh, he nods. "You used to be more fun, Ruby."

"Yeah, well, you used to have scruples."

He drops his napkin on the table along with some money. "True. But one day I realized how much more fun I could have without them." Pressing a kiss to the top of my head, he whispers, "Later, Ruby."

I nod, keeping my eyes trained out the window to the car park. It would be my luck that of all the days, this would be the one Harold would decide to return to the café. After a few minutes, I relax and finish my salad that I was too nauseated to eat with the PDA going on between Nellie and Oscar.

The waitress clears the table, and I check my watch. Nellie

has been in the loo a long time. Physically she's good, but I worry about her making some mental mistake. Maybe's she's stuck with no toilet paper.

Sliding my handbag over my shoulder, I make my way to the back of the café. As I start to push open the door to the loo, someone opens it from the inside.

"Oh, Nellie, I was checking to see—"

She has lip gloss smeared all over her face. Her hands work to tuck her blouse back into her skirt that's completely twisted around.

"Are you O—"

Fuck. Me. Sideways.

My name is Scarlet Stone and very few things in life shock me.

"Enjoy the rest of your afternoon, ladies."

My jaw plummets to the ground as Oscar walks out like the fucking cat who's got the cream.

"Lunch was especially good today." Nellie smiles like she has no idea that I feel as discombobulated as she looks right now.

I cup a hand over my mouth to keep from screaming or crying or … something as I nod slowly.

THE DOOR TO my flat creaks on its hinges as my anger sends it flying into the wall. "You wanker! I can't believe what a complete fuckwit you are!"

Oscar eyes me over the top of his reading spectacles, wetting his thumb then turning the page to his book. "I had a lovely day, Ruby. Thanks for asking. How was yours?"

"You bellend, I'm not playing this game."

"Can't say I've ever heard you speak to me like this. What happened to respecting your elders?"

"You have to be worthy of my respect. What you did to Nellie is *not* worthy of my respect."

He shrugs, returning his attention to his book. "I didn't hear her complain."

Every cell in my body grasps for a breath, a shred of control, a way to calm down. This is not good for me. This is exactly why I had to leave London. "You need to go. I can't have you here. You told me to choose myself and it wouldn't be selfish. I'm asking you to leave … for me."

"Don't you want to know what Nellie said to me in the loo?"

My stomach clenches as my nose wrinkles. "No."

He frowns. "Not about that. She said Harold cheated on her once and it ruined everything."

I grunt, taking a few steps toward my bedroom before stopping again. "*Once?* She said he cheated on her once?"

"Now, that's my girl. What does that tell you?"

I turn. "That's what happened. She caught him cheating on her, but …" I shake my head. "That doesn't drive the average person to completely lose it. There has to be more."

"Well, I'm happy to help get more out of her if you need me to."

"Go away. You can't stay here," I call before shutting my bedroom door.

CHAPTER TWENTY-NINE

My name is Scarlet Stone, and I know the difference between right and wrong. I just haven't mastered the art of giving a shit about it.

DREAM OF Theo again. I wake up in a sweat again. And …
with my hand in my knickers. This is not a life.

To my surprise, the man who refuses to follow instructions
is gone. I tear the sticky note off the fridge.

Ruby,

*I'm off doing some sightseeing. I'll be back—when
I'm back. Then we can talk about our living ar-
rangements after you've had time to reconsider.*

~Oscar

"Please be sightseeing in Alaska," I mumble to myself as I
throw the note in the bin.

After a quick shower, I juice, pack my rucksack, and bike to
the Moores'. There aren't enough miles between my flat and
their mansion to work out the right thing to say to Nellie when
I see her.

Oscar.

Nellie.

The loo.

There are no words.

"Good morning, Miss Stone."

"Scarlet," I correct her.

"Scarlet." Sofia smiles. "Mrs. Moore is taking a bath."

Brilliant idea. She needs to wash everything about the British bloke from yesterday clean from her body—and her mind. I wish I could do the same.

"I'm going to check on her, maybe choose something for her to wear today."

After several unanswered knocks on her bedroom door, I open it a few inches. "Nellie? Hello?"

A crack of light peeks from the partially-shut bathroom door. Nellie's voice mixes with the running water. Each butchered note of a song I've never heard before makes me cringe. I give her some privacy, opting to explore her wardrobe for something that doesn't say "crazy lady" nor "adulterous twat." Something wholesome would be nice.

"Is it too hot for a turtle neck and cardigan?" I grin, sifting through rows of hanging clothes and drawers of jumpers, hosiery, and lingerie. "Nellie Moore ..." I whisper and shake my head, holding up a red lace teddy. Folding the tiny and no doubt expensive bit of nothing, I return it to the drawer. The drawer won't close. Something seems to be behind it.

Nellie's harmonic catastrophe continues—the nerve-grating sound of a donkey braying infused with a heavy dose of monkey screeching. It's really the most unexpected noise coming from a woman who, on the outside, is quite stunning.

After some tedious manipulating, I manage to pull the drawer completely out. Threading my arm in the empty hole, I fish out the culprit. It's a honey and bronze leather journal with a latching strap.

"Put it back," I whisper, tracing the strap with the pad of my finger. Curiosity drives the discovery of new frontiers. Okay, that's what Oscar always tells me. However, acting on it all the time is a disease—one for which I have yet to find the cure.

My name is Scarlet Stone, and I know the difference between right and wrong. I just haven't mastered the art of giving a shit about it.

Before reason can jump in and rescue my unscrupulous impulse, I have the journal open, my eyes tracking the first sentence of the first entry.

> *Bell,*
>
> *I was prepared to leave Harold today, but the psychiatrist declared me insane. Do you think I'm insane?*
>
> *~Nel*

I flip the page.

> *Bell,*
>
> *It's official. I'm insane. I decided not to leave Harold, assuming he would leave me, but he's still here.*
>
> *~Nel*

Next page. This is so wrong.

> *Bell,*
>
> *I can't let that cheating bastard get away with it. Do you understand? Well, I'm sure you do.*
>
> *~Nel*

> *Bell,*
>
> *I busted a seven-thousand-dollar mirror today because I couldn't stand my reflection. Did you ever think about your mortality? Suicide isn't always selfish. Sometimes it's making the hard decision so other people don't have to make it for you. It's crazy how much I've envied you lately.*
>
> *~Nel*

There are too many entries to read them all right now, so I skip to the last one. Bell—who is Bell?

Bell,

I cheated on Harold. I had sex in a public ladies' room with a British man who made me come with his tongue.

"Ew. No, no, no!" I slam the journal shut, wrap the leather strap around it, and slip it under the folded lingerie at the back of the drawer then fit it back into the dresser. There are more words to the final entry, but my stomach can't bear to read them all right now—or ever.

Karma. There she goes again, punishing me for my wrong doings.

My ability to think vanishes. I grab the first outfit that matches and wait for Nellie, perching myself on the cream bench at the end of her canopy bed with spindle wood posts carved in intricate detail. I shake my head, looking over at the fireplace. Her bedroom is three times the size of my flat.

"Oh!"

My head whips around. "Good morning!"

Nellie tightens the sash on her plush white dressing gown and adjusts the towel wrapped around her head. "I didn't know you were here. You should have said something."

"I didn't want to disrupt your bath. Here." I hold up the gray trousers and white blouse.

"Maybe I should wear a dress today. Will we be seeing your father?"

No. Never again will you see Oscar or his tongue. A grimace attempts to consume my face in spite of my effort to appear neutral on this disturbing situation.

"I'm afraid he's left."

"Left? To go where?"

This lady has not cared about a single thing other than coupons, secondhand-clothes shopping, and talking about dead people as if they're still alive. Now—now she's interested?

"Just away. I'm not sure."

Oh. My. God. Are those tears in her eyes? She's married and mentally not right. Why? Why is she fighting back tears over sex in the loo with a man who is no good for her? Nolan thought she'd be devastated if Harold left her. This is the face of a devastated woman, but not because her husband left her. Oscar Stone. That wanker has worked his magic again.

"Actually, I think he said something about doing some sightseeing before he leaves. It's possible he could pop by again in a week or so."

Relief evaporates her tears and a huge smile grows across her face. I should never have introduced them. Never. Ever. Ever.

"Do you work out?" She tugs the towel from her head and dries her matted hair some more.

"Sorry?"

"Jogging? Pilates? Swimming?"

"Um … I used to run quite a bit. Now I enjoy walking and sometimes yoga and meditation."

Nellie frowns. "I think I'm going to need a bit more than that to whip this saggy body back into shape."

"You look perfect. You're not a bit over weight."

"Thank you, sweetie, but I really need to firm things up. I didn't realize how loose everything was until …"

No, no, no … Why is she blushing? Stop blushing. Stop implying things that make me nauseous.

"So, how did you and Harold meet?" He's a total arsebadger, and I really don't care, but I can't sit idle while this whole thing turns into a clusterfuck under my supervision. The house, the money, everything is Nellie's. If she doesn't love him, then cut the weasel off at his bollocks and send him packing.

The frown reappears. "My Debutante Ball. He was one of my two escorts. Carlton was bred just for me." She rolls her eyes.

I've never seen her roll her eyes.

"I told my parents I wouldn't go unless I could also invite a boy from school, Harry Moore. I only invited him to piss them off. That's the same reason I gave him my virginity."

The Nellie Moore before me, sharing her past with complete lucidness, is not the Nellie with whom I've been spending my time with over the past few weeks.

"Is that also why you married him?"

She laughs. Not a crazy, childish laugh—an evil laugh laced with a bit of sarcasm. "I married him because I gave him my virginity. The pissing off my parents was just a bonus, much like the baby we had months after our shotgun wedding."

My lips form into an O as I nod. Every bit of understanding raises fifty new questions. My curiosity level flies off the meter. I can't ask her, and it's killing me. If her past is connected to some sort of trigger, I don't want to be the one to push the damn button. She needs to discover it on her own—with maybe a nudge from me.

"These are nice clothes." I hold up the trousers and blouse, perfectly-pressed, expensive fabric hanging from wood hangers. "Where did you get them?"

"Probably one of the stores we've been at over the past few

weeks." Her gaze diverts to her wedding ring, like she's admiring it for the first time.

"Do you feel guilty about Oscar?" I can't help it. The truth is right there. I can feel it with the tips of my fingers, but I can't quite grasp it. Her sanity. It feels like her sanity.

"What do you mean?" Just like that. She flips on me.

"Nothing. Let's get you dressed and do your hair and makeup."

THAT JOURNAL HOLDS the answers. I need to steal it, but she still writes in it, so I can't take it. She'll know. More than anything, I need to meditate—try to meditate. I haven't forgotten that I have cancer. It would suck to die before I solve this mystery, before I make peace with the part of myself that wants for the bearded man from Tybee, before I ride a real horse, or unravel the true wonder of being someone's song.

"Wow, so much for giving me space." I'm too exhausted to even be that exasperated with Oscar lounging on his bed, the bed that should be gone, next to the chair that should be gone. I shut the door.

He glances at his watch. "I've given you a solid ten hours, Ruby. You're usually much more efficient with your time. What's wrong?"

"Nice watch." I continue to the kitchen.

"It's new." He follows me.

"It's stolen."

"Borrowed."

I grab a drink of water and turn toward him. "Really? You're going to return it?"

"Swap it. Yes."

"Whatever." I gulp down the whole glass of water.

"Aren't you going to ask me whose watch it is?"

"No." I put the empty glass down and give him the piss-off look because I'm really not interested in playing his games.

He sighs, letting his hand fall back to his side. "It's Harold's. I swapped it for an exact replica that has a tracking chip embedded in it."

I close my eyes and shake my head.

"I thought you'd be proud of me. Now, I'll know where he is at all times so we won't get caught."

"We? Really? Now you and Nellie are a 'we?'"

"Alright, Ruby, tell me what's bugging you."

"You're bugging me. Missing Theo is bugging me. Having cancer is bugging me. Nellie's secret journal is bugging me. Living in this tiny flat instead of my house on the beach is bugging me. Needing *me* time but not getting it is bugging me!"

"Nellie has a secret journal."

Yes. I said that. Why did I say that? "Yes."

"Did you take it?"

There's nothing left to offer but a painful laugh. "No. I can't take a journal she still writes in every day."

"Why is it bugging you?"

"Because it's filled with cryptic stuff that doesn't make any sense yet something tells me if I could read the whole thing it might make perfect sense."

"I'll get it for you."

"Sorry? No! You're not going anywhere near her. Watch or no watch. Were you not listening to me? She still writes in it. If it shows up missing, there's a short list of people who could be accused, and I'm on that list."

Oscar nods—but it's not a nod that I like. It's a nod that tells me he's planning something.

"Promise me you won't steal it."

His gaze shifts to mine. "I promise."

"Oscar."

"What? I said I promise. What more do you want?"

"Time. I need you to leave for real this time. I need some time to focus on me and do what's best for me. Nellie already knows I'm taking a few days or maybe even a few weeks off. Go home. Please. I'm going to look for that place I was at before everything ended." Minus Theodore. Can that place exist without him? I hope so.

Oscar pushes off the worktop and brings me into his embrace. "As you wish, Ruby."

CHAPTER THIRTY

My name is Scarlet Stone and for my twelfth birthday, Oscar gave me a signed first edition of Sherlock Holmes *by Sir Arthur Conan Doyle, an Inverness cape, and a deerstalker cap.*

LIFE DOESN'T HAVE an off button, at least not one you can press and still be alive. The truth is, I could leave. I could go anywhere in the world. I could find places and people who would nourish my body and my mind and maybe this fucking leach called cancer would vanish for good. However, I fear the damage it would do to me to get there.

The lies.

The manipulating.

The stealing.

I may not have told Theo the whole truth, but even my lies were wrapped in dreams of reality. That has to count for something. Six months of being a Scarlet Stone that I didn't recognize was part of what started to cure my cancer. I can't prove it. True miracles don't need to be justified. It's my truth and that's all that matters. I will never need anyone to believe me as long as I'm my own living proof.

Filling the Theodore Reed void in my heart makes concentrating, meditating, eating, sleeping, and *breathing* feel impossible. One breath. One day at a time. It's been a week, and I haven't heard from anyone, not even Oscar. He left with a kiss, a smile, and a nod. No goodbye. I suppose the most personal relationships in life eventually live on their own—without words, without explanation. He knows I love him and I know he loves me. That's why we're here … I think.

I still steep herbs Yimin gave me. I drink carrot juice. I

avoid alcohol. I eat unprocessed foods. I meditate for hours. I read and read and read. Some days I feel quite inspired. Some days I think of Theo and smile instead of cry. Some days I wake with my hands folded under my chin, very angelically, instead of down my knickers molesting myself.

Today I wake late to a knock at my door.

"Scarlet Stone?" The delivery man asks.

"Yes." I cover my mouth with my fist to hide my yawn.

"Delivery. I just need your signature." He hands me the tablet and I sign for the small parcel.

"Thank you." I shut the door and rip into it.

A mobile. It's like sending an alcoholic a bottle of vodka. When I open the actual mobile box there's a note on the inside.

For your reading pleasure.

Taking a deep breath, I turn on the phone. There's a document waiting for me. I open it.

"Bloody hell …" It's scanned pages of Nellie's journal.

Oscar. He was in her house. *In her bedroom!*

I'm mad as hell and … curious. I've been doing so good. Okay, maybe not "good," but not bad. Sometimes not bad can be a really good day. It's all perspective.

The journal gobbles up the rest of my day. Hundreds of entries, some short, some quite long, but they're all written to Bell. A lot of them don't make any sense and in some ways they confirm Nellie's diagnosis. Other entires remind me of my last day with her, the lucidity, the moment I questioned every day before with her. By the time I reach the end of the final entry, I don't feel the enlightenment that I had hoped I would find. I wanted to know more about the "incident" that led to her mental state. One thing I know is that something happened to

Bell, and Nellie is responsible.

However, the last entry, which was three days ago, is most shocking. She's *not* insane—at least not in the way her family believes she is. And I think Bell is the woman with whom Harold had an affair. I don't know if anyone else would read these same words and come to the same conclusion, but I feel it in the space between words. Bell and Nellie were friends who betrayed each other. That much bleeds through every page of the journal.

> *Bell,*
>
> *I'm done. The lie has to end. I don't know if the truth will set me free, but I have to try. I've found someone who makes me want something more than revenge. I'm not even sure if revenge was ever mine to give. That's probably something you would know. What about forgiveness? Have I earned that? Have you forgiven me? I've forgiven you. I think I could even forgive Harold if I thought it would give me true freedom.*
>
> *~Nel*

My name is Scarlet Stone and for my twelfth birthday, Oscar gave me a signed first edition of *Sherlock Holmes* by Sir Arthur Conan Doyle, an Inverness cape, and a deerstalker cap. It was more than a gift; it was symbolic of my duty to solve mysteries.

Nellie and I need to have a chat. I grab my bag and open the door. "Nolan." I gasp.

"Scarlet, we need to talk."

"Oh, um … okay. Come in."

He steps inside and looks around my tiny flat, specifically

at the bed and massage chair that consumes the room.

"Have a seat." I nod to the massage chair.

His brow tightens.

"You don't have to turn it on if you don't want to." I return a half smile while grabbing my picnic chair, unfolding it, then taking a seat. It would feel too weird to sit on the bed.

Never mind. Nolan's gaping-mouth assessment of my place has already maxed out the weirdness level. I should have just sat on the bed.

He eases into the chair like each inch he descends is the final crank to a Jack in the box. "Your father," he begins once he's convinced a scary clown is not going to jump out.

For me, the clown is already out and his name is Oscar. Tapping my finger on the plastic arm of my chair, I bide my time. It's too early to jump to any conclusions.

"He and my mother were …"

Here it comes: horrific tales of the trouser snake. The small smile on my face feels pained. I can only imagine what it must look like.

"…having dinner last night. They seemed *close.*"

As long as he wasn't eating her for dinner, then I can handle this. It's still manageable. "Dinner at your house?"

Nolan nods.

"With your father?"

"He's out of town."

I swallow a hard lump then clear my throat. "What … what were they eating?"

Nolan narrows his eyes. "I don't know."

My sigh of relief is a bit louder than intended.

"He said you asked him to keep her company while you took some time off."

Of course he did. Wanker.

"My mother seemed …" His lips twist to the side.

I hate how he keeps baiting me with fragmented sentences that leave me hanging. It's like he's waiting to see if I will jump in and … what? I don't know for sure.

"Different."

"Different how?"

Nolan shrugs. "Normal. Too normal."

I laugh a bit. "Too normal? I'd consider that progress, a good thing. Isn't it?"

"I know you're going to take this wrong. My intention is not to sound like an awful son who doesn't want to see his mother get better, but … I don't want her memory of the incident to come back if it means she could spiral out of control to the point where we could lose her forever."

"This incident. I don't understand this 'incident' that you and your father seem so determined to keep from her and everyone else. You're so afraid of me triggering her memory, snapping her out of her delusional state, but you won't tell me what it is you don't want her to remember. So how can I tiptoe around some invisible trigger?"

Resting his elbows on his knees, he cradles his head in his hands. "I don't know," he mumbles.

"What does that mean?"

"I don't know!" His head snaps up.

I flinch.

The last time I saw so much agony etched into Nolan's face was when he told me about his ability to sense other people's pain.

"My accident. That's what caused my mother's condition. She thought I died and something just broke inside of her. She doesn't remember it. Not once since her mind has gone to its 'safe place' has she mentioned it."

"But if it was an accident—"

He shakes his head. "It was her fault. I still don't know all the details because my own memory of it is so sketchy. I have these fragments, but when I try to piece them together, they don't make sense. We were going somewhere. My father was out of town. She needed to make a quick stop." He shakes his head some more. "I waited in the car. It was taking her too long, so I went to look for her."

I wait for him to continue, but he doesn't. His eyes remain fixed to his interlaced fingers.

"Where were you?"

"I don't remember where we were. My father said it happened at home. That doesn't fit with what little I do remember—or think I remember."

"So he's lying?"

"I don't know."

"Tell me what happened, Nolan."

He nods slowly. "I was shot. I lost a lot of blood. I died on the operating table. But they brought me back to life."

"Nellie shot you?"

He nods.

"Why?"

"My father said it was an intruder. She grabbed a gun from their bedroom. When I walked around the corner at the top of the stairs, it spooked her. She shot me."

"What did the newspapers say?"

"Nothing."

"Nothing? That doesn't make any sense. The only son of a prominent family gets shot by his mother and *nothing* gets printed in the newspaper?"

He shrugs. "My father didn't want her to end up in prison for an accident. He didn't want it to tarnish our family's name. He made it ..."

"Go away," I whisper.

He nods.

"So, you live or come back to life, with an abnormally heightened sense of feelings, only to discover that your mother has lost it."

"Yes."

"So your father stays with her, in spite of what seems to be a broken marriage, because he wants the money."

"Yes."

"And when did he start cheating on her?"

"I'm not sure. He claims it didn't happen until several years after the accident."

"You're pissed off he cheated on her."

"Yes."

"But you think she still loves him and it would crush her if he left?"

"Yes."

"And he gets the best of both worlds—the money and other women. Tell me, what does she get?" Revenge. She gets revenge, but I don't know how or why ... yet.

"She gets peace. Peace of not remembering what she did to me. Peace of knowing her family is still together."

"This is messed-up."

Nolan doesn't respond.

"I did not tell my dad to keep Nellie company for me. He bullied his way to work with me a while back. I introduced them. Your mother—the innocent doe-eyed Nellie? She took an instant liking to him and he to her."

"That doesn't make sense. My father said she's like a child when it comes to intimacy. That's what drove him to cheat on her."

"Oh yeah? Well, the British bloke I sadly have to claim as my dad, he's corrupted that child you call your mother and as much as it disgusts me, she's enjoyed every bit of it."

Nolan narrows his eyes. "What? You're saying—"

"Yes. Please don't make me go into detail. But ... yes."

I told him Father Christmas does not exist.

Blink.

Blink.

Blink.

He didn't see the epilogue of the loo scene like I did. Clearly, he doesn't understand how lucky he is at this moment.

"Is Oscar at your house right now?"

More blinking. "Uh ... no, I don't think so. When I left, my mother was in her room."

"Alone?"

He flinches. Welcome to my world, Nolan, where some things cannot be unseen or unheard.

"Let's go." I stand and grab my bag.

CHAPTER THIRTY-ONE

My name is Scarlet Stone, and I can't remember ever feeling a connection to normal, well-adjusted people. My reflection has always been in the many faces of dysfunctional souls.

NELLIE IS ALONE in her room. The look of relief on Nolan's face makes me smile.

"Are you announcing your engagement?" she asks, setting her book on the bedside table then swinging her legs off the side of the bed.

"We're not dating, Mother."

Nellie frowns. I don't buy it.

"Can you give us a few minutes, Nolan?" I ask.

"Sure. I'll be downstairs." He shuts the door behind him.

"Scarlet, how have you been, dear?"

"Did you shoot Nolan at home or somewhere else?" There it is. I pulled the pin on the grenade. I'm *that* sure she's not going to have an epiphany—a sudden remembrance of her past.

Zero. There is absolutely no shock in her expression. Nellie didn't forget. She's not crazy—at least not in the way everyone thinks she is.

"My journal." She nods. "You read my journal. I wrap the leather tie left to right, but the last time I opened it, the tie was wrapped right to left."

Not Oscar's mistake. Mine. He wound it back the same way it was when he found it, after *I* wound it the wrong way. That's why I do best behind a computer. I don't see the physical details that he does or that my grandfather did.

There's nothing in her journal that would lead me to think

that she shot her son. We both know the journal only proves she's been acting for years.

"I had a hunch that Harold was cheating on me. Intuition, I suppose. Harold said he was going on a business trip. He had this brown leather briefcase that I bought him after he graduated college. It traveled everywhere with him, especially on business trips. I found it in his office a few hours after he left. Of course, I knew I'd be getting a phone call with him all in a panic over leaving it."

Nellie shakes her head. "The call never came. My mind wandered places a proper southern lady's mind should never have to go. I made fools out of my parents when I married him. I wasn't going to let him make a fool out of me. He had a handgun in a wooden box in our closet. I shoved it in my purse and headed to the car. I knew where he was. A day earlier, I wouldn't have known."

She laughs. "It's funny how we already know certain things but our mind won't let the images into the light until something else triggers it. I saw *them*—the subtle looks, the accidental brush of their hands in passing that was anything but accidental. I saw it. I should have known before then. I just didn't want to see it."

"And Nolan?"

She focuses on me for the first time, every word until this point had been spoken with her eyes glazed over into the past. "He pulled up as I was getting ready to leave. It was his birthday. I'd forgotten my only child's birthday. He offered to take me to dinner. I couldn't say no, so I told him we needed to make a quick stop before going to the restaurant. He asked why we were going there? He knew them. We all knew them. I said I had a luncheon invitation to drop off and it would only take a few minutes, so he stayed in the car like I asked him to do."

With one blink, Nellie's tears fall. "I didn't knock. The door was unlocked, so I opened it. I knew. It's so hard to explain that slow ascent up the stairs knowing that everything in life is about to change forever. When I eased open the door, Bell shot up out of bed, holding a sheet over her naked body. No one was in bed with her. For a full three seconds I doubted myself. I heard the bathroom door open, and I prepared to explain to her husband why I had let myself uninvited into their house. But it wasn't her husband … it was mine."

I haven't blinked. I'm not sure I've taken a breath the whole time.

"I pulled the gun from my purse and aimed it at him." Nellie pinches her eyes shut for few silent seconds, releasing more tears. "My hands were shaking so much I could barely keep my finger on the trigger."

Even now, her hands shake folded in her lap.

"I was crying because my world seemed to be ending before my eyes. He was my husband. She was my friend. With each blink, I became more and more blinded by my emotions. Bell's pleading voice was a mere echo. He … said nothing. I closed my eyes, and pulled the trigger."

Biting her lips together, her body trembles in silent sobs. "Sh-sh-she jumped in front of him."

I draw in a shaky breath, blinking back my own emotions.

"Harry yelled my name as he caught her limp body collapsing to the ground. When he looked up at me, all I could see was murder in his eyes. The gun fell from my numb hands. I didn't move when he dove for it. Then I realized what he was doing, and I took a step backwards and then another. When he lifted the gun like an extension of his arm, I turned and dove toward the door. The pop of the gun sent a chill up my spine at the same time my shoulder connected with something— someone—as I tried to escape."

"Nolan," I whisper.

Nellie nods.

"I-I t-told him to w-wait in the c-car." She sobs.

The two people who were meant to die that day, lived. I grab a tissue from her bedside table and hand it to her.

"And Bell?"

She shakes her head.

Nellie is responsible for someone dying. I hate that I know how that feels, but I do.

My name is Scarlet Stone, and I can't remember ever feeling a connection to normal, well-adjusted people. My reflection has always been in the many faces of dysfunctional souls.

"Why does Nolan think you shot him?"

"Because that's what Harry told him. Since Nolan didn't remember much at all, it was easy to tell him what Harry told the police."

"But you told Nolan it was a burglary at home. This didn't happen at home."

Nellie blots her eyes. "Money can buy just about anything. It bought …" She sniffles.

"The police."

She nods.

"Clean up."

She nods.

I feel nauseous.

"Whatever story you want?"

"Yes," she whispers. "I killed the woman he loved, so he

made me take the blame for Nolan, justice in a twisted tale.

"But you were declared insane."

She shrugs, taking in a shaky breath. "I've seen a psychiatrist for years. Truthfully, I *did* feel like I was having a mental breakdown after they told us Nolan's heart stopped beating on the operating table. *That* Nellie … her heart stopped too. They brought Nolan back. *I* didn't want to come back. I was on suicide watch for weeks. Harry wanted me to be evaluated to determine if I was of sound mind." Her eyes hold firm to mine, silently pleading for me to understand. "It was an out. A way to live without accountability."

"How did you get your psychiatrist to declare you—" I know the answer before I ever finish the question. "Money," I whisper. "All these years …"

"Crazy was just easier. And I had the lead in all the school plays. I can play any part."

I shake my head. "The secondhand shopping … the coupons …"

"Harry didn't grow up with money. Everything he owned was secondhand. Nothing was purchased without a coupon. He swore he'd never go back to that life. I wanted to prove him wrong."

"It was an illusion."

She laughs. "I know. I know about the women. I know he's one man with me and another man the second he walks out of here. I know no one else sees the clothes I buy for him. I know he's only here because of the money—my money. I also know that Nolan's fear of me remembering something that he himself can't remember is what has kept him from kicking his father's philandering arse to the curb."

I'm speechless.

"I'm observant. People talk over crazy people. They think I can't hear them one room away."

"Oscar ..." Eventually, I'll talk in full sentences again. My mind is spinning way too fast, throwing out a word here and there.

Nellie smiles like a giddy school girl. "He's the first breath I've taken in years. Do you have any idea what it's like to physically feel your breath? It's like your heartbeat. It's there doing its job, but we take it for granted until we almost lose it or until something or *someone* unexpectedly crashes into your life, making you *feel* absolutely everything." She rolls her red eyes. "You must think I'm a stupid woman saying such non-sense."

One.

Two.

Three.

I count them all the time. With Theo each breath felt like life. Without him, each breath is nothing more than a chemical exchange necessary to keep my heart beating. Without him, I can imagine I might eventually take them for granted and stop counting.

"Oscar has a past that's—"

"He's told me about his past, *Ruby*. Prison. His 'profession,' your mom, and ... your cancer." Nellie grabs my hand and squeezes it.

I blink away my own tears. Oscar is in love. He's *never* told another soul about my mum.

CHAPTER THIRTY-TWO

My name is Scarlet Stone and when I was fifteen, we had to disappear for a while.

TAKE ALL THE stars, Theodore Reed. You own all the breaths that have mattered most to me. Why would I think that anyone but you could claim every. Single. Dream. The idea of living without you seemed much more bearable when I thought I wouldn't be alive. *This* ... is a skeleton of existence.

Every new day should be a celebration—complete gratitude—of life. Instead, it's just another day I've survived without you. When loneliness takes its occasional break, guilt takes over.

Guilt over needing you.

Guilt over needing anything but a heartbeat.

No one wants to be the last human living on Earth. Why do I feel like that person? What's wrong with me?

The first of November ushers in a few brisk mornings, so I pull on a jumper and go for a walk this morning since I have a few days off. The Moores left town today for a wedding in South Beach. Nellie plans on telling Nolan and Harold everything.

My father has moved back in with me, but just until Harold is gone. I'm not sure if Nolan will welcome Oscar Stone into his house—his mum's bed.

After I get a stone's throw from my flat, an unexpected shower spoils my walk, so I duck into the library for shelter until it lets up.

I browse through the aisles, pulling this book and that book off the shelf.

I look at the rows of computers.

I browse some more.

I think of Theo.

I look at the rows of computers.

I go to the loo and browse some more.

It's still raining.

I ease into a chair by a computer, just to rest.

My hand bumps the mouse and the screen lights up.

I fist my hands. Maybe I can just do a search for live radar to see when the rain will let up. That's no big deal. I did read Nellie's journal on my phone, but I haven't touched it since then. I can do this.

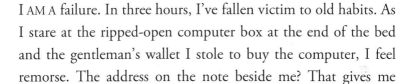

I AM A failure. In three hours, I've fallen victim to old habits. As I stare at the ripped-open computer box at the end of the bed and the gentleman's wallet I stole to buy the computer, I feel remorse. The address on the note beside me? That gives me hope.

Theo's mobile was a dead end. As I suspected, he must have destroyed it after I texted him from Nolan's mobile. Credit cards? Nope. I did that one to myself. It would appear that Theo has been paying cash for everything. However, a DMV search gave me his registration number and since then, I've accessed every traffic camera and building security camera starting in Savannah to piece together his whereabouts.

He's in Lexington.

Where? I'm not sure yet but for the past week, he's been caught on a bank security camera getting coffee at a Starbucks next to the bank.

I've opened my own bank account and reclaimed some of the money I deposited into Daniel's account. He'll have to understand. I refuse to take any more money from Oscar. I can do this on my own. Okay—starting now.

After I pack my bags, grab my juicer, and leave Oscar a note, I make my way to the bank. *My* bank. Withdrawing money is as quick as pouring a cup of cold treacle. Banks tend to be sensitive about major withdrawals.

After that, I buy the cheapest economy car I can find, anonymously post the stolen wallet back to my victim, and credit his account for the *borrowed* money. Then I set the sat nav for the Starbucks next to the bank in Lexington.

I'm coming for you, Theodore Reed.

<hr />

NINE HOURS AND four stops later, I arrive in Lexington. Starbucks is closed. I get a hotel room for the night and return in the morning. The moment I see him, I will want to leap into his arms. But I can't. First I need to know why he's here.

Parked across the street, I sit low in my seat with a cap on my head. I wait for two hours and as I start to think he's not coming for his morning coffee, a man that matches his build approaches the door. It's him but … his beard is not long like Theo's. It looks like a few days' worth of thick stubble. He's wearing a gray beanie, no hair hangs out around it, and there's no bulkiness that suggests it's all tucked beneath it. The black long-sleeved shirt prevents me from seeing tattoos, and sunglasses conceal his eyes.

I know it's him as much as I don't believe it can be him. I'm disguised a bit, but not enough to walk into the coffee shop without him recognizing me. "Theo ... is that you?" I whisper to myself.

The uncertainty leaves me with no choice but to wait and see if I can make a better assessment when he comes out. A few minutes later, he emerges, taking a sip from his takeaway cup. I squint, but ... I don't know. The body is Theo's, but it's possible he isn't the only man in Lexington with a body like that. Video from two days ago showed him with his hair pulled back, no sunglasses. This might not be him. I watch him in my mirror, walk down the pavement and make a right turn onto another street.

My focus returns to the Starbucks, but a few seconds later, I happen to glance in my mirror again. "It's him." I sit up in my seat and fumble with my seatbelt as his truck turns on the main street going in the opposite direction as my car is parked.

I do a U-turn onto the street and gun it, slowing up as his truck comes into sight again. After weaving his way through town, he parallel parks on the street. I've already passed my best spot to park a few cars behind him, so I have to go around the block. I tuck my chin and pull on the bill of my hat when my car passes his truck. A few minutes later, I secure a spot four cars back from his truck.

I was worried he'd be out of his truck, but he's not. His window is cracked and he's looking straight ahead, sipping his coffee.

Six hours. He sits in his truck for six hours. I'm dying. My arse is numb, and my bladder is ready to burst when his brake lights illuminate.

"Oh thank God." I wait a few seconds after he pulls out before following him. He doesn't go far, just two streets. A blue car pulls into an angled parking spot in front of an old block of flats. Theo pulls in a few spaces back from the blue car. I do the same behind Theo. Bloody hell, I need to wee!

Theo's head moves slowly. He seems to be following the man getting out of the blue car. The man walks across the street. Theo's head turns in his direction. Once the man disappears into another tall block of flats, Theo gets out of his truck. I scoot down low in my seat, peeking at him through the steering wheel. The locks on his truck beep, and he uses a key to get into the block on the same side of the street that we're parked.

Wee. Dammit, I need to wee, but I don't want to get out yet. Theo could be looking out a window and see me. I'm not ready for him to see me yet. Desperate times ... I grab an empty disposable cup from the holder between the seats, unbuckle, and move my seat back as far as it will go. Then I maneuver my feet onto the seat into a squatted position. After a quick look around the area, I shimmy my leggings and knickers down just far enough to get the cup upright between my legs and ... ahh ...

I won't apologize. At the moment, this release feels almost as good as an orgasm.

My name is Scarlet Stone and when I was fifteen, we had to disappear for a while. Oscar feared for his life, so we holed up in this warehouse for two weeks until the threat was eliminated. No plumbing. We bathed with baby wipes and became experts at the art of weeing in a cup. The first few times didn't go so well for me. My aim wasn't nearly as good as the male porcupine's.

Plastering my face to the window, I look for lights on in any of the flats but it's still too light out. I dig my computer out of my bag to see if I can find some information on the man that Theo seemed so interested in following.

A registration plate is a great start.

"What. The. Hell?"

The blue car was recently registered to Braxton Ames. That's the name from the newspaper clipping in Theo's trunk.

Braxton Ames arrested in the murder of Kathryn Reed

I search his name.

Investigators reopen the Kathryn Reed homicide case.

Braxton Ames's attorney claims he was coerced into confessing to the murder of Reed and lack of evidence will prove his claim of not guilty. A judge will rehear his case in October.

Judge finds Braxton Ames not guilty for the murder of Kathryn Reed. Police are now searching for the person responsible for her death.

October. October was the end of our six months on Tybee. Theo's here for Braxton. He doesn't believe he's innocent. Theo's here to kill Braxton Ames.

"Think, Scarlet." Before I can plot my next move, Theo comes out of the block. He's still wearing the gray beanie but no sunglasses. I can barely breathe. He looks so different with his trimmed facial hair and that hat.

He gets into his truck and pulls out. As much as I want to know where he's going, I need to stay here. Braxton is in his flat across the street. For now he's safe. After Theo's truck turns the corner, I jump out, depositing my urine cup in the bin by the entrance that's locked.

I'm getting faster at breaking in, just like old times. The main door opens for me in less than ten seconds.

"Great," I mutter as I look up the stairs. There must be seven floors of flats. How the hell am I supposed to find which one is his?"

He wants to keep an eye on Braxton, so his flat has to face the street. That still doesn't narrow it down enough, but it's a start. I begin at the top floor, assuming he'd want to be up a ways. Door after door, I knock and knock. When I'm lucky enough to get an answer, I go through my spiel describing him, but no one knows who I'm talking about. Of course he's not exactly going to be the one in the block throwing parties, but he's not exactly someone you don't notice either.

I'm running out of time. Without knowing where he went, I have no idea when he'll be back, but it's been over an hour since he left. I knock on the last door on the fourth floor, feeling a bit defeated.

"Yes?" A ponytailed blonde answers the door, jogging in place. "Sorry, you caught me in the middle of a workout."

"Oh, sorry. I'm looking for Theodore Reed, he's about six—"

"Yes, Theo. Nice guy. His apartment is that one." She points to the door just to the right of hers. The one I just knocked on, and of course, no one answered.

"Are you okay?" she asks, bouncing up and down.

I must look a bit dazed. I'd given up on finding it. "Yeah. Thanks. I knocked. He's not home, so I'll come back later."

"Do you want me to tell him you stopped by if I see him?"

I don't really want happy, bouncy tits to see him at all. "No. No need. Thank you."

As she waves and starts to shut her door, I notice something familiar behind her, near her window. *Phoebe!* I recognized the green ceramic pot.

"Wait!" I bang the toe of my shoe into her door to prevent it from closing.

"Yes?"

"That's my plant!"

She glances over her shoulder then back at me. "Excuse me?"

"Theo gave you that plant, didn't he?" Bastard!

"Uh ... yes, but—hey!"

I shove past her, stepping over her minefield of clutter to rescue my peace lily. "It's mine. Sorry, he had no right to give it to you." I grab the doorknob and slam her door shut before she has a chance to protest anymore.

New plan. I'm going to kill him.

I glance at the door to the stairwell and then the door to the lift. He could show up any minute. He could also put a bullet in Braxton Ames's head before morning. I pick his lock and shut the door behind me, locking it again. I can't help but grin. It's bare in here except for a folding chair. Then I look at Phoebe in my arms and my smile vanishes.

Bastard!

With one shift of my gaze to the window, even the plant is forgotten. There's a rifle mounted onto a tripod. I open the door to the right. It's a bathroom. I put Phoebe in the bath and run a little water. The poor thing looks like a dead jelly fish. Bouncy tits is clueless.

The other door is to a bedroom—mattress on the floor, trunk next to it. I can strip down naked on his bed and wait. He'll see me. I'll give him a bollocking for giving Phoebe away—*again*. We'll fuck like rabid animals. He'll forget why he came to Lexington.

Yeah, right.

I tug on the trunk. It must weigh several hundred pounds, so I unlock it. Everything looks about the same, except the missing rifle that's now perched by the window. I run back out and tug open drawers and cupboards in the kitchen until I find a bin bag. Then I hustle back to the bedroom and start filling it with weapons.

"The rifle." I frown at the bag that's full and remove some of the knives. Figuring out how to remove the rifle from the tripod eats up almost ten minutes. I can disarm a state-of-the-art security system in less than sixty seconds but a simple tripod has me completely perplexed.

I'm sure the rifle comes apart, but hell if I know how to do that. I shove it into the bag and lift the heavy thing up. The end of the rifle busts through.

"Shit." I grab another bag and double bag everything. Then I glance out the window. No Theo, yet. Lugging weapons in bin bags is not ideal.

"Need help?" A young man with scraggly dark hair and a pathetic excuse for a beard asks as I heave it into the lift.

"Thank you. I'm good. Just some … stuff I'm donating."

He nods as the lift starts to descend.

"After you." He holds out his arm when the door opens.

Manners can have a downside. With my luck, one of the guns is loaded and will go off, killing this poor bloke before I get the bag dragged out of the building.

"Thank you." I grunt, lifting the bag.

"Here."

"No!"

Before I can stop him, he has the bag hoisted up. I hold my breath.

"Where's your car?"

Gulp!

"Uh, follow me, but please be careful … some of it's fragile."

He follows me to my car.

"Here, put it in the boot."

He laughs. "The boot?"

"Uh …" I shake my head. "The um … trunk I believe you call it."

He puts it in the boot—trunk. "You're not from these parts."

I return a shaky smile, surveying the area for Theo's truck. "Just moved here."

"What apartment are you in?"

"Sorry? Oh, uh …" I laugh. "Gosh, I can't even remember, I just walk right to it. Um …"

"Well, it has to be four-something."

I nod. "Yes." I wave my hands around. "The uh … door down the hall like, second or third from the end. Sorry, it's been a long day and I'm …"

He laughs. "No problem. I'm Kyle, apartment 512. Don't hesitate if you need help with anything or…" he shrugs "…if you want to get a drink sometime."

"Lovely. I'll keep that in mind. Thank you." I open the door and give him one last smile before closing it, starting the car, and getting the hell out of here.

CHAPTER THIRTY-THREE

My name is Scarlet Stone, and I'm not afraid of death. My mum waits for me with open arms.

NOTHING MAKES ONE drive like an eighty-year-old woman quite like a bag of weapons in the boot of a car. I drive to the hotel, cursing every twat that feels the need to ride my arse. The last thing I need is a crash. Tied for the last thing I need is to be pulled over for speeding and land in jail when they check the boot. I want the weapons out, but I can't risk lugging them to my hotel room or worse: having someone else do it for me. My only choice is to leave them in the boot and deal with them tomorrow, so that's what I do.

Another sleepless night ends in a sunrise that's blinding and daunting. Now what? I need to figure out who killed Theo's mum. That's the only way to keep him from killing Braxton Ames and risking life in prison or worse. The problem is I can't leave him unattended. It won't take much to replace his weapons. Americans show great pride in worshiping their Second Amendment like a religion.

Gathering my computer, I put the *Do Not Disturb* sign on the door and head to Starbucks. Like yesterday, I park across the street. Parking next to his flat is too risky, especially since he's probably on high alert after returning last night to the scene of a weapons robbery. I hope he needs his coffee this morning.

A big pair of black sunglasses cover most of my face. I thought I needed to add them to my hat disguise. I spy him in my mirror, so I scoot down a bit even though he's on the other side of the street. Again, he has on a long-sleeve shirt, beanie, and sunglasses. He looks around before opening the door to Starbucks. I tip my head down when his head turns in my direction.

When the door shuts behind him, I release the breath I've been holding. A few minutes later he comes out, but instead of walking toward his truck the way he came, he heads in the opposite direction, disappearing around the front of the building.

"Where are you going?" My teeth dig into my bottom lip as I contemplate following him versus waiting for him to come back around the corner. A tracking device would be much easier. That's what Oscar would do. I might have to acquire one so that I have more time to devote to Kathryn's murderer. I'm not used to leaving my house or hotel room to conduct my business. Mobiles and tracking devices usually do the job, but I don't have help on this, so here I am, following Theo the old-fashioned way. I'm completely rubbish at it.

"Shit!" I jump when something shakes my car like someone ran into the back of me, but when I look in my mirror, I don't see anything except the vacant car that's been parked behind me for the last forty-five minutes. There was a crushing sound, I know something hit me. "Fuck it, what the hell was that?" I mutter, releasing my seatbelt then glancing at the corner to check once more for Theo. As soon as I unlock the door, it opens.

"Ah!" My scream is silenced by a large hand over my mouth.

"Over," Theo's gritty voice sends prickly bumps along my skin.

He doesn't wait for me to move before lifting my body

with one hand while keeping my mouth covered with his other hand. My bum lands in the passenger seat.

"Fucking scream and I'll shove the lone knife you left me right into your heart. Understood?"

No, I don't understand, but since his massive hand covers both my mouth and nose, I nod because my lungs crave some oxygen. He eases his hand away from my mouth, testing my response. I have no response. What's happening?

Theo starts the car and pulls out into traffic. The only sound in the car is my heart hammering in my chest. I am his song.

He can't stab his song in the chest!

"How did you know?" I whisper, *not* wanting to be stabbed in the chest. But if I'm honest, it already feels like that's what he's done.

He gives me a quick, menacing sideways glance, the one where he bares his teeth a bit. "I smelled you. The second I walked through my door, I smelled your fucking scent."

Scent. Hmm … most experts solve crimes with fingerprints or eyewitnesses. Nope. Theodore Reed is a bloody hound dog. That's why I like to work from my flat where no one can smell my scent.

"And there was a fucking plant in my tub."

Phoebe. How did I forget her? Oh, that's right … I had a bag of weapons that needed to be hauled to my car.

He pulls into a parking spot outside of his flat and shoves my car into park. "If you run, I will catch you and it won't be pretty."

The last time he caught me, it changed everything. Our *nothing* became a very real *something*. I don't think if I run this time it will end with him worshiping my body in the shallow moonlit waters of the Atlantic.

"I mean it. Whatever you thought you knew about me no longer exists. I'm not that guy. If you want to live, you'd better let every fucking memory go. They are all dead."

Who is this man? I physically feel nauseous. I came here because I didn't want to live without him, only to find out it's the only chance I have to live at all. Bloody great.

"Wait right there." He gets out and walks around to my side and opens the door. "Get out."

I get out, feeling quite wobbly.

"Ow!" I groan when the tip of his knife digs into the small of my back.

"Shut up and walk." He leads me into the block and into the lift.

I blink back my tears. This cannot be happening. I'm his *song*. His tears didn't need to fall for me to see them. I saw the emotion—the love—in his eyes when we made love. It was hard and brutal, but it was love. Painful … beautiful love.

"Hold the elevator!" a voice calls.

I reach out to push the open button, but Theo yanks my arm back. The frantic woman, with her arms full of groceries, manages to make it in time to stop the doors with her foot.

"Close call." She smiles stepping into the lift. Then she frowns. "Are you okay?"

Theo scowls at the tears running down my cheeks then his face softens. "Her grandma died." After tucking the knife into the back of his trousers, he cradles my face and wipes away my tears with his thumbs.

"Fu—" He cuts off my "fuck you" by kissing me. I can sense the woman's discomfort with our display of affection that is not at all fitting for grieving the death of a loved one. I try to push him away, but he grabs my wrists and backs me against the wall, shoving his tongue further down my throat.

The lift stops on the third floor.

"Uh ... sorry about your grandma." She hurries off and the doors close.

He pulls away, both of us breathless.

Smack!

My hand connects with his face. He narrows his eyes and reaches for the knife but pulls his hand back without it as the doors open to the fourth floor. I tumble into the lifeless hallway with his hand clutched to the back of my neck—hard—guiding me toward his flat as my feet stumble to keep up. After unlocking the door, he shoves me inside, sending me stumbling to the ground. The door slams shut, and he locks it as I scramble to my feet.

This man has *crushed* my heart. I'm not even sure it's still beating. Reaching around, I press my fingers to the area on my back where he held the knife to me. It stings. Holding my hand out, I focus on the blood. It's not a deep cut, but it's still bleeding.

My gaze lifts to his, but he's staring at the blood on my fingers.

I wait.

I watch.

Show me the slightest twitch of regret, Theo.

"You cut me."

Cold, hard eyes snap to mine. "You followed me. You broke into my apartment and stole my things."

"I'm your song." I tip my chin up and bite back my emotion.

He shakes his head. "You're nothing."

I look down, hiding from the hate in his eyes while focusing on the blood as I rub my fingers together. "You're worse than the cancer." I don't care about the cut, even if I were bleeding to death. *We* are dying and that is … indescribable.

When I look up again, the muscles in his jaw flex as he returns his gaze to the blood on my fingers.

"I hope your dirty knife gives me some flesh-eating infection so you can watch me slowly die. My rotten, putrid stench filling the air around you. When that happens, just remember … her name is Karma and she's one unforgiving bitch." If we're dying, it's going to be with guns blazing. I will not censor a single emotion.

He looks at me, not a crack to the iciness in his stare. "Sit." He nods to the folding chair.

"Go to Hell."

He barrels toward me. Six months ago I would have retreated until my bum landed in the chair. Not now. I refuse to fear this man anymore, even if he takes my last heartbeat.

"Sit. Down." His black boots hit the toes of my neon yellow trainers.

"Go. To. Hell." I squint at him.

Grabbing my shoulders, he shoves me back until my arse does in fact hit the chair. The back of it scrapes against my wound. I try not to grimace, but I can't completely avoid it.

"You shouldn't have come." He grabs several rags from the kitchen and rips them into strips.

I bite back my words. He's not worth them.

He ties my arms behind my back, and then he binds my legs to the chair before disappearing to the bathroom. A few seconds later, he returns with a bottle of hydrogen peroxide, some tape, and gauze.

"Leave it," I say with absolutely no emotion to my voice.

Theo squats down behind me and eases the back of my shirt up.

"I said LEAVE IT!" I heave my body to the side, sending the chair and the mad woman attached to it crashing to the ground.

"Jesus!" He grabs the chair to put us both upright.

"DON'T TOUCH ME!" I scream as loud as I can.

He jumps to his feet, nostrils flaring, hands fisted, and teeth bared. I don't blink. I'm the fucking queen of stare offs. Bring it on, arsebadger.

Theo stomps off.

Door slam.

Bang!

Something hits the wall in his bedroom.

Bang! Bang! Bang!

I close my eyes and let my cheek rest against the dirty gray carpet.

Twenty minutes—hell, it could be an hour later, I've lost sense of time—Theo comes out of his bedroom. I turn my head enough to see him filling a glass with water. His other hand has a T-shirt wrapped around it. The fabric around his knuckles is tinged with blood.

How did this happen? In a matter of days, I've gone from wanting *everything* with this man to wanting nothing—not even my next breath. It's as if I was on life support and he pulled the plug. Again, I close my eyes and wait to escape this moment—sleep, unconsciousness, death—it no longer matters. I'm ready to tap out.

My name is Scarlet Stone, and I'm not afraid of death. My mum waits for me with open arms.

THAT VOICE. IT comforts me. In my dreams it wraps around me like a warm cocoon. Guarding me. Saving me. Loving me.

"You need to eat and drink."

I blink open my eyes. It's dark except for the small lamp on the floor in the corner of the room, glowing yellow. It's night or early morning. I don't know. My chair and I have magically found an upright position again. My shoulders burn but my hands and feet tingle with numbness.

That voice. It's the one from my dreams. But it's no longer warm. It's dull and lifeless like the eyes staring back at me. It's no longer guarding me. Saving me. Loving me.

Why can't this be a nightmare?

Why can't I wake up?

"Eat." Theo holds spaghetti twirled around a fork in front of my face.

I turn my head to the side.

"You're going to eat."

He's so very wrong.

"Drink." He jabs a straw at my lips.

I bite them together.

"So goddamn stubborn," he mutters as he stands.

I grunt when he clutches my chin, tipping my head back enough to part my lips. Some sort of sugary juice runs into my mouth and down the sides of my face as I reject his attempts. As soon as he releases my chin, I spit it in his face.

Theo's expression hardens even more as he lifts his shirt to wipe his face.

"I will not eat. I will not drink. I will not live for you."

I hate him. He made me love him. He made me want to live. And then he took it all away.

The muscles in his arms shift as he clenches his fists over and over.

"Hit me. Beat me. Cut me. Rip my fucking world apart if that's what you need. You want the guns? They're in my car. Go get them. Load the clips. Shove the barrel down my throat and pull the trigger. But I will not let you bandage my wounds, give me food, or make me drink anything. I. Will. Not. Live. For. You."

He launches the glass of water at the sink and it shatters. I don't flinch. I'll be his song. I'll be the song that people play when they're ready to end their life. Theo can plant his fist into the wall until his hand falls off. He can break every glass in the cupboard. He can self-destruct before my eyes, but I will not live for him.

My eyes close and minutes later I hear the shower. I fade back into the world where this is all a terrible illusion. When I wake again, the glass is cleaned up and the door to Theo's room is closed. The light in the corner still flickers its yellow glow but behind me the sun peeks in through the blinds, giving more light to everything—except my life.

Navigating this world is beyond grueling sometimes. I keep waiting for my mind to wonder if Oscar will find me, if he will save me, but it won't go there because I don't want to be saved. Fighting the cancer. Fighting my emotions for Theo. It's too much. I'm so tired. I want everything to be over.

A creak in the hinge of the bedroom door announces my captor's approach. Where is my fear? It's died already.

The door to the bathroom closes. The toilet flushes. The door opens.

My gaze stays glued to the floor.

"You need a bathroom break."

Looking at him feels like too much effort, but I inch my eyes up to meet his anyway. "I needed one hours ago. So, I wet myself." My eyes drop back to the floor.

CHAPTER THIRTY-FOUR

My name is Scarlet Stone, and on the day Oscar was arrested, he told me to remember that letting go takes far more strength than holding on.

H OW DOES THIS happen? How does the man I fell so hard for just—disappear? This revenge of his has washed away the memories of us—the love.

I can no more stop loving him than he can stop hating Braxton Ames. Both of our uncontrolled emotions will likely escort us to our graves.

"Come on, motherfucker," he mutters as he looks through the rifle scope, his finger steady on the trigger.

Someone has been in the boot of my car.

He hasn't given me a second of his attention all day. I smell like piss, that's probably why. It's soaked my leggings right down to my ankles. I can't even stand the smell of myself. There's been two times in my life that I've honestly wanted to die. Both of them have been in the presence of Theodore Reed. Only this time, I can't pull the trigger.

Why does life without him seem so unlivable? Oh, the questions. I want to know if he ever really loved me. I want to know if taking another man's life will give him any sort of peace. I want to know if taking my life will leave him with regret.

I want. I want. I want.

However, my words have been silenced by the grief over losing him and the clock, once again, counting down— numbering my breaths left on this earth.

My throat itches. I try to stifle my cough. He glances over

his shoulder, his hands still poised on the rifle. I've seen that look many times. It was his favorite look for months when I moved in with him—the you-are-not-worthy-of-oxygen look. So here we are. We've come full circle. Nothing is forever, especially not love. It is for now. Some people get more nows than other people.

"Communal underwear." I laugh. I've heard the appetizer to death is a nice serving of delusion. I'm there. "You'd better kill yourself after you kill Ames and me. No one wants to wear communal underwear."

He adjusts his grip on the rifle and presses his eye to the scope. "Shut up."

"Ma'am. Shut up, Ma'am. You've always had rubbish manners. Not Daniel. He was a gentleman. The sex was a bit vanilla, but he loved me. He was such a catch." I laugh and cough, then laugh again. "Oh, Karma … she doesn't miss a thing. I've done a lot of things in my life that I should not have done. I've shown disregard for the law, and even life. How did she know? How did she know I'd follow you into the arms of Hell?"

A fit of coughs takes over; each time it constricts, it feels like sandpaper lodged in my throat.

"Jesus fucking Christ!" He stomps over to the sink and fills a glass with water. "Drink." He tips my chin up. Some of it makes it into my mouth, despite my efforts to pinch my lips together.

I choke on the water. He keeps pouring, most of it running down my face. When he stops. I spit what's in my mouth onto his shirt.

He's angry. I should care. But I don't. Why? Oh, that's right: heart ground into the soles of his boots. After putting the glass on the worktop, he shrugs off his shirt and throws it onto the floor.

"Will you tattoo my name on your other arm under a gravestone?"

He glares at me for a few seconds before returning to the rifle.

"Ask them to use san serif script. I'm quite fond of it."

"Shut up."

"Maybe they could draw—"

"Shut. Up!"

After only two seconds of silence, I continue. "My ruby pendant necklace draped over the gravestone and—"

"Shut the fuck UP!" He whips around and has me in a headlock with the blade of his knife pressed to my throat.

"Do. It," I whisper. "But … don't be a fucking coward." Each breath gasps for life as I try to speak past the lump in my throat. "My heart. Stab me in the heart like you promised."

My lungs get yet another unexpected breath of air as the knife vanishes and Theodore Reed turns into a tornado of anger—stabbing the knife into the cupboard door, ripping the one next to it off its hinges, breaking the glass on the worktop, while growling profanities.

I flinch with each outburst. He grabs the knife from the cupboard and rushes toward me, gripping the knife in one hand and my neck in his other, our faces mere inches apart. "If you speak again. I will put this in your heart."

He won't. Theodore Reed doesn't hate me—he hates that he loves me. He hates that I came into his life when I did. Loving me is killing him. We are two wounded creatures suffering from unspeakable pain that has marred the decent people we once were. But right now, my existence is too agonizing for both of us, and I no longer want to be here.

"Do. It." I narrow my eyes.

I swear he winces like I stabbed him. "Fuck!" he roars, bringing the knife above his head as his grip on my neck tightens to the point that I can't breathe.

I close my eyes. It's time … I'm ready. *Do it, Theo. I'll still love you.*

The chair jerks, almost tipping over. All I hear is his panting. His hold on my neck loosens. I peek open one eye. The knife is lodged in the seat of the chair between my legs.

I guess he is a true sadist. Killing me would be less torturous. He squints down at the floor. I've wet myself again. My body begins to shake with uncontrollable sobs.

"Just kill me, *p-p-please*." I don't recognize my own voice. It's like part of me is already gone.

THEO GRUNTS, BUT he won't have to worry about it happening much longer if I'm not eating or drinking. He unties me and lifts me from the chair by my arms. My dignity disintegrates as he peels my soiled leggings and knickers off me, followed by my shirt and bra; my arms fall limp to my sides. If I could muster a single emotion it would be humiliation, but I can't even feel that. He shoves my dirty clothes in a bin bag. Then he carries me into the bathroom and puts me in the bath.

I jump when the cold water from the showerhead hits me. He stuffed my peace lily upside down in the bathroom bin by the sink. Poor Phoebe.

"Wash up." He closes the curtain and leaves the bathroom.

I remain unmoving except for the uncontrolled shivering from the icy water. Fuck you, cancer. I came here to die. You indiscriminately pluck souls from this world all of the time. I didn't fight you. I surrendered. What more do you want?

Losing the will to live cannot be understood until—it happens. It's not that the pain is too much; it's the ability to feel *anything* has been suffocated by the pain. It's literally *mind-numbing*. Complete detachment from life and reality.

My name is Scarlet Stone, and on the day Oscar was arrested, he told me to remember that letting go takes far more strength than holding on.

Later—when? I don't know, just *later*—Theo comes back into the bathroom and opens the curtain. I hug my knees, feeling more numb than ever before. My lips have to be blue.

"For fuck's sake ..." He adjusts the water and squirts shampoo in my hair and all over my body. Then he scrubs me down as the warm water begins to erase the chills.

I'm wrapped in a towel and carried to his bedroom where he lays me on the mattress and dresses me in a long-sleeved T-shirt and boxer shorts that he has to roll over at the waist several times and even then they slide from my hips.

The man with remnants of my heart embedded in the bottom of his black boots on the floor a few feet away squats in front of me as I hug my knees, resting my chin on one of them. I stare at the frayed hems of his jeans brushing along the top of his bare feet. Theo has pretty feet. Does he know that? I bet it's from walking in the sand and swimming in the ocean everyday. I would tell him that, but I'm done talking. I'm done caring. I'm done worrying. I'm just ... done.

CHAPTER THIRTY-FIVE

THEODORE

MY MOTHER WAS shot in the head at close range. We didn't have an open-casket funeral for her. My father took his own life two weeks later. We didn't have an open-casket funeral for him either. Braxton Ames confessed to murdering my mom, but when he decided he couldn't handle prison anymore, he fabricated some story about being coerced into confessing to a crime he didn't commit. He knew the evidence against him was weak to begin with so I had no doubt that when the judge granted a retrial, he would go free.

It's not right. It's not fair. A man cannot take away my whole life and then walk. I cannot live knowing that he is enjoying freedom while my parents reside six feet under. Everyone has a calling in life. This is mine. Seeking revenge—justice—for the death of my parents is my calling.

But ...

The woman before me could quite possibly kill me before I get the chance to avenge my parents' deaths. Loving her hurts ... Some days I swear it hurts worse than the loss of my parents. Today is one of those days. I've said the unimaginable and done the unforgivable. And now I'm the one with the knife lodged into my heart. With every look she twists it a little deeper.

Every time she refuses to eat.

Every time she refuses to drink.

Every time she refuses my touch.

Every word. God ... the words. She's obliterated me with words.

It's not just the words; it's how she says them. Her voice, the vacant look in her eyes. It's that she means them. I can't find an ounce of life in her expression.

"Drink." I lift her head and tip the glass of water to her mouth. She doesn't even blink. She also doesn't fight me. I keep tipping the glass until she drinks the last drop of water.

Show me some fucking life.

She hasn't been here that long. The woman before me is not suffering from starvation or dehydration. She just fell in love with the wrong guy. It's true—I am worse than the cancer.

"I'm leaving. You're not tied up. Your purse is over there on the floor. Your car keys are in it. The guns are not in your trunk anymore."

Please leave.

Save yourself.

Hate me. I need you to hate me so that you can let me go.

Then go ...

CHAPTER THIRTY-SIX

My name is Scarlet Stone and kids make fun of my name. I don't understand what's wrong with my name.

SCARLET

THEO LEAVES. I collapse onto the mattress and close my eyes. When all the life inside is gone, there is nowhere to go except in dreams. What happens when dreams die? What happens when the mind can't find any more stories? What happens when thoughts die before they ever truly form?

Time passes. Minutes? Hours? My mind can't make sense of it. I stopped counting: minutes, seconds, *breaths*.

"Goddammit! Why are you still here?" Theo is so mad at me. Why is he mad at me? I love him. I'm his song.

"If I find you passed out, when I find you passed out, I'm not calling for an ambulance. If you want to kill yourself, a gun would be a helluva lot easier."

"You have to leave! Open your eyes." Pain. There's so much pain to that voice. I can hear it, but I can't feel it. I can't feel anything. I like not feeling anything.

Fuck you, cancer.
I pull the trigger.
Nothing.

"I take your life. You don't get the fucking choice. Do you understand?"

Calloused hands grip my face. I fight the heavy weight, the bright light, and blink open my eyes.

"You," I whisper. "You take it."

Theo's forehead wrinkles, eyes squinted. "Take what?"

"My life."

His jaw clenches and I see something I never thought I'd see—tears. They fill his eyes like he's choking on his next breath. "Jesus ..." He presses his forehead to mine, squeezing his eyes shut, and his tears fall onto my face and become mine. Silent sobs wrack his body. "I can't take your life ..." The words rip from his throat. "So, fuck you..." more tears "...because you've already taken mine." He grips my face harder. "You've ruined the man I need to be..." more sobs "...You've turned me into a fucking failure because all I want to do is this."

Theo kisses me, slow at first, then more urgent. I don't kiss him back. I can't. Everything is still too numb—my lips, my hands, my *heart*.

His mouth moves to my cheek, my jaw, my neck.

Nothing.

He releases another sob. My heart tries to feel it, but it can't. It's too late.

"Don't ... don't do this." His mouth covers mine again.

Nothing.

I should cry. I've waited so long for him to give me this. I blink.

Nothing.

Pushing away, he kneels by the mattress, sitting back on his heels. He rips off his gray beanie, exposing his closely buzzed hair. His hands cover his face, shoulders curled inward, body shaking. "No ... no ... no... *Scarlet* ..." He whispers my name like he's using his last breath to say it.

I gasp as if his last breath is my first. One blink and tears run down my face. My heart drums with so much pain … pain that I *feel*.

Theodore Reed has *never* said my name. Not. One. Single. Time.

Until now.

Inch by slow inch, I bring myself to sitting on the edge of the mattress in front of him. My hands wrap around his wrists. He sucks in a shaky breath and holds it as I pull his hands away from his face. When he releases his breath it's *everything*.

"Scarlet," he whispers again.

Chills. I never thought it was possible for someone to whisper life back into another person. I was wrong.

He swallows hard. Eyes red. Cheeks stained with emotion. "*Live* for me."

Love?

Hate?

It's love. Love wins.

Biting my quivering lips together, I nod once.

Theo cradles my face. I cradle his.

He kisses me. I kiss him.

He tears at my clothes. I tear at his.

He moves down my body, bringing it back to life one kiss—one bite at a time. My back arches as my hands move to his head. I curl them into fists, finding nothing to hold. I miss his hair.

Sucking in a sharp breath, my fingers clutch the sheets next to me instead. His tongue drags between my legs so…

Very. Slowly.

I feel my pulse right where his tongue stops.

Feeling.

I feel again. His name lingers on my lips, but I don't have the breath to bring it into existence. There's too much emotion in my chest. Breathing is its own feat.

He nips and sucks at my flesh all the way up to my lips again, thrusting his tongue into my mouth, claiming all of me.

The swollen head of his cock teases between my legs. What if it's a dream? What if I'm dead?

I have to know if this is real. "Hard…" I breathe as he sucks the sensitive skin along my neck "…unforgiving…" I pant "…or not at all."

His forehead drops to the mattress above my shoulder as his hands hook behind my knees. Pulling my pelvis off the mattress, he drives into me. *Hard.*

I cry out, pinching my eyes shut.

"It's the only way I know how," he whispers in my ear between labored breaths.

MY LIPS PRESS to his chest, relishing the warmth of his flesh against mine, our limbs tangled, the sheets twisted in chaos. The physical questions have all been answered with sex. *But …* to exist in this world together, we have to acknowledge emotion and reason.

I wanted to die, and for a moment in time, I honestly thought he wanted me dead too. Some things—certain emotions—cut so deep they become physical wounds to the soul. They bleed into the next life. Words can't heal. Time can't erase. At best, love can make them bearable.

We took each other to the breaking point, and I don't know about him, but I think I actually broke. I resented every breath my lungs took, every blink, every heartbeat. I found peace in not wanting to exist. The darkness no longer felt cold. The pain evaporated.

"I need you," I whisper.

Theo kisses the top of my head.

"I need you to help me *not* need you."

He pulls back to look at my face, his head resting on his folded arm, confusion a roadmap on his forehead.

My fingers pinch my bottom lip, tugging at it gently. I feel as much confusion etched in my own face. This is so hard to articulate. "I want to beat this cancer for you ... but I *need* to beat it for me. I'm living for you at the moment because I ..." Tears sting my eyes. Rolling my lips together, I blink them away. "I've lost the will to live it for myself."

This is the lowest of all lows. Admitting I don't want to live. I've never felt so weak, so pathetic, so *nothing*.

The pad of his thumb catches my tear before it gets away.

"I need you to teach me to walk again. Show me how to live *with* you, not *for* you." I shake my head, swallowing past the remnants of my pride. "I thought I had it. On Tybee, I felt peace, strength, grounded, unafraid. The cancer started to shrink. I was happy. I was different, and I loved the new me. I loved *life*."

His thumb brushes my cheek again like its sole purpose in life is to catch every piece of me to do what he does best: put things together—put *me* back together.

"But then you left, and I started to fall apart. That's when I realized everything I did on Tybee was tethered to you and the farther you were from me, the more I unraveled. I was the bird who built my nest in a beautiful oak tree. I was so proud of my nest, my home. Then a storm came along and knocked down the oak tree."

"I'm your tree," Theo whispers.

I nod.

His thumb moves to my lips. There's so many unspoken emotions in his expression.

"Scarlet …"

My name. Will the day ever come that my name passing his lips doesn't bring tears to my eyes?

My name is Scarlet Stone and kids make fun of my name. I don't understand what's wrong with my name.

I didn't recognize the man who threatened to kill me, and I don't recognize the man before me with so much regret in his eyes. The muscle in his jaw ticks and his nostrils flare on a long exhale like his silence is the only thing holding him together.

There is nothing I can do to take away the things he did to me. Nor is there anything I can say to make it okay.

"There are no words for what I've done to us—to you." Sorrow deepens in his eyes. "You will be my greatest masterpiece. I will build you with the strongest materials. Nothing will be rushed. Even if it takes a lifetime … every little detail will be *perfect.*"

No human has ever said "I love you" as poetically as Theodore Reed just did.

He ducks down and brushes his lips over mine. "Scarlet," he whispers with choked words. "I am so … incredibly…" his voice cracks "…incomparably … infinitely sorry."

My lips part when his tongue brushes along the seam.

"I will spend a thousand lifetimes making it up to you."

<p style="text-align:center">~~~</p>

AFTER I DRIFT off to sleep, Theo retrieves my stuff from the hotel and brings it back to his flat. In the morning, we lie silent in the emotional rubble. I slip out of bed; we share sad smiles. What's left to say? I grab some clothes.

"Scarlet?"

I stop before rounding the corner to the bathroom. Without turning back toward him, I just listen.

Nothing.

He may live. I may live. We may overcome this. But ... part of us died. Every day will be a test to see if *we* hit our tipping point. Did the cancer of revenge and lies take too much? I hope not. Theo doesn't have to say any more. I feel the same fear that's in his voice.

"I forgive you," I whisper. It's impossible to forget. This is all I can give him. It may feel like nothing, but it's all I have. It's *something*.

When I get out of the shower, he's in his room loading all the weapons back in the trunk. I pause a second to admire his body, no shirt, beautiful ink, dark jeans, and the minimal hair on his head and face. I do miss his hair.

"Now what?" I ask, draping my bath towel around my neck.

He locks the trunk and turns, taking a seat on top of it, hands folded between his legs. "Food. I show you where I grew up. Maybe we happen upon a horse or two and I teach you how to ride."

Can we step over the remnants of destruction and move forward? I smile because Theo is trying to lay the foundation for the life I never even imagined. I think it could be a good one.

My smile falters. "And Braxton Ames?"

He blows out a long breath. "I have no direction right now.

I've spent years feeding on rage, existing in an aftermath of regret, living for revenge. If I let Ames walk … then what?"

I shrug as I straddle his legs and drape my arms behind his neck. "Then us."

His brow wrinkles with what I know is pain. Asking him to choose us probably feels like he's letting his parents down. I don't want him to let them down. I want him to let them *go*. This is not a life, and Theo is too young, too talented, too *loved* to not have a life that's worthy of rock-star status.

With a slow nod, he whispers, "Then us," like he's searching for the true meaning of those two words.

There may never come a day that he can completely let go. I think revenge is a very animalistic part of human behavior that is ingrained in all of us from birth. Even on a very basic level of a mother's instinct to protect her child, humans have that capability. And like certain animals, we can tame it, control it, but it never completely goes away.

CHAPTER THIRTY-SEVEN

THEODORE

THE SMILE ON my face screams pathetic schmuck. For a brief moment in time, I forget that inside I'm still at war. Is it—*can* it be—possible that I got it wrong? Is my purpose the woman before me? Because I seriously cannot stop grinning. The Scarlet Stone on Tybee was a glimpse of the woman who insisted she have her own horse to ride—the woman who rode it with such command it made my dick hard, the woman now hugging the gentle giant, giving me the can-we-keep-him look.

"Say goodbye."

"I want to steal him." She gives me a Cheshire cat grin.

If anyone else said that, I would laugh. Something tells me, if given the chance, she could steal that thoroughbred. I don't give her the chance.

"I have something else you can ride."

Two perfect eyebrows perk. "I'm listening."

"Maybe we leave the horse and steal a riding crop."

She kisses the horse and struts toward me with purpose. "Leather riding boots would be fun too."

My fucking zipper is about to bust. "They would."

"Meet me in the truck, Mr. Reed."

She brushes past me.

"Where are you going?"

"To steal a riding crop."

Hooking my finger through the belt loop of her jeans, I tug her toward me then flip her little body over my shoulder.

"Hey!"

"Shh. You're going to scare the horses." I smack her ass.

She fights for all of two seconds before her body goes limp. I love her surrender.

I cut her back.

I held a knife to her throat.

I threatened to kill her.

Yet … she gives me everything. Why, Scarlet? I will never fully understand how you do it.

Her hands tug at the back of my shirt, inching it up until I feel the warmth of her lips on my skin. Ambling to the truck with the best part of this world hanging over my shoulder, I close my eyes for a few breaths. Can a hundred and fifteen pounds of sexy, sass, and stubbornness save me? I swear to God … I think it's possible, and I have no idea what to do with that possibility.

I unlock the truck and ease her from my shoulder, setting her in the seat. She grabs my shirt and pulls me to her lips. There's no one more undeserving of this moment than I am. Scarlet likes the idea of Karma. Not me. Karma would never give this woman to me. It will be fine with me if Karma dies in a cosmic accident before my name comes up on her Scores to Settle List.

Pulling back, I try to hide the fucking fear that's eating me up inside. The moment I surrendered to her was a drop-all-weapons-raise-the-white-flag moment that's left me scared shitless—completely vulnerable. "I'm—" I can't even speak past the fear. It's a living thing pulsing in my throat.

Her hands press to my cheeks. "You're forgiven."

I don't deserve her.

"But not forgotten," I whisper. She'll never forget what I did. It's not humanly possible. Sometimes I want the impossible.

Her expression doesn't change. "My head is undiscriminating with the memories it keeps, but my heart has already forgotten."

I don't want to move. Hell, I don't want to blink. I think if I could stay lost in her long enough, I could let go of everything and my past would truly not matter.

"Let's go." I bite her bottom lip, tugging at it until she laughs.

"Where are we going?"

"You'll see." I grin and shut her door.

SCARLET

"WHERE ARE WE?" I look around at the tall, tangled trees and overgrowth of weeds hiding the gray-sided two-story house.

"This is where I grew up." He turns off the truck and stares out the window as if he's waiting for something. Courage?

"Who lives here now?"

"No one."

"Who owns it?"

"I do." He frowns, eyes still trained straight ahead.

"Are you trying to sell it?"

Theo shakes his head and then gets out. I follow him as he plods through the tall grass that's overtaken the brick walk to the front porch.

"Siblings?"

He shakes his head.

"How old were you when you moved here?"

"I lived here my whole life until I moved into an apartment my first year of college." Resting his boot on the first porch step, he shifts his weight forward like he's testing it. The white paint has weathered leaving rotting planks with cracks and holes. It creeks when he steps up.

"When was the last time you were here?"

Gripping the column at the top of the porch, Theo releases a sigh. "The day I found my father's body." He lowers his head while his knuckles turn white with his tightening grip on the column. "His face was unrecognizable," he whispers.

The bottom step creaks again as I step onto it.

Theo turns and holds out his hand. "Here. Careful. The place was in need of renovation before they died. The years since haven't done it any favors."

We test each of our steps until we reach the door. Theo fishes his keys from his pocket and unlocks the front door. It, too, whines as he eases it open.

"Oh, wow." The inside of the house doesn't match the outside at all. The dark wood floors have a layer of dust blanketing them, but it's easy to see that beneath the dust, they are flawless. The elaborate trim work of the stairway bannister, crown molding, and built-in bookshelves in the study to our left all scream Theodore Reed.

"My father and I were in the process of remodeling the whole house when ..."

I nod. "Is that how you learned to do this? Your father?"

"Yeah." He takes my hand and leads me up the solid stairs, not one single creak. Theo wraps his hand around the doorknob on the right but his gaze drifts to the closed door at the end of the ginger-painted hallway adorned with black frames—the Reed family story in pictures.

I imagine that story ended in tragedy in that room at the end of the hall.

"Is this your room?"

His head jerks back to the door before us, back to the present. "Yes." He opens it.

With one step, my mind is blown by what I see. This isn't a lie. This is real. This is *Theodore Reed.*

"My mom decorated it after I moved out." He laughs through the palpable pain in his voice. "I'm not this vain."

Who is the boy in all of these pictures? Shaggy, blond hair and a smile that could light an entire universe.

Theo as a baby in the arms of his beautiful mum. She was truly stunning.

Theo holding his first hammer as a toddler, standing next to his father, both wearing overalls and tool belts.

Theo riding horses.

Theo playing American football in school.

Theo in a deep red suit with a black tie, standing next to a girl with long blond hair, dressed in a strapless black dress. Maybe a school dance. I smile.

"Your band," I whisper as my fingers wipe away the dust from the black and white photo of The Derby performing on stage. Just like the video Nolan showed me, Theo is zoned into his guitar.

He wasn't always *the law.* Theo lived a normal childhood. He had girlfriends, loving parents, and a beautiful life. It's so perfectly ... heartbreaking.

I turn and study the vulnerable version of *my* Theodore Reed perched at the end of his bed, hands fisted on his jean-clad legs.

"You had a normal life." I exhale a whisper of a laugh. "I think. Actually, I'm not sure I know what that means. I never had normal. Nothing about me has ever been relatable. Oscar told me to just be me. I'll be thirty-two next month, and I still haven't got a clue who I am." I roll my lips between my teeth, easing my way to Theo. His mouth stays firm; his eyes sparkle with something hopeful.

He grabs my hips and straddles me over his lap. I lace my fingers together behind his neck.

"Maybe you could just be mine—the naked body I worship, the mouth that sucks my—"

"Stop!" I pinch his lips together like a duck's. His grin makes my grip on them slip.

"No gag reflex." He shakes his head.

I shove him back on the bed. His body vibrates with laughter. I'll let him make crude comments all day if it means I'm rewarded with smiles and his endearing chuckles—so uncontrolled and innocent.

My face hurts. I think my grin could crack it.

Theo squeezes my legs with a firm grip. "Scarlet Stone?"

There it is again.

His voice.

My name.

It forms a lump in my throat and makes my eyes burn with tears.

"Hmm?"

"I don't deserve you."

My grin chases the tears away. "You really don't."

"Can we keep that little secret just between the two of us?"

Twisting my lips, I cock my head to the side. "Yes. But I'll need it in writing."

"In writing?"

I nod. He interlaces his fingers behind his head. It makes his white T-shirt pull up just enough to expose a few centimeters of his abs.

"Like a contract?"

I shake my head. "Something more *permanent*."

His right eyebrow peaks. "Such as?"

I trace my finger along the wide waistband of his black briefs, to the left of his happy trail. His erection grows firm, inching closer to my finger. My lips curl into a smirk that matches his. His muscles tense, tipping his pelvis up a bit as if he thinks I don't already see how turned on he is right now.

"Right here." My finger dips under the waistband.

He groans as I tease his skin so close to where he's most begging for my touch.

"This is where I want you to put in *permanent* writing that you don't deserve me."

Theo's eyes narrow. "You want me to get a tattoo?"

I nod.

"About you?"

I nod.

"Right there?"

"Yes. Right here. My name in red, everything else in black."

Stealing my breath, he sits up, stopping when the tip of his nose touches mine. "We'll see," he whispers.

"Will we?" I breathe back, a little more breathless than intended. I'm rubbish at hiding how much he affects me.

"Yes. Now … what else do you want from me?"

Forever. I want all the days. All the smiles. All the breaths.

"I want to hear you play."

His gaze goes through me. A contemplative side I've seen a million times.

"There's one of my first guitars ... in the attic. I think."

My eyes roll to the ceiling. "How do we get up there?"

CHAPTER THIRTY-EIGHT
THEODORE

THE PULL-DOWN ATTIC ladder is right outside of my parents' bedroom. I haven't opened their door since my dad was taken out in a black bag. The room was cleaned. I know behind the door there no longer exists a drop of blood, yet I can't open the door. Not today.

I pull on the chain and bring the ladder down. Scarlet focuses on the closed bedroom door. She's smart. I don't have to tell her why it's shut and why I have no intention of opening it.

"Don't stare at my ass. It makes me feel violated," I say as I climb the ladder first to turn on the light and access the attic that's been undisturbed for years.

She laughs. "But it's such a lovely arse."

"Arse? Really? How long before you stop fucking up the English language?" As I stretch up to reach for the string to the single light bulb, a sharp pain radiates from my junk to my stomach. "Mother fucking hell!" I bend at the waist, pressing my hands to the unfinished wood floor to keep myself from falling down the ladder and landing on her. But holy fuck, my knees feel weak.

Scarlet has part of my junk clawed in her hand, squeezing it like she's trying to extract my dick and at least one testicle from my body. I've underestimated her size and her *grip*.

"Sorry? Could you repeat that?"

Once I can find a full breath, I reach down and grab her wrist, prying her hand off me. "Only one person on the ladder." I pull her lithe body up next to mine and set her *ass* on the floor of the attic, her legs dangling down the hole.

"There's nothing wrong with the way I speak the English language." She crosses her arms over her chest.

It squeezes her breasts together, pushing her cleavage up a bit. I don't mind at all.

Her finger lifts my chin up an inch. "My eyes are up here."

I shrug. "For now."

"For now?" What's that supposed to mean?"

I lean in until she holds her breath. This is my favorite part. The high I get from stealing her complete attention should be illegal. "It means later your eyes will be looking up at me while I fuck your mouth."

She gasps. I like her gasp. It relaxes her jaw even more, making my dick hard and ready to slip inside that sexy mouth of hers.

"Crude. *Beyond* crude." Her eyes narrow. "Touring with your band … 'getting laid …' Did brash comments like that really work for you?"

I lean in closer. Her breath hitches again. Full lips part. That cherry tongue of hers makes a lazy swipe along her bottom lip. Why do I do this to myself? I'm fucking hard right now.

"OW!"

I grin with my teeth still clamped around her nipple, my tongue leaving a wet mark on her shirt. "Yes, it does work for me," I whisper after releasing her nipple.

"Not for me."

"Liar." I climb the rest of the way up then grab her waist to pull her to her feet.

She winces, a quick breath seething through her teeth.

"What's—" It hits me like a ton of bricks dropped on my chest. I release my grip on her waist and slide up the back of her shirt, revealing the cut on her back where *I* cut her.

"It's fine."

It's not fucking fine. I cut her. It wasn't an accident. Nothing about that is fine. Even as she says the words, the look on her face contradicts them.

It's not fine.

"Why?" she whispers. Her gaze lowers to her feet as she drops her chin.

I knew it was coming. Scarlet Stone is a lot of things, but she's not stupid. It wasn't domestic abuse. I didn't hit her in a fit of rage then fall to my knees and beg for forgiveness. The sex. The apologies. Even her willingness to forgive me can't replace what she deserves most—an explanation.

"I hated life—my life."

She looks up, disbelief morphing her face in tight lines and a painful frown.

"I wanted you to hate me. I *thought* I wanted you to hate me." I shake my head and turn toward the wall hidden behind piles of boxes covered in dust and cobwebs. "Ames stood at his window, probably a dozen or more times. The shot was there. All I could see through the scope was you. I'd close my eyes, trying to erase you from my mind, that's when I'd hear the click." I brush my hand along one of the boxes, dispersing the dust into a thin cloud.

"What click?" The defeat in her voice resurrects the pain I've tried to suppress for the past twenty-four hours.

"You." Something between a grunt and a laugh rips from

my chest. "You pulled the fucking trigger. *Click.*" I close my eyes. *Click.* I can hear it as clear as I did the moment she did it. Scarlet lived. I died that day. "I didn't know about the cancer. You..." my eyes pinch shut "...you made me pause. It was a long blink, a deep breath, a spark of doubt. Our *nothing* was that pause, a glimpse of an alternate future, a breath of hesitation."

"I made you question your purpose," she whispers.

"Yes." Opening my eyes, I swallow past the constricting pain in my throat. "You were this light. Warm. Blinding. Breathtaking. For an incredibly short moment, I thought you could..." I clear my throat "...save me."

Her body presses to my back, hands sliding up my chest. I hug her hands to me. There's that warmth. She's alive. I don't ever want to let her go.

"But I pulled the trigger."

Click.

I nod. "My father said when he found my mom there was so much blood. Her head was just—" Fuck, this is still so raw. "I imagine it was very much like how I found my father after he—"

"I'm sorry."

I shake my head. "I never really understood why my dad did it. He had me. He had *something*. You shattered my whole fucking world when you pulled the trigger."

"Theo ..." She hugs me tighter, her body shaking in silent sobs.

"I knew what made a person want to kill another. I lived and breathed that hatred every day. But I never could understand the amount of self-loathing that brought someone to take their own life. Until ..."

Scarlet releases a strangled sob. I squeeze her hands and press them firm to my chest.

"Until Daniel told me you were dying."

SCARLET

LOVE IS A brutal emotion. That's how I'm certain, beyond a shadow of doubt, it's our sole purpose in life. Love is the heartbeat of our existence—the essence of humanity. In every life we try to do it better.

Harder.

Longer.

More completely.

Unconditionally.

Love is maddening. It robs all reason and leaves us drowning in desperation and fear. Desperate to hold on to everything that makes each breath worth taking. Fearful that the very air that fills our lungs is that love. One cannot live without air. Can one live without love?

The reason there is such a fine line between love and hate is because both require a deep emotional investment. Both emotions make us *feel* very deeply.

Theo loved me.

Theo hated me.

I will accept both his love and hate, as long as he never stops *feeling* so deeply for me.

"I didn't pull the trigger because I wanted to die. I pulled it because I was no longer afraid of not living."

Releasing my hands, he turns toward me. I've never seen so many unspoken questions in his eyes.

Fear. Regret. Love. It's all there in a chaos of emotion that makes me love him that much more.

"And yesterday?" He cradles my face, erasing my tears with the pads of his thumbs. "No more lies."

I'm not sure if I'm more afraid to admit the truth to Theo … or myself. The truth is in the tears that continue to slide down my face. "Yesterday … I wanted to die."

There are two options: I can be fearless and steadfast in everything I do. I can wear the illusion of a strong, independent woman like a merit badge, priding myself on being the woman whom all women should strive to be. Or … I can love Theo. Navigating a minefield with my unprotected heart.

For thirty-one years, I was strong and independent. Oscar built me up. He gave me a suit of armor and told me to conquer the world. I did. I owned it. Now? I want my greatest strength to be letting go of control. Giving my heart to another. *That* takes courage and fearlessness.

"Truth." I fight to give him even a hint of a sad smile. I am only weak if I can't admit my imperfections.

Theo's posture is stiff, jaw clenched, eyes glassy. "Why?" He shakes his head.

"There were just…" my unfocused gaze slips to his chest "…too many emotions—all at once. Life and death. Love and loss. Anger and regret. Too much to feel. I just…" I shrug "…broke. And in a blink, all feeling disappeared. It was like finding sleep after a lifetime of insomnia." My eyes shift to his again. "The only thing I truly felt was the arms of death. Weightless. Peaceful. Silent. *Perfect.*"

He swallows over and over, maybe searching for the words to say or the strength to say them. I'm not sure they exist. Theo struggled with loving me and hating me. He wanted to take a life. I wanted to let one go. It's a million ways of fucked-up.

There's no explaining that.

"You..." he tightens his grip on my face as he presses his forehead to mine "...are *mine* now. I build you. I give you life. I make you perfect again."

"You are the law," I whisper with a smile growing along my face. It feels good. *Feeling* feels good.

He smirks. "Damn right." His lips make a firm claim to mine.

His hands slide down my neck, pausing with his thumb pressed to the side of it. My heart constricts. *He's feeling my pulse.* I'm counting breaths ... Theo's counting heartbeats.

I moan when his tongue plunges deeper into my mouth while his hands move over my breasts, continuing on to my jeans. He fumbles, tugging hard at my button, his moves growing impatient. I push his hands away and unfasten them before he rips them apart.

He growls and squats in front of me.

"I'll get—"

He cuts me off with a firm look. Shoving my hands out of the way, he yanks down my jeans and knickers like he's bloody pissed off that I'm even wearing them. One shoe gets pulled off, then the other. I grab the edge of the box behind me to steady myself as he tugs my jeans and knickers the rest of the way off.

My ribs tell my heart to calm the fuck down. I'm in humming-bird mode as Theodore Reed stands, eyes filled with a hunger for me like a lion mere inches from its dinner.

He takes a step toward me. I take one back. Several boxes fall to the floor, sending me stumbling back another step. Theo doesn't flinch. The wall saves me from falling on my arse. As I begin to suck in a breath of relief, Theo crashes his mouth to mine, his deep groan sending chills along my skin.

He keeps me pinned to the wall with just his mouth. My hands claw the side of his head, missing his hair so damn much. The sharp hiss of his zip lets me know I'm seconds away from being fucked into the next century.

Expecting nothing less from this part-man-part-beast, the one I have literally decided to *live* for, he leaves me gasping for breath as he licks his fingers, swipes them between my legs, and then lifts me up a second before burying his hard cock in me to the hilt.

"Fuuck ... Theo!" I yell.

No. Acclimation. That's never been his style.

He bites my neck, leaving his first of what will be many marks. Then his lips curl into a grin along my skin as he drags them to my ear. "Yes ... that's *exactly* what you're going to do."

CHAPTER THIRTY-NINE

My name is Scarlet Stone, and I was not put on this earth to judge anyone.

"CAN I OPEN this box?"

Theo glances up from his spot, perched on an upside-down milk crate, tuning his guitar. We've been in the attic for almost an hour, most of it spent discussing the madness of our relationship and righting the world again with our favorite answer to all questions—sex.

"Go for it." He shrugs before returning his attention back to his guitar.

I rip off the tape and open a box marked *Photos and Letters.* My eager hands shuffle through them. The Reed family photos depict the all-American family with their Christmas pictures by the tree, holidays, birthdays, sporting events ... it all paints a perfect story. How did it end in such tragedy?

"Are these love letters that your parents wrote to each other?" I take a stack of letters held together by a thick elastic band.

"Doubtful. My mom was the letter writer, but I don't imagine she wrote anything to my father, knowing the chances of him writing something in return was nil. She loved fancy stationary and calligraphy pens. Most of the time she wrote to friends, even some that lived nearby. Just pick up the fucking phone. Right?" He shakes his head. "So those must be return letters from her friends."

The elastic band is dry and disintegrating, so I ease one letter out. Theo has no idea how giving me total access to these boxes is like Christmas for my curiosity. I unfold the letter.

My heart stops.

All air vanishes.

Dear Bell,

My hands begin to shake. I can hardly read the words. "Wh-who is Bell?" My eyes skip to the closing signature.

Sincerely,
Belle

It takes a few moments to register Theo's voice. The rush of blood in my ears drowns out all other sound.

"Nellie Moore. She and my mom were friends. Their maiden names were both Bell, but spelled differently. Everyone used to joke at how fitting the names were. My mom grew up on a farm with cow *bells*, and Nellie grew up in a rich family like *belle* of the ball." He continues to focus on his guitar strings. "They used to call each other Bell."

Every word is an echo. This isn't real. This can't be real.

Th-thump. Th-thump. Th-thump.

"Oh my god," I whisper.

"Scarlet?"

This can't be.

"Scarlet?"

No. No. No. This isn't right. It's not real.

"Scarlet!"

My head snaps up to Theo, hunched in front of me. "We have to go," I whisper, the letter falling from my hands.

"Go where?"

Blink. Blink. Blink. This isn't real.

"Savannah. We have to go back to Savannah. My dad—

Oscar—I need …" I scramble to my feet.

"What are you talking about?" Theo grabs my arms, forcing me to look at him. "He's in prison."

I shake my head. "He's in Savannah. We … we have to go."

"What … I …" He shakes his head. "What's going on?"

I wriggle in his grasp until he lets me go. Then I climb down the ladder. "We have to go. Now." Down the hall, down the stairs, out the front door, I can't get out of here fast enough.

"Scarlet!"

Theo's call to me is muted by the cracking of boards. My feeling of desperation to get back to Savannah is replaced with a shooting pain in my ankle and then my bum. Dusty shadows surround me.

"Scarlet!"

I look up to the light filtering through the jagged hole in the porch. Mucky weeds and dirt cover me. Theo grimaces then extends his arm into the hole.

I grab his hand as tears sting my eyes. The pain is excruciating.

"Can you stand up?"

I release a desperate sob and shake my head.

He lets go of my hand. With a grunt, he rips off several rotting boards with his bare hands, then he offers his hand again. I take it and he slowly pulls me up.

"Easy."

I try to stand, but I can't. "My ankle," I seethe.

"Dammit." He scoops me up.

"Ah!" The pain is blinding.

"Sorry." He presses his lips to my head, standing still for a moment until the pain becomes bearable again. Then he navigates us off the porch, testing each step. "Let's get you checked out."

"I'm f-f-fine. We n-need to get back to S-Savannah."

"Your fucking teeth are chattering like you're going into shock. You have a gouge on your leg that's bleeding and you can't walk. We're going to the emergency room. At the very least, you're going to need a tetanus shot and some stitches."

What the hell, Karma? This isn't fair.

THEODORE

FUCKING PORCH. I never should have taken her there.

"I don't want the surgery."

The doctor and nurse glance at each other.

"You'll never walk again if you don't have surgery," the doctor says.

"I have somewhere I need to go."

She can't even speak without gasping from the pain with each word.

"She's having the surgery. Please give us a few minutes."

The doctor nods, then he ushers out of the room behind the nurse.

"You don't understand," Scarlet says with so much anguish in her voice.

Taking her hand in mine, I press a kiss to the back of it. "You're right. I don't. Why don't you explain it to me? Because I can wrap my head around the cancer going away. I just don't see the two complete fractures in your ankle mending on their own if you meditate, or drink shitty smelling tea, or suck down gallons of carrot juice, or—"

"Stop! I'm not saying that. I just don't have *time* for this. I *need* to see Oscar. It's—"

"Not happening."

"Theo—"

"Fine." I step back. This is laughable, yet so damn frustrating. "I'll drive you. Your clothes are right there." I walk toward the door. "I'll meet you in the truck."

"Theo ..." This time my name is a broken sob followed by more sobs.

This woman breaks my heart. A heart that, not long ago, I didn't think still existed. "Scarlet ..." I take her face in my hands and kiss away her tears. "I'll make this right. Shh ..."

She covers my hands with hers and claws at my skin, like she's trying to crawl inside of me—desperate, broken.

"Is your dad's number in your phone?"

She sniffles then nods.

"I'll make sure he's here by the time you're out of surgery tomorrow. Okay?"

"O-O-K."

Eventually, they give her enough pain meds to help her drift off to sleep. Her phone is locked, so I press her fingers one at a time to the lock button until it finally unlocks. Oscar Stone is the only name in her contacts. It only rings once.

"Ruby, why haven't you—"

"It's not *Ruby*."

"Who is this? Where the hell is Scarlet?"

"My name is Theo. Scarlet is sleeping. She broke her ankle in two spots and they're doing surgery on it tomorrow."

"Did you hurt her?"

Yes. I've hurt your daughter in ways I can never completely mend.

"She fell through an old porch. She asked for you. I'll text you the address."

I end the call. "What the hell is going on, Scarlet?" I whisper. Why is your father out of prison? Why did you suddenly need to see him? It makes no sense.

～～

SCARLET

MY HEAVY EYES make several attempts to open before the blurred figures come into focus. The tray table in front of me has a glass of water and a bottle of something orange.

"Carrot juice. Freshly pressed."

Oscar.

"Hey." My fuzzy mind feels as lethargic as my voice sounds.

Bell.

Belle.

Theo's mom.

Nellie.

Harold.

Something beside me begins to beep over and over. A nurse comes in the room.

"What's going on?" Oscar asks with panic in his voice.

"Her heart rate is a little high. Are you in pain, Scarlet?"

It all comes back. The affair. Murder. "Oscar … I have to tell—"

"Shh." The nurse brings the back of my bed up a bit more. "The doctor is on his way."

"No. I have to tell—"

"Ruby, calm down. You're going to be fine." Oscar rests his hand on mine.

My eyes dart around the room.

Oh my god. Nellie is in the chair by the window. When our eyes meet, she smiles.

"Hey, sweetie."

"Th-Theo."

"He left to get something to drink. He'll be right back."

"No." I shake my head.

"Look who's up." The doctor smiles as he walks in the room. "The surgery went well." He frowns at my monitor.

"Is she reacting to the anesthetic?" Oscar asks.

The doctor shakes his head. "No. How are you feeling, Scarlet?"

My gaze returns to Nellie. Theo is going to kill her. He's going to find out, and he's going to kill her and Harold too. I continue to stare at her until she begins to squirm in the chair.

"I'm scared."

Nellie's brow furrows, and if I could drag my gaze away from her, I imagine both the doctor and Oscar have the same look of confusion.

"Bell," I whisper.

All the color drains from Nellie's face. Why did Oscar bring her with him? She can't be here.

"I think we're all overwhelming the poor girl." She stands and clears her throat. "Why don't y'all let me and Scarlet have a few minutes alone. Let me work a mother's touch."

She's not my mum. Oscar can stuff his trouser snake into her fanny all he wants, but she will never be my mum.

"Is that okay, Ruby?"

Oscar can't have her. Not now. Not ever.

"Ruby? Did you hear me?"

I nod slowly. Oscar squeezes my hand once. Then he kisses

Nellie on the cheek before following the doctor and nurse out of the room.

Nellie rubs her non-orange-lipstick-covered lips together and stares at her feet. This is completely sane Nellie. Has Theo seen her? Did she already tell Nolan and Harold?

"How?" she whispers.

"He's going to kill you."

Her head snaps up. "Why would you say that?"

I stare at her for a few moments. This is something so far beyond a nightmare, I can't even begin to make sense of it. "Because he came here to kill Braxton Ames."

She sucks in a breath as her hand covers her mouth, eyes wide.

"Your friend had an affair with your husband."

Tears fill her eyes. "It was—" she mutters behind her hand, unable to finish her words.

My name is Scarlet Stone, and I was not put on this earth to judge anyone.

"An accident. I know. And another man went to jail for years for a crime he didn't commit." I'm thinking aloud, that's all. I can't judge her, not one bit. I took a life. I may not have pulled a trigger, but someone died because of what I did, and I let someone else do the time for my crime. I'm Nellie.

"Does Theo know?" She moves her hand from her mouth to her cheeks, wiping the tears as fast as they fall.

I shake my head.

"Braxton?"

"He's alive."

A bit of relief washes over her features.

"Does he know? Does Braxton Ames know who hired him to go to prison?" I want to ask what the going price is for willingly accepting life in prison for a crime he didn't commit. I don't ask. My previous profession gave me too much experience with putting a price on things that should be priceless—untouchable—sacred.

She shakes her head. "Harold handled everything. Money buys a lot of dead ends. No one will ever know unless …"

I close my eyes and exhale. This is all on me. I am the gatekeeper. "I can't." She doesn't understand this is exactly the type of life that nearly ended mine. This is a secret that will kill me.

"What if Theo …" Fear paints her face.

"Then turn yourself in." I can't believe those words came out of my mouth. I'm such a bloody hypocrite.

She bites her lips together, her gaze fixed to mine. What's going through her head?

After a long silence, she nods. "OK," she whispers and turns. Before she reaches the door, she stops. "Thank you, Scarlet."

"For what?"

"For giving me back a life, even if it was only for a brief time." She opens the door and disappears.

"Nellie."

I stiffen at the sound of Theo's curt greeting to her a few seconds before he appears in the doorway. He smiles. I fight back my emotions, the ones that could one day make another attempt at my life and succeed.

"Hello."

He moves to the bed. "Surgery went well."

"So I hear."

"Your father knows you." He nods to the bottle of carrot juice then opens the lid, drops the straw into it, and brings it to my mouth.

I take a sip. The cool juice feels like heaven on my dry throat. "He does, but don't let him hear you say 'father.'"

"Did you get your urgent matter settled with him?"

Him? No. Settled? Hardly.

"Thank you for calling him and getting him here."

Theo nods, taking a seat in the chair by my bed. "You get to go home tomorrow."

I laugh. "Home? Where is that?"

"Good question." He smirks. "I don't think my mattress on the floor is conducive to your compromised physical condition."

"Brilliant observation, Mr. Reed."

We smile at each other for a few long moments. It feels good. In spite of everything, and even if I don't have one damn good reason to do so, I love this man with every fiber of my being.

"So … Nellie. She's better? And your father? They're together? I don't understand."

I wait. Maybe if I wait long enough, he'll ask me to lie to him.

He doesn't.

"Nellie, she—"

"Ruby?" Oscar peeks his head around the door. "We're going to go back to the hotel for a few hours. Can I have a quick word with you before I leave?"

Theo sighs and stands. "I'll be back," he whispers in my ear before biting my earlobe.

"Thanks." I smile at him.

As soon as he leaves the room, my smile dies.

"Interesting bloke."

"Sorry I wasn't awake to introduce the two of you."

"He doesn't say much."

"And he's not even British."

Oscar smiles. "Do you think he's a good choice for you?"

If he only knew. "I love him."

"You loved Daniel."

"Not like this."

"And what is *this*?"

"It's mad love. The kind that makes no sense. The kind that is bigger than anything I've ever experienced. The kind that ensnares your soul and never lets go."

"Sounds dangerous."

I nod slowly. "It's ... *necessary.*" I'm not sure I'll ever be able to tell Oscar Stone that his Ruby lives and dies by the hands of one man that's not him.

"We need to talk." I feel the mood shift. We're no longer talking about Theo. *Nellie.*

It only takes two seconds of looking into his eyes to know. "You knew."

"It was an accident."

"Oh my god ..." I shake my head. "She told you before today?"

"She's catholic, Ruby. Did you know that? It's been years since she's been to confession. I think she was dying to share *everything.*"

I refuse to look at him. "Then you know if you cheat on her, she will try to kill you."

"Ruby ..."

On a heavy sigh, I look at him with a slight wince as the pain from my surgery makes a claim for my attention. "I don't blame her. Not for any of it. You know that's not me. But ... it's not just about her."

"Theo."

I nod. "This has consumed his life." *And it nearly took mine.* "I can't know what happened and not tell him. It would ruin us."

"You want her to turn herself in."

I close my eyes.

"You're in pain. We don't have to talk about this now." He takes my hand. "You are my priority. Always."

"But you have feelings for her. I can tell and they're not like anything you've had for other women." He went to prison for me—for Daniel. Communal underwear. Oscar would do anything for me. My mother died thirty years ago. He's been in prison for a decade. I'm torn between two men who I love so damn much.

"*You're* my priority," he whispers before pressing a kiss to my head. "Now, get some rest. I'll have the nurse come in and make sure you have what you need for the pain. We'll be back later."

CHAPTER FORTY

My name is Scarlet Stone, and I don't like indecisiveness. I make a decision and stick with it. Consequences be damned.

I N THE MIDDLE of the night, a half-stifled cry jerks my body from sleep. "Help ..." It takes a few labored breaths to realize the agonizing plea is mine. I broke a couple of bones. They repaired my ankle with some pins and a metal plate. I'm on pain medication. Why does it still hurt like a motherfucker, making me nauseous with its throbbing intensity?

Theo jumps from the chair and runs out the door, returning with a nurse. He stayed. For a brief moment that realization is its own analgesic.

The nurse increases my pain medication. "This should help you sleep again." She smiles. Why is she smiling? I want to punch it straight off her face. Clearly the pain has me a little on edge.

When she leaves, I turn my attention to Theo, trying to hide my grimace. "You stayed."

He leans down and rests his cheek on my hand for a few seconds before brushing his beard back and forth across it several times. Then he presses his lips to it, letting them linger—easing my pain. "You're mine. Where else would I be?"

I think my dad is falling in love with the woman who killed your mum. My heart claims some of the pain. I'm not sure the meds will ease that.

"I'm worried you're going to sue the home owner for your accident."

An actual smile tries to overtake my grimace.

"Nellie offered to pay for all your medical expenses. She's obviously taken a real liking to you."

I close my eyes. "That's ... *generous* of her."

His lips press to mine. "Sleep, beautiful ... just sleep."

Beautiful ...

I will always love you, Theodore Reed.

<hr />

I'M IN BED with the devil. Again.

Oscar insisted I come back to Savannah to recover. Theo insisted I stay in Lexington.

I'm back at my flat in Savannah. Oscar won. Nellie paid to have a private jet transport me "home." Theo arrived a day later. Fuming.

My instinct to kick and scream, insisting I stay in Lexington, was trodden by a lovely air cast and crutches. I still had a verbal tantrum. Oscar Stone is his own kind of *law.* Law number one: no tantrums.

Oscar's bed is gone, but he left the massage chair, and I can't deny my gratitude. The rest of my flat has been completely furnished as well. Thanks to Nellie Moore—the devil.

"It's not a bribe."

I laugh.

Oscar answers my sarcasm with a reprimanding scowl as he hands me a cup of tea. He takes a seat on my new sofa. Theo took off as soon as Oscar arrived. Two alphas in one room is not a good idea.

"Nel is not like that. She'd turn herself in tomorrow if that's what you really want her to do."

"You mean, if I'm going to tell Theo."

He takes a sip of his tea.

"Do you love her?"

Oscar stares into the cup, eyes squinted a bit. "I would miss her if we weren't together."

"Can those eight words be decoded to mean love?"

"Do you miss Daniel?"

Everything always goes back to Daniel. He seems to be Oscar's favorite measurement for my emotions.

"You said you love him and that you'll always love him. But do you miss him?"

Now, I stare at my tea. It's quite mesmerizing.

He clears his throat. I look up as he glances at his watch. "Your Mr. Reed has been gone for a little over an hour. Do you miss him?"

"Yes." Dear. God. I can't believe how quickly that answer came out of my mouth. There was no thought, it was instinct.

"Well, there you have it."

Yes, there I have it. Oscar cares for Nellie very deeply. If she went to prison, he would feel how I felt when Theo left for Lexington and I never thought I'd see him again.

This man spent a decade in prison for me. He's my family, my blood. My love for him is eternal. But Theo has become my *life*.

"If I tell him, he could try and kill her. That's worst case. Then there's all of the other scenarios that feel nearly as devastating: I don't tell him and my cancer gets worse, I tell him and he doesn't kill her, but you and I can never see each other again because the people we've chosen to be with can't ever be together."

I shake my head. "There's no good answer. So tell me what to do." This is not me. Why can't I make this decision?

My name is Scarlet Stone, and I don't like indecisiveness. I make a decision and stick with it. Consequences be damned.

He puts his cup down on the coffee table and leans forward, resting his elbows on his knees. "I can't make this decision for you."

"You make decisions for me all the time! I'm here because you decided I needed to be here. I stole a heart because you decided I needed to save Daniel. I've lived with the guilt over you going to prison for a crime that I committed because you decided my freedom was more important than yours. All the time! You make decisions for me all the time! Now, when I *need* you to make a decision, you don't have a bloody opinion on the matter?!"

My heart pounds in my ankle as tears race down my face. Never in my life have I been such a clusterfuck of emotions, crying all the damn time. I'm lost and out of control, scared, and confused.

He stands and grabs a handkerchief from his coat pocket. "My love for you will not waiver one bit with your decision." Bending down, he puts the handkerchief in my hand and whispers in my ear, "The only person I truly cannot live without in this world is you."

Squeezing my eyes shut, I hold my breath and all the sobs ready to explode as he kisses my cheek. A few seconds later, the door closes and I fall to pieces.

THE DOOR CREAKS open. My puffy eyes feel like they could creak trying to open as well.

"Sorry. Didn't mean to wake you." Theo closes the door behind him.

"Where did you go?" I rub my eyes and my throbbing sinuses.

"For a drive. Have you been crying?"

"Yes. I'm rather emotional right now. I hate being so incapacitated. It took me ten minutes to make it to the toilet and back for a wee that took less than ten seconds."

"Sorry, I wasn't here." He kneels down next to my chair and rests his head on my good leg. His desire to feel close to me, always touching me like he needs the reminder that I'm still here—it tightens the noose around my heart.

"I can't have children."

He doesn't move.

"I'm not implying anything. Just stating a fact."

He nods slowly against my leg. "I've been told I snore."

My finger traces the lines of his face. His eyes close.

"My first time having sex, I faked four orgasms. Apparently, faking one is believable, two is questionable, by four, the bloke loses his erection, runs out the door shoving his pork sword back in his trousers, and never calls again."

Theo smiles, eyes still shut. "You know if a horse is cold by feeling behind its ears. Cold behind the ears. Cold horse."

"I have no gag reflex, like ... at all."

I'm not sure which I love more: Theo singing or him laughing. Right now, his laughter feels like a fuzzy blanket on a rainy day, with a cup of tea, a handful of Jammie Dodgers, and a good book.

He sits up and interlaces his fingers behind his head. "I have some money."

"Yeah? Did you steal it?"

"No." He smirks. "I want to build a house."

I shrug. "Well, you've got the skills."

"I want to build it for you—for us. Maybe buy a plant or

two and possibly a dog ... a goat ... a horse."

Karma. Karma. Karma. What am I going to do with you? My world is right there. Something so far beyond my dreams, something completely perfect, it's on a silver platter. Yet it's out of my reach by the width of an ocean. And all I have is a boat with a single broken paddle and a bloody huge hole in the bottom. I'll never be able to cross it. *Ever.* I'll be left here, in the distance, watching it disappear into the sunset.

"And Braxton Ames?"

His jaw clenches as he swallows hard. "He'll have to build his own house."

He chose me over revenge. He just ... chose me.

"Where are you going to build our house?"

Theo smiles so big my heart's reminded it never stood a chance.

"My grandfather left my father twenty acres of land in North Carolina, just outside of Asheville. It has 365 degrees of the best mountain views. The beach is a half-day drive away."

"How are you going to fit building a house into your tour schedule?"

Taking my hand, he presses my index finger to his lips, giving it a soft kiss. "I might stick to a private concert for one."

The decision has been made. I will take Nellie's secret to my grave, even if that happens sooner rather than later. Oscar gets his chance at happiness. Theo lets go of his past. I get as many breaths with this man as I can possibly steal. And if the burden becomes too much to bear, I'll get to die in the arms of the man who I was put on this earth to love.

"When do we move in?"

He chuckles. "In about a year, if I do everything myself."

"And the interim?"

"We rent someplace nearby."

"How do we make money?"

He shrugs. "I do some side jobs to supplement us if my savings dips too low. You most likely lift a few wallets when we run errands or look for shopping companion jobs."

"You know me so well." I laugh.

"Say, yes."

Jump, Scarlet. Jump off the fucking cliff.

"I can't have children." This needs to be iterated. I need him to understand this reality.

"I want *you*."

Tears fill my eyes. "I have cancer."

"I. Want. You." He leans forward, sliding his hands through my hair while pressing his lips to mine.

CHAPTER FORTY-ONE

My name is Scarlet Stone. When I was seventeen, I got in an argument with Oscar and ran away. It felt like the end of the world. The next morning I awoke curled up next to my mum's gravestone.

T AP. *TAP. TAP.*

I rub my eyes open. Theo comes into focus. There's only a ghost of light filtering through the curtains. It's early. I'm sick of sleeping in a chair but sleeping in bed is still worse, in spite of the company.

Tap. Tap. Tap.

His body swallows up half the sofa, long legs spread wide, mobile resting on his thigh, *finger tapping it.*

Tap. Tap. Tap.

Why does he look so menacing this morning? Maybe this is a dream, a throwback to the early stage of our relationship.

Tap. Tap. Tap.

My gaze refocuses on the mobile. It's mine. Not his.

"Good morning." I struggle to push myself up a bit. "You're up early. Did I miss a call?"

"When were you going to tell me?"

The tapping stops, but my gaze remains on my mobile. No question is a better hook than that. I can't afford to take the bait. He will have to be more—very—specific before I offer any sort of answer. If my world is going to implode, I'm not going to be the one to light the fuse.

My eyes make their way to his. I say nothing.

"Nellie Moore."

Strike.

A constant rhythm of blinks. That's all I give him.

"You have pages from some diary or journal of hers on your phone."

Flame.

I nod slowly, just once.

"She killed my mother."

Implosion.

"Yes," I whisper.

He draws in a slow breath, holds it, then releases it, nostrils flared, jaw firm, every visible muscle constricted to the point his whole body shakes. "When…" his voice trembles like it's taking everything he has not to rip something—or someone—apart "…were you going to tell me?"

"Never." I don't think it's possible to shatter a person's world without scarring your soul.

I brush my thumbs along his cheeks. "Daniel, I won't be responsible for your missed opportunity. Do this for me. It's my dying wish."

"Jesus Christ, Scarlet…" his voice breaks "…I'm not leaving you to die alone."

"If you don't leave … I will."

Theo throws my mobile against the wall. The pieces of it clink on the wood floor. I know how it feels.

"Lie to me, Scarlet." He towers over me, chest heaving, teeth bared. "But don't fucking tell me that you were *never* going to tell me this!"

If he read every page of her journal, he'd know Nellie killed his mum. But no where in the journal does she disclose the actual affair. It was just a *feeling* I had when I read it. I have no idea what to say. This isn't us—we are no longer a lie.

"Say something!" he roars.

I wince. The ache in my heart is not a metaphor. It's real, tangible, and all-consuming. "Nothing I can say will bring back your parents. Nothing I can say will make what happened okay. Nothing I can say will change the facts."

"The facts? THE FACTS?!"

I swallow past my fear, which is hard with him inching closer to me, hands clenched, body vibrating with so much anger.

"Please, enlighten me."

I'm not sure he really means it. But since he said it, I'm going to do what I seem to do best: shatter worlds.

"Your mum and Harold were having an affair."

His head juts back, eyes narrowed. "No." He shakes his head.

Now does he see all of the unwritten words that I saw in the journal?

"Nellie found out. She drove to your house with the intention of killing Harold."

"Stop." He continues to shake his head.

"She caught them together and aimed the gun at Harold—"

"Stop!" Theo presses the heels of his hands to the side of his head.

"Your mum jumped in front of Harold right as the gun went off."

"STOP!" He buckles at both the waist and the knees, with his face buried in his hands.

"Theo …" I bend forward, reaching for him, but he stumbles backwards, collapsing onto the sofa.

Averting his red, glassy eyes, he reaches for his pocket.

"What are you doing?"

"Calling the police."

"Please, don't."

He freezes, then slowly looks up at me. "What did you say?"

"It was an accident."

"My mother is *dead*," he says through gritted teeth.

"Oscar loves her." Theo can't understand what that really means in the scope of my life and my relationship with Oscar. And at this exact moment, with his finger poised to press *send*, I can't convey it quick enough for him to comprehend.

"My. Mother. Is. DEAD! My father is DEAD!"

I swipe at my tears and nod. "I'm sorry."

The vacant look in his eyes says all there's left to say.

No more begging.

No more bargaining.

No more lies.

He presses *send*. I hear his voice, but the words don't register past the grief of mourning the loss of his parents, Oscar's future, Nolan, Nellie, but most especially ... Theo.

A few minutes later, he ends the call. Holding his mobile in his hands, he stares at it—head bowed, shoulders turned inward. How long before the police arrive at the Moores'? How long before Oscar arrives at my door?

I support my air cast with one hand while I lower the recliner's footrest.

"Don't," he whispers as I reach for my crutches.

The idea of Theo never looking at me again, never touching me again is so unfathomable it feels like a special kind of pain saved for the worst of humanity. I bite my trembling lips together and nod, tears blurring everything. There's no question about it, I'm far from perfect. I've taken things that weren't mine to take. I've hurt one person to save another. I've made impossible choices, and I've lived with the consequences—as I am now. But I have to believe that I'm not unredeemable. I have to believe that there's something inside of me that's worthy of love.

Theo slowly stands. I sniffle and swallow back so much pain it nearly chokes me. I wait for it—pray for it.

Nothing.

Not a single glance.

He turns and opens the door.

"Why were you looking at my phone?" It's not a plea. I know I no longer have a case. I need to make sense of what just happened. *How* it happened. I need closure.

Theo keeps his back to me, but pauses halfway out the door. "I was going to ask for your dad's blessing before proposing to you."

The door closes.

I hug my stomach, collapsing back in the chair as sobs wrack my whole body.

CHAPTER FORTY-TWO

My name is Scarlet Stone, and I am alive.

TRUE TO HIS word, Oscar doesn't blame me. Four months ago, Nellie pled guilty to manslaughter. Harold was arrested and charged with aiding and abetting in the conviction of Braxton Ames as well as attempted murder. After Nolan testified, he sold the mansion and all of his other property and moved to the West Coast.

Oscar walks around Savannah from sunrise to sunset, stopping at book stores and coffee shops. He says very little, but always gives me a warm smile and kiss on the cheek like I'm still the light of his life. I'm not sure if he's avoiding me or just searching for a new direction.

I feel quite lost myself. Theo disappeared. I haven't looked for him. What could I possibly say or do to change what has happened? He has the truth. I didn't stand in the way of him turning in Nellie, and I won't stand in the way of him grieving the news of his mum cheating on his dad. He is unequivocally the love of my life—of every life I will ever have. He's branded into my scarred soul.

I wish him well.

Oscar encourages me every day to love myself enough to continue what I "originally came to Savannah to do." I remind him that I came here to die on my own terms. His response is always the same: "Exactly." I think I finally understand what he means. Death is inevitable for everyone, but we can make choices in life that increase our chance of taking lots and lots of breaths before our time expires.

I have juice. I have tea. Meditation starts my days, followed by physical therapy. My ankle is better, not perfect, but close. With my new and affordable car, I drive to Tybee several days a week to walk along the shore. It's difficult with my ankle still healing, but I feel better when I can walk by the house where it all began. Sometimes I think I see Theo swimming in the distance but it's never him, just wishful thinking. I guess if I have 70,000 thoughts a day, I might as well make as many of them as 'wishful' as possible.

"How was work?" Oscar asks as I come through the door. He's sprawled out on the sofa that he's been sleeping on for the past several months.

I told him he could get rid of the sofa and haul his bed back in, but Nellie picked out the sofa, and he doesn't want to get rid of it.

"Just fabulous." I smirk with an eye roll.

"You're a genius, Ruby. What more could you possibly want to achieve in life?" He keeps his gaze on his book. It's Tolle. I told him there's a lot of comfort in Tolle and Dyer.

"I'm not sure tech support at the Apple store really qualifies as being a genius."

"But they call it the 'Genius Bar.'"

"True." I ease into 'my' chair on a long sigh.

"It's a waste of your potential, Ruby."

"It's temporary, until I literally get back on my feet. And I'm close."

He flips another page. "Then what?"

"Well, according to the oncologist—anything."

Oscar slaps the book shut, raising a single eyebrow. "You saw the oncologist today?"

"Yes, sir."

"And?"

"They can't find any cancer. Blood tests, scans ... every-thing looked perfect."

Oscar Stone doesn't cry, but I swear I see tears in his eyes.

"Ruby, that's ..."

"Crazy? Insane? Incredibly unlikely? Inexplicable? Those were the words the doctor used. He couldn't explain it, not that I was asking for an explanation. He kept asking me if I was sure I hadn't had some form of treatment. Like a round of radiation or chemo could slip my mind." I grin.

"I wish your mum—"

I shake my head. "Don't say it. She made the decision she needed to make. If a hundred people with the same diagnosis I had did the same thing I did, I don't know how many, if any, would still be alive."

That will always be the hardest part for me to explain. I had terminal cancer. Surviving it, no matter the means, is a miracle. Over eighty-five percent of the world's population believes in a higher power, yet very few people believe in miracles. It makes no sense.

"For me, it worked. Today it became my truth. I'm not going to write a book about my story, or make any miraculous claims that I've figured out the cure for cancer."

He throws the book aside. "Well, you could. You're a geni-us."

I laugh and like always, it quickly fades. I'm existing. I ha-ven't had a single suicidal thought since being in Lexington with Theo, but what I'm doing is far from truly living and that's okay. Visiting the cancer wing of a hospital and sitting in the waiting room of the oncologist's office has given me some much needed perspective.

Not every day is a parade with fireworks, but every breath counts. Life is incredibly fucking hard, rarely fair, and always unpredictable. Most days, surviving is as good as it gets. Today I watched a healthy little girl sitting next to her mum, with a lovely pink scarf wrapped around her head, give her doll to another little girl sitting across from me, with no hair and a portable oxygen pack on her back. I shall never *ever* forget the smile on her face.

Love. It's why we are here.

SPRING.

I'm ready to put away my jumpers and dig out my flip-flops. Oscar took off two weeks ago for an epic "bucket list" road trip. I asked if he's dying, and he winked at me. I know the answer. *"We're all dying, Ruby."*

As soon as I'm within a block of my flat, the skies open up. Yep, it's definitely spring. I sprint—OK, a slow jog with my ankle—then I put on the brakes just enough so I don't slip on the stairs leading to my flat. Once I reach the top, where I'm protected by the roof, I shake the water from my hair like a dog and glance up while pulling the key from my handbag.

I halt. Every part of my body, including my breath, just … stops.

I've had dreams like this—too many to count. This one is much more vivid than any of the other dreams.

"Hi." His voice is not echoed like it's been before in my other dreams. His golden blond hair is longer, not quite long enough to pull back into a ponytail but close. The beard. It's longer too. Shorter than it was when we met but longer than it was … in my last dream. Because … this has to be a dream.

Blink. Blink. Blink.

"Mind if I come inside?" He nods toward my door, a small smile spreading across his beautiful face.

Blink. Blink. Blink.

"Hi," I whisper.

Thunder rumbles, vibrating the floor beneath us.

Theo's smile grows a bit more. "Is this still your apartment?"

I shake my head. "Sorry. Uh … yes." I unlock the door and step inside, shrugging off my jacket.

Theo closes the door behind him and leans up against it, shoving his hands deep into the pockets of his jeans. "You live alone?" His gaze trails around the room.

I rub the goose bumps along my arms and nod. Words still evade me.

"How have you been?"

How have I been? Is that a real question? "Good." I relinquish a polite smile.

He nods.

The awkwardness sucks the oxygen from the room. My heartbeat is sporadic like it doesn't have a clue what to do.

"You just get off work?"

I nod.

"What do you do?"

"Um …" I fiddle with the hem of my shirt.

He chuckles.

I narrow my eyes then look down. "Oh." I laugh at my blue shirt with an apple on the front.

"Sorry." He pushes his hands deeper into his pockets. It brings his shoulders closer to his face. He looks so young, handsome, and ... *happy*. "I've seen you at the Genius Bar."

"You have?" I narrow one eye.

He looks down at his feet. God ... who is this man? Is he embarrassed? Shy? I've never known this side to Theodore Reed. "Yes. I've been in town for a few days."

"Stalking me?"

He glances up. "Just ... seeing how you're doing."

I try to decide what that means as I return a slow nod.

"You look amazing."

I smile. "So do you."

We stare at each other in more awkward silence.

"Uh, can I get you some tea or ..."

"Tea?" He chuckles. "Just say it. You only have tea or water to offer me. Maybe some carrot juice?"

I shake my head, biting back my grin. "I'm out of carrots. I need to go to the supermarket."

"I'm good. I don't want to keep you. I just wanted to say hi and see how you're doing."

Theodore Reed, if you walk out that door again, I'm certain I will die right here in this very spot. It still feels like this is a dream. I'm so afraid if I move an inch, I'll wake up and he'll be gone.

I point toward the kitchen. "Maybe there's still one of Oscar's beers in the back of the fridge. I can go check."

Theo shakes his head. "It's fine. Really, I don't want to keep you." He turns and twists the doorknob.

"Do you miss me?" I ask in unapologetic desperation. I don't need to know if he still loves me, just if he misses me. That's all that matters.

He drops his forehead to the door, slowly rolling it side to side. My fucking feet won't move. Maybe it's my heart pounding in my throat. Maybe it's the fear that if I touch him and he still leaves, the heartache will start all over again.

"So much I can barely breathe," he whispers.

Tears flood my eyes. "Then maybe you should want to."

He slowly turns, eyes red and glassy with emotion. "Want to what?"

"You…" I blink and the tears release "…you said you didn't want to keep me. But if you miss me even a fraction of the way I miss you…" my voice shakes as my words struggle to claw past the lump of emotion stuck in my throat "…then maybe you should want to keep me."

His forehead tightens. "Scarlet …"

Scarlet …

I close my eyes. My name on his lips brings my mere existence back to life again. When his hand presses to my cheek, I open my eyes.

"I don't deserve you."

I rest my hand on his chest. I've never felt his heartbeat in dreams. "You really don't." I grin through my tears.

He smiles back. It's sad and filled with uneasiness. "Can I keep you anyway?"

Leaning forward, I rest my ear next to my hand on his chest. It's such a beautiful sound, such a perfect feeling, such an unforgettable moment.

"I've always been yours, Theodore Reed."

My name is Scarlet Stone, and I am alive.

EPILOGUE

THEODORE

"**A**RE YOU NERVOUS?" Scarlet asks as I grab my faded jeans and slip them on.

"Of course not." I'm fucking terrified.

She hops off the stool and saunters toward me. My dick's hard in less than three seconds. It's not a good time to get an erection. Her finger traces down the lines of my chest, over my abs, stopping at the waistband of my briefs.

"I'm not jealous," she whispers, looking up at me through thick eyelashes.

"You shouldn't be." I hold completely still.

Why is she sliding her finger past my waistband? I glance at the clock on the wall next to the door.

Four minutes. I have four minutes. I need more than that to properly fuck her.

"Just remember…" she tugs the waistband down an inch, her hand totally ignoring the pulsing head of my cock "…when bras and knickers land on the stage…" her finger traces the script "…you belong to *me*."

I close my eyes. For the love of God … this woman likes to torture me. But I love it when she admires my tattoo.

I don't deserve Scarlet …
but she's still mine.

Scarlet is in red. The rest is in black.

"Now, finish getting dressed and go be a rock star."

I look up at the ceiling and shake my head. "Sure, Scar ... I can't fasten my fucking pants now, but I'm sure the over 18,000 fans in this sold-out venue won't notice."

She presses a kiss to my chest then digs her teeth into my tense muscle.

I groan. "Not helping."

"How much time do you have?" She kisses her way down my chest.

"Not enough." My chin drops to my chest, jaw slack. I thread my fingers through her long curls, ready to protest.

"How. Long?" She frees my cock as she gets on her knees.

Fucking hell! "Two minutes," I pant.

She runs her tongue along the hard vein then circles the head of it, her wicked intentions twinkling in her eyes. "I only need one."

"Fuuuck ..." I grab the wall next to me with one hand and fist her hair with my other hand as she proves, once again— No. Gag. Reflex.

THREE YEARS AGO, when I walked out Scarlet's door, I never imagined I could overcome the feelings of betrayal, grief, and hatred for everything and everyone in my life. I made a piss-ass attempt at building a house on my acreage, because building it for myself gave me little motivation.

Instead, I turned to my first love—music. My old manager once told me there's nothing more magical in the music industry than a broken heart. So I wrote and wrote and wrote. Thirteen songs later, I felt a helluva lot better. I packed up my stuff and drove back to Savannah to get the girl.

I waited a week to ask her to marry me, without asking Oscar's permission. Asking for it seemed like a bad omen. She pointed to my guitar and the tattered stacks of paper with the scribbled lyrics to all of my songs and said, "I want to marry a rock star. When you're a rock star. I'll marry you."

Seven months later, I signed a record deal and my marriage license.

My wife beat cancer. She's my hero, my friend, my lover. Scarlet is the reason I'm living my dream. I nod at the crew as I make my way to the stage, with my guitar in one hand and her hand in my other. We stop at the bottom of the backstage stairs, both of us grinning at the thunderous roar of 18,000 fans chanting my name.

"Tell me a story, Theo." She says the same thing before every concert.

I kiss her long and hard until I know she's gasping for air. "I'll sing you a song, Scarlet."

"Make it a love song." She releases my hand.

I take several steps up toward the stage. The adrenaline begins to burn in my veins. "It's your song. They're all your songs." I wink and take my spot—center stage at Madison Square Garden. Tonight, I will perform every song from my debut album, *Songs of Scarlet.*

SCARLET

Two Years Later

MY NAME IS Scarlet Reed. I enjoy counting breaths, observing the diversity of the human condition, and witnessing miracles.

Oh … and I'm married to a rock star.

"Let me guess … you thought you couldn't get pregnant?" Mary, our adoption agent, peers over the frames of her reading glasses, zeroing in on my baby bump. Theo signs the adoption papers then hands me the pen.

"How'd you guess?" I rest my hand on Theo's leg. Six months ago I feared the worst—that my cancer had returned. After a trip to the doctor, we discovered I didn't have cancer and my infertility from endometriosis was no longer an issue. I was diagnosed with a healthy case of pregnancy with the side effect of morning sickness. I didn't speak for days, I was so gobsmacked. Theo, on the other hand, strutted around like a cock, claiming he had super sperm.

"I see it all the time, honey. Years of failed attempts leads to adoption. Then … boom! Once you stop actually trying, it happens. Most don't go through with the adoption when that happens."

I shrug, placing the pen on the paper after signing it. "We've been Maya's foster parents for a year. She's already family." I smile.

Two years ago, Maya lost both of her parents and her older brother to gang violence in Chicago. Her closest living relative is a grandmother here in Nashville. Last year, her grandmother suffered a heart attack and was moved to an assisted living facility. Maya was put into foster care.

Theo met her through a school-sponsored music outreach program shortly after her parents died. At seven, she is nothing short of amazing. Theo calls her a music prodigy. Although, I think he fell in love with her smile before she ever played a single note. He said she has a small dimple on her right cheek when she smiles really big, just like me. I don't have a dimple.

We agree to disagree.

"Well, she's a lucky little girl. Often times, black, adolescent children can spend their entire youth being bounced around in foster care until they turn eighteen."

With everything finalized, we thank Mary and hurry to the car. Maya will have finished school in an hour which means we need to get our *adult activities* done before she gets home.

"Don't speed."

Theo shoots me a sideways glance. "I'm not."

"You're ten miles an hour over the speed limit."

He returns his eyes to the road. "If you must know, I'm fifteen over."

I laugh. "We're not talking about how fast you're going, are we?"

"He said four days and it turned into over two weeks."

I roll my eyes. Although Oscar let Nellie go without so much as one guilty look at either one of us, Theo hasn't forgotten that I was going to let Nellie get away with murder so that Oscar could have a chance at love and happiness. Theo claims he understands why I did it, but I don't think he ever understood how anyone could fall in love with Nellie. He never had the chance to see that side of her.

"He visits us two or three times a year."

"Too many," he grumbles.

Fifteen days. He's gone fifteen days without sex.

When we pull onto our private property, I smile at Thor, our retired thoroughbred, and Queen, our goat, both grazing by the barn. Our two-story house on the outskirts of Nashville isn't a Theodore Reed original. It's a thirty-year-old house that he's making his mark on one room at a time. It's in need of love and rebuilding—I was in need of love and rebuilding. I am his greatest masterpiece. I see it in his eyes. I hear it in the words he sings.

"Down, Derby," Theo scolds our rescued pit bull terrier when he goes to jump on me.

"You're fine, baby." I squat down and scratch behind his ears. "He's just overprotective."

Theo hooks the truck keys on the hook by the door then walks into the living room. "Derby knocked over another one of your plants."

I stand, resting my fists on my hips. "Derby."

He cocks his head to the side.

I narrow my eyes. He drops to the floor and rolls on his back.

I shake my head. "No. You don't get your belly rubbed if you didn't play nice with my plants."

"Do I get my belly rubbed?" Theo shrugs off his shirt and tucks it in the back of his jeans.

I admire his arms and all his new tattoos. Lots of song lyrics—about me. When we decided to adopt Maya, he added her name to his back, each letter connected with notes.

As much as my pregnancy hormones scream for me to rip off my clothes and sprawl out on the worktop for Theo to love every inch of me, I let myself enjoy the moment, counting breaths and staring at the man that was made just for me.

"What's with the sappy look, Mum?" He refers to me as Mum and it makes me smile every time.

I think it's because my life has found a perfection beyond anything I ever thought to dream of that I find myself reflecting back so often.

"We nearly destroyed each other."

Theo nods, a bit of tension wrinkles his forehead.

"We nearly destroyed ourselves."

Another nod. He slides his hands into his pockets and it does all kinds of wonderful things to the muscles in his chest and arms.

"Sometimes I feel like we broke together, and some of your pieces mixed with mine, and some of mine mixed with yours."

He crooks a finger at me. I grin and walk to him, my whole body feeling quite *itchy*.

"I think I like it when our pieces mix together." He rests his hands on my belly.

I wait for them to move, make haste with removing my clothes, the sound of my gasp when one of his fingers slides into me—his tongue and teeth torturing my nipples. *I'm so horny.*

But … he doesn't move. It's just my beautifully inked husband—my rock star—holding our baby in his hands and me in his eyes.

"She's moving," he whispers, wide eyes focused on my baby bump.

I cover his hands with mine. "We did it, Theo." Emotion builds inside of me. "After many dinners and small talk, me saying things that made you grin, and you saying things that made me laugh. After countless walks on the beach in the shadows of the night, too much wine and conversation—some of it lies, some of it truth—we finally managed to find a real life and feel … *human*."

Theo's eyes shift to mine. I feel like his whole world—like his song. Then he takes this perfect life, perfect day, perfect moment, and makes it even better by saying that one word that still reaches my soul. "Scarlet …"

THE END

Acknowledgements

Four years. Ten Books. I've built quite the village.

Thank you to my husband and three children. You are my every breath.

Thank you, Leslie and Kambra, for enduring my weakest moments and messiest manuscripts.

Thank you to Jyl for thirty-three years of friendship. Our "girl time" is my sanity!

Thank you, Shauna, for days filled with random messages and emojis. I've come to need them!

Thank you to my amazing assistant, Jennifer, for making me look far more creative and organized than I really am. I've stopped counting how many times you've saved me on things.

Thank you to my Jonesies Facebook group for reading my words, supporting me, sharing my books with the world, and pretending to enjoy my videos.

Thank you, Sian and Arabella, for making Scarlet truly British. In so many ways, you brought this book to life.

Thank you to my editor, Maxann, for blowing my mind. I love your brain!

Thank you to my beta readers for what has to feel like muddling though my unedited manuscript. You never get to experience my words at their best for the first time. I will forever be grateful for your sacrifice.

Thank you to Monique and Allison for joining my proof-reading team *over a holiday!* I had seven proofreaders for this book. If this book was not perfect, blame them—kidding.

Thank you to Sarah Hansen for the AMAZING cover!

Thank you to Paul for always giving my books a professional look with your formatting and awesome customer service!

Thank you to my readers for choosing my books to read. It's such an honor to write for you.

Thank you, bloggers, for sharing your love of books with the world. You're this fabulous bridge connecting readers to new authors.

Thank you to every person who has inspired me to think beyond the norm, value my health, question everything, and live my own truth. You are the spiritual leaders who bring out the best in humanity, the healers who nurture the human body, and the warriors who protect the earth and its resources. I owe you my life.

Also by Jewel E. Ann

Jack & Jill Series
End of Day
Middle of Knight
Dawn of Forever

Holding You Series
Holding You
Releasing Me

Standalone Novels
Idle Bloom
Only Trick
Undeniably You
One

jeweleann.com

About the Author

Jewel is a free-spirited romance junkie with a quirky sense of humor.

With 10 years of flossing lectures under her belt, she took early retirement from her dental hygiene career to stay home with her three awesome boys and manage the family business.

After her best friend of nearly 30 years suggested a few books from the Contemporary Romance genre, Jewel was hooked. Devouring two and three books a week but still craving more, she decided to practice sustainable reading, AKA writing.

When she's not donning her cape and saving the planet one tree at a time, she enjoys yoga with friends, good food with family, rock climbing with her kids, watching How I Met Your Mother reruns, and of course…heart-wrenching, tear-jerking, panty-scorching novels.